I0656381

The Comforting Weight of Water

Roanna McClelland is an emerging writer of fiction and non-fiction with a background spanning environmental policy, law, politics, media, and research. Her debut novel, *The Comforting Weight of Water*, won the Arts South Australia Wakefield Press Unpublished Manuscript Award in 2022. She is currently completing a PhD in environment and water law. Her work explores conceptualisations of climate, the environment, identity, and human nature in modern society.

The Comforting
Weight of Water

Roanna McClelland

Wakefield
Press

Wakefield Press
16 Rose Street
Mile End
South Australia 5031
www.wakefieldpress.com.au

First published 2023

Edited by Maddy Sexton, Wakefield Press
Book design by Duncan Blachford, Typography Studio

ISBN 978 1 74305 958 6

A catalogue record for this book is available from the National Library of Australia

Wakefield Press thanks Coriole Vineyards for continued support

*For Alfred and Madeline: around all
the galaxies and back, always.*

*And for Ruth McCance, who taught me
the joy of wonder. Miss you every day.*

This book was written on the traditional lands of the Wurundjeri people of the Kulin nation, and the Kaurna people of the Adelaide Plains. The author acknowledges the Traditional Owners and custodians of the lands on which she works, and pays respect to Elders past and present.

1.

I PISS ON THE LEAVES IN THE MORNING.

My aim is so good now that I can stand on the old brown rock in the middle of the River, my bare arse flashing anyone stupid enough to walk by, and just point and shoot those suckers down. I love to see them shudder and fold under the swirling grey water, then pop back up seconds later at the edge of my vision, propelled that quickly by the current. The short time every morning when the Wet stops is the only time I can really see my piss, so I let out an extra loud crow with each sinking leaf. No one's going tell me to be quiet so I might as well.

It's strange to hear my voice travel across the churning River and between the scraggly trees of the forest; usually the Wet suffocates every noise in a big, sloppy hug, but in this moment every day, I reckon everyone in the five villages can hear my whoops. So I add in a ripper fart, for their pleasure.

The weak shafts of sun feel strange on my bare arms. Not unpleasant, exactly, just peculiar. I can feel the light heat drawing the moisture out of my skin. It's a weird sensation, when you are wet the rest of the time. I shudder a little on my rock; blink a few times as my eyes adjust to the glare off the choppy waters. The River spreads wider than a hundred of my body lengths to either side of me; a great, writhing mess of glinting peaks and foam.

Gammy doesn't know why it stops raining at the same time every day, and Gammy knows most things. In fact, I think the last time I asked why the Wet only stops in this period every morning she said 'fuck knows', which just goes to show that she really doesn't know. Normally she bangs on about everything and anything; probably makes half of it up, but how would I tell the difference? She's the only person I talk to around here, so I have to take her word for it.

I have a theory. I reckon the earth took pity on everyone in the five villages and gave them that one window of warm sun every day as a gift. A short period of time without the water drizzling down and filling every part of the air, to make sure they could dry out and see their own piss, and to stop the River finally taking over and swamping the lot of them. When I told Gammy my brilliant theory she looked at me strangely, and asked why I didn't think that gift was for me too? Which seemed like a silly thing to ask – she knows the Wet doesn't bother me like it does them.

Or maybe, the Wet lets the sun out for that time once a day just to mess with them, give them a taste of what they can't have before continuing with the torrential drenching of their mouldy old huts and their soft, wrinkled skin. As Gammy says, fuck knows, and really, why would I care?

Even with the sun's soft light streaming down onto the mud covering the River's banks at the edge of my vision, trickles of water make their way down every branch and drops fall off every leaf, splashing into the pools of water weaving around the sticky black sludge below. The Wet never stops, not really. Every mossy tree, every slimy rock, the rotting piles of mulch I crush with my dirty feet, all of them are circled by dribbles of water, even when the sheets of rain stop falling from above.

The leaves glisten and sparkle with silver droplets, shining in a way you never notice when the Wet batters them downward. As far as I can see, through the wooded plains, sloping branches shimmer and steam in the now clear air. My eyes aren't used to the bright light and I squint uncomfortably. It's a bit irritating actually, this sun business, Gammy.

Then with a sharp hiss, the sun slides behind a sheet of thick grey clouds and the Wet sets in again, filling the air with the water that will cloak our little world until tomorrow's yellow ball comes out for its quick visit.

I stay on the rock for a bit longer, watching the sharp edges and colours of the boulders and forest soften and blur until everything is a slick of dirty grey; no clear lines between the River and the wall of water above.

I'm whistling when I slide off the now slippery rock edge and just like that, I am under the water where everything is clear again. My whistle is muffled by the big old River. This time my fart explodes with a wet bang and bubbles to the surface, and I am literally pissing myself under the water, watching the bubbles from my open, cackling mouth join my fart bubbles in a wild and swirling dance above my head.

IT DOESN'T REALLY TAKE ME LONG TO COLLECT THE long, silky brown reeds from the bottom of the River for dinner, but because I stuffed around longer than usual on the rock this morning, the day is getting darker when I finally emerge, and I've got to hurry up. Not that it's obvious; Gammy says there used to be sunrises and sunsets but here it's just grey, then darker grey, then black. It happens painfully slowly and it makes no difference to the Wet so I don't know why we all rush about to get back in our huts before the black. The villagers are just shit-scared of everything.

My scratchy woven reed basket is overflowing with slimy tendrils and just the damp smell of them is making my stomach growl. My eyelashes bat the Wet from my eyes as I run back through the forest, ducking and weaving under the large canopies groaning with the weight of water. I can almost hear the trees moaning about their load above my head, complaining like everyone else in this place.

Sometimes, I think our whole world is melting slowly under the constant onslaught of the Wet. I see trees that stood proud and tall when I was a skinny little kid now stooped and grey; mud slicks inching down every jagged pathway; the surface of the earth looking a bit more disfigured every day.

I reckon I am the only one who stops long enough to see these creeping changes, though. The villagers just scurry about, desperately trying – and failing – to avoid the Wet and clinging to each other inside their rickety stilted houses – which they would see are also melting into the mud, if they ever bothered to look. Not like me; I see it all.

I'm rushing to get back to Gammy, a trail of spray in my

wake and damp green cloak flapping wildly behind me, which is why I almost miss the lizard. I'm pretty much on top of it before I see its yellow eye; have to stop so quickly I almost go arse up. Lucky no one is ever out in the forest or they would have seen me skidding through the mud like a right fool, basket full of slinky reeds flapping wildly on my arm. I can't believe he hasn't heard my bell; the Wet muffles everything, but that damn bell on my ankle always seems to cut through.

This old lizard is bloody huge. He would feed Gammy and me for days, so I've got to be careful to catch him. He sits there rigid on the side of the tree, water pouring all around him, blinking like a dumb fucker. Like he doesn't realise he's probably one of the only giant lizards left in the forest. Maybe on the whole earth. Like he doesn't realise he's going to be in my belly soon.

I slowly unravel a dirty old rag from around my wrist and wrap it around the bell on my ankle to muffle it. He might be deaf from the constant rain, but I can't take any chances, not with what could be the last lizard on earth.

Stay there, my pretty.

I reach carefully into the rags draped across my chest and pull out an old knife, mottled with brown rust, ready in case he puts up a fight. Not that anything in this bloody place fights anymore. All too wet to care. But Gammy is getting weaker and she needs some real meat, so I'm ready for anything.

No need though. When my hand darts out of the Wet to grab his thick green neck he just looks at me with those shiny dead eyes and doesn't move a muscle, beads of water rolling down his scaly face. Given up like the rest of them. I let out a long sigh. It feels wrong to take advantage of him like this, but we've got to eat so them's the breaks. When I slit his throat I only see the bright red blood for a second before it disappears into the rain.

I wonder if he used to be an energetic lizard that fought and hunted for bugs and thought he was King of the Forest, and if he is sad that even his blood has been lost to the Wet.

2.

YOU'D THINK GAMMY WOULD BE GRATEFUL THAT I brought back the last fucking lizard on earth to eat but she's just *yap yap yap* in my ear about bringing water into the hut, and won't even let me show her until I have taken off my soggy cloak. She's bonkers – it's bloody wet everywhere. It's thick in the air inside even where the sheets of rain aren't falling. It drips through every crack in the ceiling and trickles down the side of every wall – what does she care if I get some water on the ground? But she insists, and so I rip off my mouldy green rags and stomp them around our one room, using them to make the puddles disappear, until she clicks her tongue in satisfaction and I can finally sit.

I throw myself dramatically, naked except for my ankle bell, onto the rotting wet floor and prop my head on my hands, trying my best wide-eyed innocent look. The soft floorboards sag a little under my weight. She can't help laughing at me but tells me to put on some clothes in her sternest voice. No way, lady. I only wear those stupid green rags outside because the villagers insist. It's mad to wear clothes that instantly get weighed down by water and chafe and drag through the mud. They never dry either, not even in that one time of sun every day. I don't understand why the villagers wear hopeless wet rags every day, their pale bodies riddled with red raw marks and rash.

'You wear that green cloak so they can see you coming.'

That wasn't what I was asking, Gammy. I know why I wear my cloak, so that the villagers can recognise my green among their black and always know where I am. I get that. But they could still put me in green and hear my bell and know I was coming, and they could throw away their rotting black rags and their bodies could feel free for a change.

The villagers are scared of nakedness, scared of their own shadows. You know it's true, Gammy. They find it hard enough to move in the Wet, with the whole of the sky trying to push them into the mud slicks below. Why else would they wear the chafing, stiff black rags that stick to every part of their skin? Perhaps they are terrified their pasty white bodies will go the way of everything else, worn down by the Wet day in and day out until they are just big puddles themselves.

They should know they look like they are heading that way anyway.

I wonder for a moment what their bodies are like underneath those piles of damp black. Pasty and wrinkled and pink-scarred from rubbing, just like their exposed ankles and necks, I reckon. I can't imagine them having proper features under the rags. There isn't sharpness to anything in the Wet, all rounded corners and liquids and peeling surfaces, and I can't picture sharpness to their bodies either. More like white, trembling blobs, wobbling together in their dank huts across the clearing.

Now that is an image I want out of my head quick smart, Gammy. I shudder and shake my head with a frown, as though I could dislodge the thought. Gammy hasn't noticed my expression. Mad old lady can't sit still, keeps pottering about our bare square of a hut, tripping over the small pile of pots in the corner and cleaning rotting wooden walls that will still be speckled with black mould tomorrow despite all her fussing. I deliberately don't rise from where I am lying on the floor to help: lady wants the stupid place clean, she can do it all herself.

A large dollop of water drops from one of the many holes in our roof. It falls directly where I lie naked on my stomach on the rotting floor and trickles down my butt crack, causing me to shiver quietly. Gammy doesn't see this either, squatting creakily as she tries to put flint to rusty knife above wet twigs in our smoke-scarred little fire pit that sits on the floor, so we can eat the Lizard King (who now looks as fucked as the villagers: pale, droopy and defeated).

Gammy isn't looking too flash herself. Her legs tremble in their U-shape, like they were made too slim and weak for her body. Every day she looks more bowed; the damp is seeping into her once-hard bones and softening them until they bend like saplings. Her bouts of hacking coughs, the ones that bring up misty water and reeds are now more regular than the period of sun each day. I want to explain to her that it feels wrong to me to lie on the floor dry and feel only one drop of water on my arse – that when I am completely wet I feel alive, but to be dry feels prickly and strange on my bare skin. But I can hardly tell an old drooping lady that, not when the Wet is stealing life out of her every day.

So I keep my thoughts to myself, grab one of the semi-dried reeds from a basket by the cloths and reeds hanging from our doorframe, and use it to pick the gums between my big front teeth. Gammy moves quickly in our tiny space, finally lighting a fire under King Lizard's funeral pyre. The smoke and steam from the damp wood combine in tendrils together and escape through the jagged edges of our walls, hissing as they hit the Wet outside.

'I USED TO SWIM.'

This is a new one. I can always count on Gammy to start prattling away after dinner but I haven't heard this story before. She swats my bare backside when I say that to her face. I roll sideways away from her, laughing, but I do listen. Because Gammy is the only person who talks to me; the idiot villagers hear my bell and slosh away as fast as their stupid soft legs will take them, and there isn't anyone else around these parts. And because she remembers before the Wet. So, with the constant rush of water bouncing off the roof of our poor old collapsing hut, I sit – moisture slipping in through every crack and hole and up through the wooden floor itself – and I listen.

'You wouldn't believe it, but I used to swim. Don't grin at me, you cheeky bugger, I did! You wouldn't catch me out in that crap now, but once, nothing made me happier than going to the local pool. A pool . . . it's hard to explain. Like the River, but . . . contained, I suppose. A square. Restricted.'

She outlines the shape on our wall. The last of King Lizard's pyre flickers and hisses in the corner, casting her small figure against peeling wood. The only contents of the hut – the small pile of pots and tools, her stool, the blackened fire pit, dried reeds slung from the ceiling – cast a bigger shadow than Gammy. I notice that her ragged fingernails are caked with mud, despite her never venturing far outside.

'And the sun shone down on us and warmed our backs and we ruled the water. We would swim, dangle our legs, do somersaults . . .' she trails off with a stupid misty look in her eyes.

I laugh at the idea of soggy old Gammy doing somersaults anywhere. She's offended, and she deliberately raises a bloody knife, covered in King Lizard's gizzards, and wipes it on my discarded green rags, looking pointedly at me as she does. Never mind, stupid old lady, she knows it will wash off in seconds in the Wet tomorrow. All our rags smell dank and mouldy anyway, with frayed, ragged edges and a crisscross of stains despite their continuous washing and drubbing from the rain. I wonder what we will do when our robes finally dissolve and fall from our bodies. There's no more material for new clothes, and only a small stash of rusty needles and thread. I've been wearing my green cloak since I was a child, Gammy diligently sewing its snagged and rotting parts back together, muttering and swearing, bent and squinting in the dim light that comes through our door. When the thread started to run low, she tried to use slim lengths of the reeds I collected, before she gave up and began to knot parts of the material together, held together by the stiffness of age. Don't know why she bothers, why she panics about dressing the way they want us to.

One day the rags will strip away – my green, their black – and fall to the earth as filthy compost, and we will have to roam around naked and free. That's probably the day the villagers decide they are never leaving their huts again – rather hole up forever in their dank houses than have to look at me strutting around in the nude.

A little snort of laughter escapes my mouth. I flick the reed between my teeth and feign disinterest in Gammy's story, but when she doesn't continue straight away, I spin my head back in her direction, which of course she notices before I can turn away again.

'Yeah, I knew you wanted to hear more, kid. Laugh at old Gammy, why don't you? Well, old Gammy was the star of the pool. I could swim like a fish, like a tadpole.' She wallops my shoulder at my latest snort. 'They thought I was destined to be one of the best . . .' she trails off, gazing past my shoulder (which still bears the stinging red mark from her nasty whack) at the shimmering sheets of rain that can be glimpsed through the door of our shite excuse for shelter. I know what she is thinking – how could someone who used to be a fish be trapped inside this rickety square on wobbly stilts, terrified by the Wet and oozing mud and the raging River outside?

Like the end of her story, she slumps back onto the stool I made her from mouldy wooden logs, deflated and tired. I skulk over to her, the rotting timber boards creaking under my weight as I move, ashamed at laughing at a sad old lady. I lean down at her knees, naked and strong, and she gingerly rests her head on my shoulder as I gouge some fat from the Lizard King's corpse with fat fingers and start to gently rub it into her skinny legs.

Her skin is soft and almost translucent, with a bulging network of iridescent blue veins. The veins seem to pulse with the crashing sound of the Wet outside as it ricochets off hastily patched together rags and branches and wooden slats and any junk we could find floating down the River to make a roof to protect Gammy from the never-ending water from above. I try so hard to rub the fatty oil on gently, but even so, sheets of her skin peel off under my clumsy fingers.

'I'm disintegrating alive,' she chuckles sadly, not moving her head from my shoulder. 'Ashes to ashes they said. Didn't say nothing about my flesh melting off me. Water to water, more like.'

I think about that, as we lay side by side on the bare floor later, Gammy shivering in the damp, wracked with coughs, my bare body shielding her from drips and draughts as much as I can. Perhaps it is water to water, really. As much as she thought she was some glorious tadpole in that past life, the minute the Wet came, Gammy and all the bloody villagers fell to pieces. They cower in their little stilt huts, terrified they will be washed away; they slink through the sticky mud but then slop back to their shelters, and rely on me to collect reeds and snails and fish to eat. Even now, I can hear muffled coughs echoing through the Wet from across the clearing; like Gammy, the water is seeping into their bent bodies and gurgling and chortling through their lungs. They were never of the water before. They tried to control it like they tried to control everything else; tried to trap it. Stupid idiots. Now the Wet is in control of them; it is peeling off layers of them, drop by drop, until they don't exist anymore. Drop by drop. Drop by drop.

I'm not sad about the villagers – those stupid cowering black-cloaked fools who can't even stay upright in the mud slicks. But I am sad about Gammy. She might be fucking annoying but she does tell a good story, and when she hears my bell chiming through the woods, she peers out of our door across our clearing and through the walls of grey rain, and smiles.

3.

THERE: THE FLICKER OF LIGHT IN THEIR DOORWAY. SEE, they *are* looking at us, Gammy. They pull the curtains aside and watch us, just like we watch them.

'Don't stand in front of that door all naked and exposed,' she mumbles, but without much hope that I will listen. Behind me I can hear the messy splash of small pink fish being gutted for breakfast. Gammy is muttering with the effort it takes to move the jagged blade between their tiny bones with her crooked, sore fingers.

I continue peering out of our door cavity, craning my neck to see through the Wet across to their side of the clearing, to the smattering of half a dozen huts. A fine mist from outside coats my flat stomach, but I am still just outside the worst of the rain. The simple square shapes of the huts seem to distort and dance under the sheets of water. As the years have gone on, the structures have become more haphazard. The old sheets of metal that sometimes appeared floating down the River have stopped washing up on our shores, so the erosion holes in the hut roofs are now covered with a crisscross of hatched and mouldy branches. Our once large cloths, shielding doors as best they could, are now threadbare rags; the timber walls rotting and thin. Each hut has just one large crawl hole in and out. Ours is high and large, reaching halfway up the wall, so that Gammy and I can see out of it. We used to have windows, but they let in mad sprays of rain, so now we have just one opening, to stop us steaming alive inside with our fires. Nowhere dry enough but inside to light them, but the smoke, along with mould and damp, doesn't do Gammy's cough any favours.

The villagers have low crawl holes, and they slither awkwardly in and out when the rain stops for that brief time every morning, like little black slugs. Probably don't want to see what is outside, scared bastards, so they keep that hole to the outside world as small as possible.

Do you think they have stories about us, Gammy? Make up lives for us, like we for do them?

She doesn't want to talk about it. With a loud grunt she heaves herself off the floor with a pot full of red and silver fish guts, skewered with white bones, and shuffles to where I stand lazily leaning against the door frame.

Hang on a sec, Gammy! She was going to chuck the fish eye out the door into the swirling mud in front of our hut. I grab her arm where it is still raised to throw out the contents of the pot, and pluck the eye out of the soft mush. She curls her lips in disgust and I flash her a grin.

Best part, Gammy!

I pop the slimy eye in my mouth and keep it open for effect as I crunch down, Gammy grimacing as sour liquid pops between my sharp little teeth.

Fussy old bird you are, considering. I gulp noisily and turn back to the clearing with a chuckle.

The villagers' huts teeter a few feet out of the mud and pooling, dirty water below, but sway and move alarmingly as the earth circles and squelches at the feet of their rickety stilts. Gammy calls the wood in front of their houses decks – but it's just a pile of old logs wedged together above the mud, making a place that they can sit when the sun comes, sheltered by a flimsy roof. If I squint, I can snatch glimpses inside the huts through torn holes, gaping cracks and missing boards. I turn away quickly though; the villagers' huts are like bleak little eel holes I wouldn't want to get too close to, just in case something black and nasty darted out and bit my bloody hand off.

Don't you ever want to see inside, Gammy? See what those daft bastards do all day?

She has moved to the centre of our hut to prepare the fish with deliberate energy and has her back to me, so her voice is muffled. 'No. Couldn't care less if they were on fire in there. I don't think about them at all, and neither should you.'

But you do, Gammy. Their presence is constantly reflected in your eyes, like my image in the River. I don't think you forget them for a second.

The fish eye has left a sharp, unpleasant taste on my tongue so I reach forward out of the doorway and cup my hands under the Wet, pulling it to my mouth. The water is almost warm as it trickles down the inside of my throat.

4.

WHO KNOWS WHEN THE SUN REALLY COMES UP. ASIDE from that one pause in the Wet every day, the slightly lighter shades of grey wouldn't wake up a baby. But they always seem to wake Gammy. I reckon the old bird just doesn't sleep. Marinates in her juices overnight until she is ready to slosh into the next day. God knows why she wants to wake up; she just hangs out in our hut all day, picking her nose probably. Except for that period of sun that toys with us daily, when she sits outside our hut hopelessly trying to dry things out that just get wet again.

Everyone needs a way to pass the time, I suppose.

The largest tree near our clearing is scarred by etchings – a mark for each daily period of sun since the village was settled, started by someone before I was born but taken over by me when I realised no one in the village was keeping track anymore. I have to do bloody everything around here. Sometimes I try to count them, make the marks match the months and years Gammy talks about, but I can't wrap the numbers she taught me around the endless lines that cover every part of the tree's soft trunk.

I am out of the hut as soon as I know Gammy is ok for the day. The moment I bounce out through the mess of rags hanging from our doorframe, the wall of Wet embraces me like a thick grey hug. The pressure of water on my back sends faint and tickly shivers down my spine. I wriggle my broad shoulders in delight, a smile splitting my dried-out mouth in two. My lips are peeled and chafing from being inside with Gammy in that hot, smoky hole, and my smile quickly turns to an uncomfortable grimace.

In the far distance on the other side of our clearing, black-cloaked villagers scurry from their sheltered decking back into their shanty huts when they hear the tingle of my bell. Fucking fools. What do they think I am going to do to them? I couldn't be bothered wandering over there anyway.

Far enough away to keep them safe from me, close enough to keep an eye on me, Gammy says. Maybe if I were the superstar tadpole Gammy thought she had been, I would swim over to them through the mud and puddles and little creeks that have escaped from the River, and scare the crap out of them in their sleep. I chuckle inwardly: like they need another reason to be scared of me. Just the sound of my bell and the flash of my green cloak turns their pasty skin even whiter.

'People have feared difference since time began,' says Gammy, grandly. I get that. She tells me stories about times through our past when that seems to have been true. But I don't think that's why the villagers fear me. And there are others like me, I know that, if I believe everything Gammy says. 'One in every village,' she claims, dramatically. The old biddy doesn't get much cause for drama these days.

Maybe even more past the five villages, if you follow the raging waters of the River upstream. No villager has been able to travel even a day upstream since I was a baby. Between the Wet, and the banks of the River that can collapse at any moment, and the mud slicks, and no food, they can't get past the clearing surrounding our huts. Plenty of water for them, but! A villager wouldn't last an hour out there without me around to build the mud walls around their huts to keep the River out, hunt for their dinner, collect the wood for their bloody shelters. I snort loudly as I walk, nearing the boundary where our ragged clearing meets the River and the woods.

I watched them once, the villagers, while I was perched in the branches of a slippery old tree. They were trying to get out there and do it themselves, to hunt and gather and build. Maybe they thought they could get rid of me if they could handle it all without me; give themselves a break from peering over their shoulders, waiting for me to emerge from the Wet like a chiming green ghost. But two of them went down screaming, dragged by the mud slicks and sucked into the River before the rest of them even knew what had happened. That's why they keep me around, even if they shit themselves when they see me.

As I skip along the River's edge into thicker undergrowth, I watch the soft bank slop into the gurgling water's surface after my feet have sprung past, the clods of mud swallowed up whole. When I check to see if the white branch I used to mark the water level yesterday is still there, I find that the swirling surface has snatched it away, as it has every morning. Every day since I can remember heading out along the River without Gammy, the water has crept up the banks, little by little. The River, where she nuzzles our clearing, now reaches a hundred or more times my body length across her slimmest part. At some parts of the River, I have stood on her banks and needed to squint to make out the other side. The trees bow lower and lower each morning under the weight of the endless rain, almost as if to greet the rising River, so that it feels like the space we live in is being compressed sideways. Flattened. Crushed under heavy grey clouds and the moisture hanging around our ears. Even I can barely tell where the River ends and the Wet begins anymore.

I glance over my shoulder, droplets spraying off my eyelashes and rolling down my neck, my green cloak already dragging and scratching between my thighs with the added water weight. How many days until we have to move the shelters further back this time? The last time we only just got them back after the River came up in leaps and bounds instead of her usual creep the villagers wearily working side by side with me – never touching me – for days until we had all of the shelters back – even if they were a bit smaller and shitter than before. Closest the villagers have ever been to me. Impending disaster makes friends of us all. Until it doesn't.

It looks like we might have to be unwilling friends again soon; the River is lapping past the previous boundaries of our clearing, laughing in her gurgling way at the villagers' efforts to survive, like the River always does. She's a bitch, Old River. Lets everyone relax for a month, a year, a week, then a surge of powerful water comes from upstream and just like that it's off with your hut, your food, your neighbour.

It's odd, though, isn't it Gammy, that they insist on rebuilding their huts within reach of old River despite her insatiable appetite? It's like they need her presence even though they fear it; need the way she claims the land and outlines her territory so they can understand theirs. Perhaps they believe they will control her again one day and when that happens, the chaos will end and they will go back to how it was before, back when the pesky Wet and the River knew their place, and the villagers were in charge. Or maybe they know there is no escaping the River, not anymore: the Wet is turning every inch of land into a little river – if they run from this one, they might run into her other thunderous friends who could turn out to be worse.

Who cares, though? If it wasn't for Gammy I reckon I would keep walking right now, reed basket slung over my shoulder; shake off my rusting bell and disappear into the Wet forever and leave them to fend off the mocking River themselves.

I sigh, my breath hissing into the warm wet air: I won't leave Gammy, and I think the Wet knows it. I couldn't bear for her to slide into the River with those arseholes. The ones who leave her in that dank hut to fend for herself while they huddle together on the other side of the clearing, whispering nonsense to each other through the crashing waves of the Wet.

'They'll never hurt you, you know. They are too busy just keeping their heads above water to bother about you.' And then she doubles over laughing at her unintentional joke. Thinks she's a fucking comedian, Gammy does.

But I've never been worried about the villagers anyway. I see Gammy sometimes peering distrustfully at their semi-circle of huts through the hole of our door, like she is waiting for something to happen. I notice the urgency with which she mends my cloak, the fear in her eyes when I laugh at them. Not me. Even when I was a little tacker, I could run rings around those idiots, darting through the Wet around their huts with my little bell rattling so much that it would slip off my ankle, and every night Gammy would sew it back on with what was left of her sewing kit. Little rusty needles she keeps tucked in the roof wrapped in stiff cloth, far away from the water but still corroding from the very air itself. Ever since I can remember I could run the length of the River around our village, my feet – scaly and hard where the villager's feet are soft – dancing on the surface of the mud slicks instead of being sucked down. My little body slicing through the Wet, untouched except for my ragged green cloak and my reed basket, raindrops rolling off me like a duck, leaving my oily arms and shoulders dry and soft. Where the villagers sank, beaten down like the poor reeds clinging to the banks, I flitted around both the River and the Wet like a manic little frog.

I used to shit outside their huts at night, so that when they got up and dragged their damp old bodies through the sliding mud and puddles at their front door, they would be wading through my little gift. They never noticed, but kept struggling through the mud, clearing it back from their houses every day in a never-ending battle with the Wet. It made me laugh though, thinking about them wading through my shit. Lord knows I need better comedy than Gammy around this place.

5.

A HOP, SKIP AND A JUMP, AS GAMMY SAYS, AND I AM DEEP
into the woods. Away from the jagged clearing that is home to
our sinking, sliding village, a solid wall of Wet between me and
them. The creeping sensation on the back of my neck that I
feel around the villagers flows out of me down through my toes
and into the puddling pools of water on the ground beneath
my feet: a release, like pissing when you really need it. It feels
good to turn my face up to the beating rain and let the droplets
make tracks against my eyes and nose and into my open mouth,
which swallows the cool moisture greedily. I slick my short hair
back from my forehead and down the nape of my bare neck, and
stand there for a few minutes, letting the sound of the crashing
torrents fill my ears with a peaceful drumming and humming of
water. No Gammy, no slinking villagers, just me and the Wet.

It doesn't take me long to fill the reed basket with curling
green and brown fronds. It never does. If the villagers could
keep their eyes clear in the Wet they could do this in minutes; every section of the bank is chock full of the thick plants,

dancing in constant motion from the wild waters raging past. Instead, the villagers choke and splutter as the Wet fills their mouths and smothers their ears and eyes, and they can't tell a reed from their own noses.

I sweep my green cloak underneath my legs and tug at the long cool leaves, leaning carefully over the River's edge, the roots sliding out of the soft wet earth like they had never been attached to start with. I gingerly pick my way across the haphazard walls of mud and broken weeds that separate the River from the rest of us: I might be a match for its raging torrents, but this is the only reed basket I have left, and I am not game to test Gammy's patience by asking her to make a new one.

I inhale the earthy, damp smell of the bank this close to the water. Gammy's hut smells of smoke and melted fat, and a little bit musty. The villagers' side of the clearing just smells like shit and decaying flesh. But over here, where the wet mud hits the River, it smells clean and tangy. It smells like old leaves and new leaves and moving waters and frogs, all at once. I grin slightly – bloody poet and I didn't know it, as Gammy would say.

I throw my basket in a corner against a moss-covered trunk and step back as far as I can from the River's edge. It's hard to make it more than a few feet; here the weeds and long grass reach up past my chest. I like the way they fight upwards despite being battered by the Wet from above, crawling toward the grey clouds even as the rain forces its way downward. But sometimes I worry that if I stand too still, the weeds and curling fronds will start to wrap their stringy fingers around my ankles like they do at the feet of our huts, and curl their way up my long legs to my stomach, covering me in slimy green like the old tree trunks. I imagine them pulling me slowly into the mud, sucking and slurping as I inch further and further under the black muck. Trapping me in this place with this lot forever.

An icy shiver runs down my spine and I shake it off. Only one thing rids me of these thoughts. So I take a deep breath and then a running leap into the River's breadth. I can almost hear the world sigh as the cool waters envelope my body, pressing all the fears and discomfort away. That is how I will spend the rest of the day. Ducking and diving with the water rushing above and below.

6.

GAMMY IS SMILING SOFTLY, HER FACE BLURRED BY THE
steam rising from our damp fire. The smell only just masks the
reek of old fish and mould in the hut. Gammy needs to clean this
place out. Burn it down, actually.

'You were a funny duffer, kid.' She leans back on her little
stool, memories misting her eyes. Here we go. Another trip down
memory lane, hey Gammy?

'Shut up. Always a bloody comedian.' But she is grinning
still, showing the remaining teeth in her gummy mouth. 'When
you were a little tacker, I used to wrap blankets around you –
back when we had them – then roll over in the night to find you
spreadeagled, blankets flung to the corner of the hut. It was like
you were defiant in the face of the Wet even then.'

I just didn't feel it like you do, Gammy. And it's not like we
could find anything like a blanket these days.

She cocks her head sideways, little strands of remaining
grey and white hair plastered greasily to her head. 'I dunno – we
could always skin you. Make a nice little leather throw.'

Yeah, really, Gammy. Who would look after you lot if I was just a blanket? You'd all starve in a day. Or the villagers would come after you for ruining their plans.

'Hmmm, you're probably right there, kid.' She peers at me across the hut, only a body length between us. My green rags are in the corner again, stiffening, ready for tomorrow when I toss them back on, scratchy and stinky and annoying as all hell. Gammy leaves her rags on all the time. Probably stuck to her body permanently by now. Grown all over her little frame like the mould on our walls.

I crane my neck to peer under my arms at the matted brown hair that has appeared there recently. Gammy was so worried when she first saw it I thought I had some strange disease. When she explained it to me, talked about the changes to my body, her concern quickly turned to amusement and we laughed and laughed at how pointless it all was. No one needs these changes in this world. Why would they? We don't need babies. Everyone has enough to worry about without bringing screaming kids into this dank place. I chuckle to myself thinking about the villagers trying to tend to a crying baby in between their periods of shaking, rocking, moaning, and generally being useless twits.

I still catch Gammy staring at me sometimes with a worried look on her face, though. Examining my bare, hard body with her craggy mouth drawn into a thin line, like she doesn't quite trust me anymore. Doesn't quite know me. Which I think is unfair. My body means nothing to me except for how it propels me across the mud slicks and through the water, how it lets me jump and climb and duck and weave through the woods. The changes just make my body taller and stronger, better able to help her and the villagers, but still I see her from the corner of my eye peering at me warily. Silly old lady.

She grins again, lost in her own thoughts as well. 'Before you could walk, you'd scramble and scuttle through the mud like a crab, on your hands and feet, little bum wagging in the air. It was such a sight.'

I giggle at the thought: little me on all fours, bum up, skating across the moving surface of the earth.

Then she sighs, the smile wiped from her face, and glares at me with that nasty glint in her eyes. The changes in her mood flash across her in an instant these days. 'Now look at you. Big stinky teenager, never grateful to Gammy, never listening to Gammy.' I notice that her neck, jutting from her cloak, is red and raw and flaking.

I'd listen if you had anything important to say, Gammy.

She huffs, crosses her arms grumpily, scowls at me as the fire flickers. The rain – or is it the River? – thunders loudly outside our walls. I stare back at her stonily, naked and lounging in the opposite corner of the hut. We stay that way for ages, neither willing to drop our eyes. A gust of wind blows our door rags to the side and a blast of cold rain sprays across the room. Gammy has to shuffle her stool sideways to avoid it, and does so crankily, staring at me the whole time. Suddenly, a snort of a chuckle escapes me before I can put my hands to my mouth.

Gammy's craggy face splits into a smile, and she drops her arms from her chest. 'Honestly. How did I end up at the end of the world with you, kid?'

You love it, Gammy. I lean back into the damp wall, smiling slyly at her through the shadows. The Wet is thrumming outside, pounding on our roof and down the outside walls. Over the years we've added long reeds, bark – anything we can find – to the door opening to keep the Wet out. Gammy used to complain about the lack of glass, but as the years went on, she reckons that's how the world looks to her anyway – like she is looking at everything through fogged-up glass, which makes no sense to me. I've offered to board some of the doorframe up with hunks of wood – use some of the green-spotted metal tools still lying in the corner of the hut – but Gammy thinks she'll be smoked alive like a cooked snail. Instead, I weigh down the bottoms of whatever we can string up there with round pebbles from the River floor, to try and keep some of the rain from splattering the inside.

'Did I ever tell you about the circus, kid?'

Warmth radiates from my chest through my whole body. I cross my bare legs and settle in. Sure you did Gammy, but you can tell me again.

7.

WHAT DO I DO ALL DAY, GAMMY? THAT'S A BIT RICH coming from you. You and the villagers, you spend your time huddled in your dank huts, staring at the flaky walls until your little window of sunlight comes out to torment you for the day. Put your damp wet cloths and reeds out for a while, let the steam rise into the golden air, and then scamper back inside when the grey fog returns. Wait for me, to bring your lordships your meals. What a day.

My days, Gammy, usually pass with the rush and rhythm of the water. Sometimes, I leave my reed basket wedged under a rock and I run, run from the lot of you. The water in the air parts like the waves in the story you told me about Gammy, the one where the man parts the waves to let all the people through. Except I part the water to leave you all behind. The centre of the wave is where I live: you are the ones cowering in the gap between its crests.

I duck and weave under low-flung branches, which look like hands reaching out to snare my green cloak, but the grasping bastards never catch me. Sometimes, a canopy collapses under the weight of water, an extra load of liquid crashing to the ground to my left or right, but never crashing onto my head. Not me. I am too quick for that. So quick you couldn't even see me – a flash of green through bent black trees.

I never run as far as the other villages downstream. I see enough sad cases here, why would I look for more? So instead I run upstream along the River, and the River runs alongside me, and, I swear to god, Gammy, the River roars at me to keep going, gurgles and laughs at me, cheers me on. I outrun my itchy cloak and stupid bloody bell and we run that way all day, and then I collapse in the mud and let the Wet dribble down my face and drag my cloak down once again.

Some days I join that cheeky, fickle River and we float. Sometimes, if she is being an arsehole, she tries to slam me into a mossy brown rock hidden below her waist, but she almost never manages to get me Gammy, not me. I can change direction in the water quicker than a little silver-tailed fish.

The days are busy Gammy. I talk to my old mate Mr Cod. I chase darting fish around rocks. I watch the rain dimple the surface of the earth because every surface is moveable now, everything can be dented. I search for your bloody dinner, and the soft, bendy wood you burn in your steamy old fire. I watch the villagers, and I watch giant trees slip out of the earth like they were never rooted in the first place, and show their undercarriages to the Wet. I pick molluscs off their perches, search under rocks for crabs cowering from the rain, scrape the lichen off the trees, pluck the reeds from the moist riverbank.

I walk through the walls of water and it slides off my shoulders like it never touched me to start with.

When you look at me like that Gammy, that half-squinting, confused look, cocking your head to the side and staring right in my face when I am telling you these things, I don't know if you don't understand what I am saying, or if you just don't like what you hear.

8.

I'M IRRITATED AS I WANDER ABOUT TODAY, MORE THAN I
have been in months. Maybe it's because I know we will have
to move the village back soon. My flesh crawls thinking about
being near the decaying old bodies of the villagers again, and
looking into their empty, red-rimmed eyes.

Maybe it's just because I am sick of the lot of them, Gammy
included.

My cloak snags on a jutting log and I swear loudly and
repeatedly, just to hear the noise. I yank on the caught fabric and it falls apart, flakes of tattered material pounded by
the rain into the swirling mud below. Gammy will be pissed,
no doubt. There aren't any new rags where those ones came
from. Would you even say they are green anymore, Gammy?
I know you and the villagers like to have your colours, your
rules, but these knotted and gnarled pieces of fabric clinging
to my body look almost as grey as the ones the villagers strap
around them in great scratchy swathes. Who can tell the difference these days?

I walk for a bit down the length of the River, parting the sheets of rain with my shoulders, practicing my whistles as I dodge collapsing clumps of riverbank. Once, long ago, I heard a bird whistle. Gammy reckons I must have heard it in my sleep, because except for the occasional duck or waterfowl, there haven't been birds since the Wet started. Squawky critters drowned in the very air that they flew in; they plunged out of the sky and fell to the earth like thousands of coloured drops of rain. But I do remember the bird whistle, whatever she says. The sound was low and long, and ever since I started fetching food by myself, I have been pushing my lips together, trying to get my mouth to make that very same noise. Low and long, long and low. I kick clods of mud from the bank into the rumbling waters of the River and head upstream, contorting my mouth and hissing through my teeth, making all the noises I know how. Up and up, following the waters as they wind upwards like an angry path, I pick my way through overturned tree trucks half covered in mud slicks. Long and low, low and long, like my walks, flitting alongside the River, bent over to dodge the drooping, dripping vines that slap against my face.

My sweet bird call doesn't get even an inch from my mouth until it is muffled by the Wet, so I soon turn my attention to kicking some old rotting logs into the raging waters instead; watch them smash against protruding green rocks as they slip and slide down the River. I wonder how long it will take until every tree in this place has been swallowed by the River, ripped from the ground and sent hurtling down the valley. The etches on my tree tell me we have moved the village three times this year alone to avoid the expanding waistline of that old Lady

35

River. Greedy bastard. Not satisfied with eating the birds and the lizards and half the villagers, she's coming for the trees too, clearing more room for the Wet to hang in the sky, unbothered.

I've only taken a few steps past the logs when I fling a particularly fat vine out of my face, and curse as I lose my footing in a mud slick and land heavily on my arse with a *thwack*. Then, before I have time to yell out or raise an arm, I am propelled toward the collapsing edge of the muddy banks. Shit.

It breaks my heart the things you won't see or hear, Gammy once said, wallowing as usual. I don't know why I think about it in this instant. Her words just rise up unbidden inside my head. She was probably squinting down at the old rags she threads her rusty needles through and muttering about the state of the earth and 'what we should have known and done' and so on. Moping about the past.

I dunno, Gammy, sliding here, arse up, with waves of mud pushing me toward the rapidly approaching River, twigs and water spraying everywhere and my hands grabbing wildly at passing rocks and branches, I reckon I have bigger fish to fry.

I skid to the bank and for a moment I am actually airborne, like those fucking birds I was getting so soppy about, and then I plunge, legs straight and tense, into the swirling brown waters of the River.

I hit the solid wall of water with a thud of pain. My basket. I need to get my bloody basket.

I'm disoriented for a moment as I plunge below the surface, murky water swirling around me, the thick opaqueness of it masking direction so that for a brief time, I hang suspended in between the walls of churning grey with no sense of up or down.

I relax and let the water flow around my body; the streams are icy this far below the surface, rushing down the sides of my face in a burst of bubbles. My eyes adjust to the dense darkness and as soon as I can make out the rocky riverbed and silvery swirls above, I kick out my legs, long and low, long and low, green cloak billowing around my thighs, and make my way upstream along the River's silent brown floor. As annoyed as I am about my basket and my uneasy surprise at being up-ended so easily and thoroughly, the water feels good on my skin and I feel strong, so strong, as my wide feet push me further and further through the dark depths.

It's impossible to know how far downstream I was swept. As I swim back up the River, I almost miss a precious cluster of shells huddling on a large grey rock, half obscured by brown reeds, so I stop, still kicking my legs to fight against the strong currents. I smack my lips together under the water: the perfect sweet flavour to accompany leftover King Lizard tonight. I wedge my foot under an old tree root, long submerged by the ever-encroaching waters, and use part of a broken-off branch to jimmy a couple of shells from their perch, the underwater currents still buffeting my cloak as I work. Little bubbles float past my nose and I squint through them. Like a bloody fool, I realise I don't have any way of carrying the shells and their fleshy inhabitants to the surface, so I cram as many as I can in my mouth, looking for all the world with my bulging cheeks like one of the codfish that hang out in the darkest corners down here.

I dislodge my foot from under the branch and then arc upwards through the water, mouth full, and bob up like one of my pissing leaves above the stormy surface. I inhale deeply through the shells rammed in my mouth, the first air in my lungs since I was so rudely dumped into the River, and peer through the grey Wet at eye level, to get my bearings.

It takes all my strength to stroke across the choppy waters to the edge of the River and the only firm-looking trunk wedged along the eroding and wetly crumbling bank. I fling myself up and over the River's edge, every vine I grasp out for too loose and slick with rain to leverage me up and out, until I finally hook my hand through a firm branch and hoist myself clear of the waters. I sit there for a bit, the stream of Wet on my back replacing the churning depths I have just come from, and I pull out the shells from my mouth, one by one, and rest them beside the edge of my mud-splattered robes. Now warm water dribbles from my nose and mouth and neck and joins the damp that is puddling at my thighs.

It breaks my heart the things you won't see or hear. But Gammy, I can come face to face with the wise old codfish that lurks below the raging surface, and hear a silence down below that you could never dream of. Don't worry about me, Gammy. You lot have enough to worry about yourselves.

It takes me half the goddamn morning to trace my steps and finally find my reed basket, thankfully still clear of the River but precariously flung across a miserable-looking shrub clinging desperately to a larger, moss-covered tree. I scrape some moss off with my long fingernails, thankful they haven't gone soft and peeled like Gammy's, and chuck the pale green carpet, along with my few rescued shells, in with the reeds. Fossicking closely around the trunk of the tree between the short ferns, I manage to find some large, juicy green snails to add to tonight's feast. The dozen or so beige fish I unceremoniously dumped in the middle of the clearing for the villagers two days ago should still see them through for another night. It's funny that while the rest of our world rots, the food stays safe for days. Something about the lack of sun and the moisture in the air, I think.

I am still making my way back to the village, arse and pride smarting a little from my trip, when the pale yellow sun slips out from behind the pillowy dark clouds and the Wet stops abruptly, as it always does at this time.

I can see steam rising off my weighted green cloak as the warm rays hit sodden fabric; I fancy it is probably rising off my short, wet hair too, and this idea makes me chuckle. Walking around like a steam monster.

When the Wet disappears quickly like this, the slimy lichen covering every surface not slick with mud becomes jarringly green, and my little bell, normally muffled by liquid, peals out loudly through bent and broken trees. Odd that the rushing of the Wet is never properly replaced by noise at this time: no scratching of other animals, no birdsong, no villagers, just me and my bell and the crashing of the River in the distance. Sometimes, the wind circling the canopies above imitates the roar of the Wet; quieter and gentler though, rising and falling, where the drumming of the Wet is constant and loud.

I spread the contents of my basket across a deep brown-coloured rock in a small clearing free of the shade of a canopy, to dry out as best they can: brown and black reeds (almost blue in the harsh sunlight), shells stuffed with briny plump meat, snails attempting their futile escape down the brackish rock side. My stomach grumbles loudly just at the sight of them as

I pick them up one by one and place them back in my basket. Cheeky little critters.

If a tree falls in a wood and there is no one there to hear it, does it make a noise? Piss off with your riddles, Gammy, no one here is interested. And of course it does. Because I am always out here listening. Even through the crashing of Lady River's torrents, I can hear the dull crack when yet another tree succumbs to the weight of the water and leans down to lie among the mud slicks. All the trees are falling, Gammy, one by one.

It amazes me how quickly the sun can suck the wetness out of the various finds I have scattered on my now warm rock. It makes me wonder about the earth before, when there was no Wet, and the River dried up, and the sun scorched everything in sight, or so Gammy tells me. 'We thought we would be burnt right off the surface of the earth,' she says quietly. She never jokes about that, the time just before the Wet. Normally she'll have a chuckle about anything, but that time makes her face soften, almost collapse like those sad old trees, and she can go quiet for the rest of the evening. Which shits me a bit; it's the only time of the day either of us talks to anyone and the sad old lady gets bummed out and just sits there in silence. Fucking boring, Gammy.

I wonder what the people from before the Wet would think now, not a dry spot in sight in the whole bloody place. When Gammy talks of a parched land, yellow and brown and scratchy, I can barely imagine it. She tells me about storms of dust and the way the heat stole the very breath from your lungs. I try to imagine breathing with no moisture in the air, but I can't. There isn't an inch of earth that isn't wet right now. Even a rock nestled deep in among the roots of a tree is pricked with condensation. Every hard surface is soft from Wet and can be scraped away.

Nothing is sharp but my jagged little teeth and my knife. And sometimes Gammy's voice when she is telling me off.

I close my eyes and try to picture open plains stripped of moisture: searing, hazy heat and burnt trees. Gammy talks about red-blistered skin and a dry that crushed their chests and fried their feet and blackened every plant and tree. An all-encompassing heat that sizzled up every drop of water, sucked up the rivers and lakes, parched the colours out of the soil. She says they thought that was what was going to get them – the angry red heat.

But all I can feel now, in this clearing, is the lukewarm rays of the sun, and all I can hear is the sound of squelching mud moving slowly under my damp feet, and when I open my eyes the world is deep green and grey and brown and slick with moisture. Dryness is a sensation I cannot even pretend to understand, not like Gammy does. I wonder if she can still feel that fierce heat now, or if the memory of the Wet arriving and never leaving has washed that feeling away.

I strip off my cloak and chuck it roughly to the muddy ground, scratching absent-mindedly at the red chafe-marks the harsh fibres have left at my crotch. It stings a little as I walk around and I curse the need for these awful rags. I should just crack the shits and refuse to wear them anymore. Who says I have to anyway? Bloody Gammy? The villagers who do nothing but squawk and run when they see me? Somewhere in my memory I know it once was the villagers, but do we see them striding over to our hut to lay down the rules these days, Gammy? I didn't think so.

The sun prickles my back; different from the heavy weight of the Wet, and not a sensation I like. It makes me feel itchy and irritated and raw. It tightens my skin and stabs at my scalp. I roll my broad shoulders back and puff out my chest a little as I saunter around my little clearing, bell chiming, poking through the debris and rotting piles of branches and moss with my feet, inspecting things I normally can't see through the heavy cloak of water. Here is an interesting flash of blue rock that is normally obscured by the grey; here is peeling bark, papery thin, the rough edges usually masked by trickling streams of water. The glare from the sun on puddles hurts my eyes and I have to shield my face to look properly. I peek in every corner of the clearing, lift every rock looking for something interesting. Occasionally I have to run back to my basket and chase my escapee snails. If I crush them now they will go bad before I get them into Gammy's pot of boiling water, so I have to constantly circle back to catch them gently sloping away from my basket, trail of slime behind them, and place them back into the centre.

A large water spider scuttles across the surface of a puddle pooling on the clearing floor. Quick as a flash, I snatch out and grab him, stuffing his flavourless little body in my mouth and munching as I continue to wander and inspect all the rocks around me.

I don't have my leaves to piss on because I am too far from the River, so I relieve myself on a gnarled old tree, my whistle travelling long and low in the now hushed wood. While the steaming yellow spray showers the trunk, I notice that what looks like an uninterrupted carpet of lichen in the Wet is actually tiny little bumps of moss in patches. I lean over, getting my nose really close to those tiny green bumps, and breathe in their damp, mildewy scent. I realise that I don't want to imagine a world without the Wet, not really.

The sudden cracking noise makes me jerk my head up, bare back instantly stiff in the sunlight, as I try to see where it has come from. I can't work out how sound travels without the usual web of mist and rain and so I spin round and round again in a frenzy, looking for the source of the noise, heart hammering. It could be a creature – dinner, maybe – but I haven't seen a big animal for years now. The heat of the sun and the pricking on my neck makes moisture appear in beads on my temples as I scan through tangled masses of vines and trees collapsed over logs, wondering what on earth is going to come at me through the streaming rays of light.

Hisssss. Just like that, the sun slips behind its thick cover and with a rush, my old friend the Wet pours down and fills the air with familiar grey. The angry and heavy sky, so dark it is almost a filthy brown, lowers so that it feels like it rests just above my head; I imagine if I reached up high enough, my hand would fold and disappear into the dense clouds.

As I move slowly back to my wet green cloak and pull it roughly over my head, I know I am alone again.

9.

THE MOON IS A SHIFTY BASTARD. CAN'T TRUST HER FOR a second, flitting about behind thick midnight clouds. The sun, he is easy. He might hide behind the Wet most of the day, but in that time he pops out every morning, he is clear and bright and simple. No tricks, no hiding, just plain old whatcha-looking-at round yellow-and-orange ball of warm light. The moon, you can never quite make out her shape. At night, the Wet is a deluge, thick and black and unforgiving. It even smells deeper than the sharp tang of the daytime rain. The sky hangs heavy and dark above the gnarled trees and you might see a shimmer of moon's silver light, you might not. Her roundness bends and moves behind opaque clouds. She hides her face, hides all her secrets.

'Can you believe we used to garden by the moon?'

I look up from the stick I am whittling in surprise. Gammy has a stupid little smile on her soft face and is staring through a crack in our door rags at faint shards of white light dancing down in the clearing. That's how she tricks you, that moon – when she does actually front up, she makes the Wet reflect her light and the whole world shimmer silver. You can enjoy it for a moment before she skims away again, leaving nothing but pools and puddles and shadows of murky blue.

Gammy turns back to me where I am squatting in the centre of the hut floor, a daft expression in her eyes. Moonstruck, hey Gammy? She'll do that to you.

'I don't even think I remember why,' she says, confused, shaking her head out of the trance. I chew my lip in concentration, trying to turn my wobbly stick into a small human figure. The head is a long oval and I can't for the life of me make it look right, but keep carving it down smaller and smaller in my attempts. Would probably help if you quit nattering, Gammy, I can't concentrate.

She sticks out her tiny tongue. 'Shhh, you.' I can tell this conversation isn't going to end soon so with a loud sigh I put the stick on the damp floor, move from my haunches to my arse, and settle in for the night. We don't have long until our smoking fire flickers and sputters out. I look to Gammy expectantly. The Wet outside is so heavy that it reverberates like a loud hum rather than single drops. Wearing down our ramshackle roof.

'There was something about gardening and planting by the moon, though. Sowing your own seeds, growing your own food, tracking the moon's phases, squatting with dirt between your toes. You felt like part of nature, *really* part of the earth.' She is always moving a little, my Gammy, even when she is sitting still. She constantly shifts in her seat to run from her pained joints and raw skin, to keep something moving in her stale old veins. She's like a messed up reflection of the Wet outside – it constantly moves too but in a whirling, swirling dance. Gammy's movements are nervous and jerky and sore, punctuated by grimaces and gasps.

Do you really reckon you were part of the earth, Gammy? If you knew what you were doing, you could have just wandered into the forest and found your food right there. Enough reeds and snails and seeds and ducks and berries and moss to feed a hundred villages. More fish and crabs and molluscs and eels than you could eat in a lifetime.

She chuckles sadly, wiping a wrinkled hand across her craggy face. 'Well, we didn't have forests like this, my dear, we had shops. Wild food was a little harder to come by, back then, and we didn't really know where to look.'

She has explained shops to me before. They sound ridiculous. I pick my whittling up again, bored by her story, and start to scrape the length of the stick with little strokes. The fading firelight forces me to squint a little harder. Lady Moon hasn't graced us with her presence again, so the black outside is quickly stealing through the hut. Through the din of the rain pelting down, I think I can hear the usual keening moans and startled coughs from across the clearing. I furrow my eyebrows and concentrate on my stick, blocking out all the sounds but the scrape of my knife and Gammy's muttering. No wonder they can't make a go of it out here – can't find food, can't hunt, plant bloody seeds in silly little rows. No wonder they spend their nights rocking and crying and coughing the Wet out of their weak old lungs. Perhaps you all should have thought of this earlier, Gammy. If you had the forests and the rivers and knew how to find food in them, you'd be bloody laughing right about now.

Gammy shoots me a withering look. 'Thanks for the enlightenment, kid. You think I had to wait to be told this by a brat at the end of the bloody world?'

No need to be fucking snooty, Gammy, geez. I roll my eyes and turn slightly from her corner of the hut, and at the same time, the last of our fire flutters and snuffs itself out. The rain sounds even louder in the black of our room. As my eyes adjust, I see Gammy is grinning shrewdly at me from her chair.

At that moment, a rolling cloud must have parted because the moon's rays break through the corner of our door and play across the floor of the hut in a flurry of silvery spots. Gammy and I both gasp with delight and leap to the door cavity at the same time to yank aside the threadbare cloths. The clearing is a sea of silver needles, every drop of water lit from above. Even the tops of the trees glisten in her light, above shadowy trunks. Gammy sighs and leans gently into my body, propping herself up against my chest. I give the sparse, knotted hair on her crown a swift kiss, then turn back to gaze at the clearing. Across the way, not a single head pops out. The villagers don't care what happens beyond their walls. Your loss, little villagers. This is bloody beautiful.

'You know we sent people to the moon?' I don't believe it, Gammy. Seems as idiotic as squatting in a garden. She giggles at that, looks up at me earnestly. 'Gammy isn't kidding, kid. We really did. We used to be able to go anywhere in the universe. Moon, Mars, Paris. It was there for the taking. I used to crave it. Used to crave sights and sounds and the way new places smelled. Used to feel uneasiness in my blood when I had been in my own space for too long. Some people felt such nostalgia, such peace in the familiar, but it used to rankle me something chronic. All I ever wanted was to get away from the day-to-day and soak up new things. Then in a matter of weeks – bang,' she raps her hand on the door pane so loudly I jump despite myself. 'Just like that, chunks of the world became out of reach. Within days, I thought I would never travel again. Like that was the worst problem I would have. Then in quick succession the world closed up more – bang, bang, bang,' rain splutters in through the open cavity as she knocks the wood. 'And the world got smaller and smaller each time. Bang. Until it was just this country, then this region, then soon enough, my world was only as large as I could see.' She is wobbling a little on her feet now, resting all her slight weight against me.

C'mon, Gammy, let's go to bed. The looming shadow of a cloud rolls past the moon and we are plunged into darkness again. The Wet hangs so dense I can barely make out the trees across the clearing.

'I never could have imagined the smallness of the world I would end up in,' she mutters sadly as we drop the curtain and move away from the door. I grab my green rags from where they were discarded when I first arrived at the hut, and attempt to mop up the water we let in as we gazed like idiots at the moon.

Do you reckon it's small, Gammy? Because there is a feeling in the Wet and the River. Don't you feel it too? The water swells and rumbles with something bigger than just this clearing, this valley, this village. I even think sometimes I can feel it swirling in my belly, telling me something older and larger than any of us could imagine. This place is bigger than you think, Gammy. It stretches far beyond us idiots.

She answers with a snore that quickly turns into a hacking cough. Without bothering to say goodnight, the old biddy has plonked herself down in the centre of the hut to sleep. I swear that she is lying on my little whittled figure and hasn't even felt its woody spike in her bony buttocks. I prod her over slightly with my scaled toe and yank out the little model, fashioned from the whitest wood I could find. My eyes haven't yet adjusted to the darkness, but I sniff in approval at my handiwork. It looks just like a real skeleton, I reckon.

I prop the bony figure up against the wall, avoiding the steady streams of water running down the inside of the hut despite my patch jobs.

Goodnight, Gammy, you daft old moonlight gardener. I laugh quietly as I lower myself to lie by her side.

10.

C'MON, GAMMY.

Her face darts up like a little tadpole at our door then disappears again into the dark of our hut.

Come outside!

Her voice is muffled. 'I'm not coming out there and you bloody well know it. Rack off.'

I chuckle and make my way to the outside of the door, the skin on my legs stretchy and tight in the sunlight. Come outside the hut, Gammy. Come into the sunshine. How often do I hang around the village when the sun comes out? Come outside, just for me. What if today is the day I leave and never come back? Get swallowed by Lady River? Then you'll be sorry. *Come. Outside.*

She is standing in our doorway now, rags pulled to the side, a bent shadow squinting into the glaring light. 'You're a little shit. Piss off and get our food.'

But she slowly moves into the light, out of the doorway. I knew she would. Her watery eyes blink rapidly as they adjust to the golden rays streaming about the clearing. I have shoved five wooden sticks into the thick mud just in front of our hut and motion to her to jump down and join me next to them. She tuts grumpily, but starts her long, clumsy descent from our deck down to the puddles below. She finally lands with a *plop!*, black muddy water streaking up her pale legs where they jut out from her robe. As soon as she has righted herself, she smooths her cloak and peers anxiously across the clearing at the other huts.

Don't worry about them, Gammy, they scampered inside as soon as they saw me playing out here.

Usually, the villagers mill about through the clearing during this time of sunshine, trying to dry out their clothes and their sweaty old crotches. It's almost the only time they emerge from their little four-walled homes throughout the entire day. Sometimes they brave their rickety decks in the Wet, but as the rain has increased and materials to patch up the holes in their shelter have decreased, they don't even hang out much there anymore. My presence in the clearing during the day would have knocked them senseless. I can almost feel the resentment drifting out of their low doors and across the blue pools of muddy water to where I stand, flexing my muscles in the warmth.

I reach out a hand and pass Gammy the circular hoop we made from thin, bendy vines before they dried. C'mon, Gammy. She is still staring nervously across the clearing. Don't wait for permission from those idiots. I give her a gentle nudge with my shoulder, which almost sends her flying and makes her drop the hoop into a mud slick circling the stilts of our hut. She scowls as it slowly floats away from us, carried by a meandering current of mulch and mud and water. I laugh out loud this time and bound off after the disappearing hoop, skimming the top of the slicks with my scaled feet and catching hold of the hoop just before it is flung into the angry River. When I turn back toward our hut, Gammy is standing as tall as she can on the slippery mud, arms crossed across her chest, her saggy face creased into a frown. Saggy face like her saggy boobs. Geez, Gammy, you sure make it hard to have a good time.

When I am back by her side I hand the now mud-spattered hoop back to her with an encouraging smile and nod toward the five staked pieces of wood, still upright despite low waves of mulch rolling around them. *C'mon, Gammy.* The Wet will be back soon and I want to play with you.

'For god's sake . . .' she sighs, but throws a hoop through the air all the same. It's a terrible shot, wobbling through the clear air and landing a body length from the first stake. I hand her another hoop with a grin and this time I notice a spark in her pink-tinged eyes when she takes it. There we go, Gammy. That's what I like to see. I smile widely as she prepares her creaky little body and raises her right arm, her cloak falling back to expose chafed skin hanging loosely above her purple, gnarled elbow. She sticks her tongue out between thin cracked lips and narrows her eyes, then takes her shot. It falls directly around the second stake and lands neatly on the mud. Gammy throws both arms in the air and whoops loudly, whacking me so hard across the back of the shoulders I splutter in shock.

'Gammy still has it, doesn't she, kid? Life in this old body yet!' she cackles. Christ, Gammy, you've got a bloody arm on you there. She nods knowingly with a satisfied grin and snatches the next hoop from my hands, ignoring my frown. It twirls through the sunny air and lands square on the third stake. This time she doesn't yell out, just raises her arms and nods cockily at me. Patting herself on the fucking back. Her pink scalp is gleaming in the sun where big chunks of white, wiry hair has fallen out, and her face is shining with delight.

When it's my turn, I take my time, carefully aiming the throw. Nothing worse than being shown up by an ancient, housebound old woman. I fling the hoop and it hits the side of a stake but bounces off awkwardly and slides away in a stream of mud headed toward the River. I can hear Gammy's vicious laughter behind me as I fetch the hoop.

This is what I get, is it Gammy, for showing you a good time? Mockery?

She chuckles evilly, and as she does, a gentle murmur of wind shakes the canopies bridging the clearing, and a thousand shimmering droplets of water spray from the drying leaves. I shield my eyes from the glare of the sun in the sky; sharp blue and so clear for this brief time before the Wet distorts it again, and the clouds roll in as a heavy grey blanket.

This is what it used to be like. Me and Gammy. Gammy and me. All the time. She would spend every moment of sunshine with me when I was a little tacker. Used to soak up the sunrays and my company. It was Gammy who taught me to play this stupid game – busying herself about in front of our hut, digging in stakes, lifting my tiny arm for me to show me how to aim. The villagers hated us being outside even back then, used to cast their sad eyes our way as we laughed and played, but they still got on with their business. Sometimes they even welcomed visitors from other villages, who would also look straight ahead and pretend we weren't there. I used to like edging slightly closer to their side of the village as the game went on; run a little closer to fetch a lost hoop, to see how near I could get before they would grunt and scuttle fearfully back into their huts in a flurry of black rags and discontent. When I would turn back to Gammy, she would have her arms folded and a worried look on her face, but it never stopped me trying again.

My next shot is even worse, and Gammy is doubled in laughter now, tears streaming down her white cheeks. I grin despite myself. It's nice to see you like this, Gammy. Nice to be with you outside. I start to take aim. It's been so long since you hung out with me out here in the sun. Or anywhere, really. Remember when I was little, Gammy, and you taught me this game? We used to play every day out here when the sun visited.

'I reckon you were better then. Gone downhill.' She lets out a craggy cough, her arm darting up to her chest as she winces in pain.

It'd help if we practiced, Gammy. I let the last hoop fly without looking at her, but I feel her silence like a wet, heavy rag behind me and know the smile has been whisked from her face like the hoop in the mud slick. I don't wait to see where my shot lands, but instead turn to look at her worriedly. She isn't looking at me, but is staring across the clearing at the villager's huts. Not one of them has ventured out since Gammy and I started our game. Probably cursing us for taking up their one window of sunshine for the day. I can see their presence as murky shadows behind ragged curtains fluttering in the light breeze, scuttling in the dark and wondering what to do about us. I haven't stayed at the clearing during sun-time for years now, and my presence would be scaring the crap out of them. Pathetic. Pathetic, right, Gammy?

She refuses to look at me, staring in silence at the little eyes peering from every door cavity at the other side of the clearing. Slowly, she starts to edge her way back toward the hut, feeling her way through the sticky black mud. I can hear her breath speeding up, rattling within her chest. Her back is hunched as she tries to shrink into her own body. From victorious queen of the game to cowering villager in twenty seconds flat. That's a record even for you, Gammy. She sidles carefully back inside the hut without even saying goodbye to me, and flicks our curtain rags back across the entrance.

Fine, Gammy. Screw you too. I trample angrily across the mud slicks, sludge spraying from my stomping feet and ankle bell ringing tinnily, and collect the stakes and hoops and throw them in a heap on our deck before storming into the centre of the clearing. With a stony stare at where I know Gammy will be peeking from our door hole, and a filthy glance at the other huts, I bend over and raise my green robes and expose my bare arse to the lot of them. How do you like that, cowering in your goddamn huts all day? I'll give you a show.

I stay that way for an age, bare arse warming in the sunlight. I laugh angrily when I feel the first trickle of the Wet on my naked backside and lower my robes. When I stomp away from the village I can feel every set of eyes boring a hole in my back, but when I look back through the now heavy sheets of rain, there isn't a single sign of life.

11.

I HATE DROPPING THE FOOD OFF MORE THAN ALMOST anything I can think of. Every few days, having to lope into the middle of the clearing, taking over-exaggerated steps to make sure my bell chimes as much as possible, because god forbid I surprise one of those idiots while they've got their head up their arse.

They are so bloody jumpy. The moment I emerge from the weeping and heaving trees, they fall over themselves to squelch back into their huts, so petrified they leave whatever they were doing outside abandoned on their mud-caked decks. The twitch of tattered curtains tells me that beady eyes are watching behind every door cavity.

Conspicuous and exposed, I try to walk as nonchalantly as possible, carefully place my basket of food in the clearing in the rain, then stroll back into the woods, staring straight ahead.

Out of the corner of my eye, I notice a flicker of movement at the closest hut, and catch a glimpse of some wood I have never noticed before piled up on top of one of the decks. That's a new one, villagers. What's going on there? But I keep slowly walking away toward the forest.

Some unlucky bastard is chosen each time to collect my food offerings, a lone volunteer shoved out into the wet clearing on behalf of the village, looking furtively this way and that like they imagine the instant they drop their guard I will launch out of the bushes, screeching.

But mostly I hate how much they reek of desperation. How much they hate me, and how much they are forced to rely on me, day in and day out. When that poor villager squelches uncertainly out into the mud and rain to pick up my basket, trembling and peering through the trees for my presence, I know they aren't just afraid. They are also grateful. Grateful that today isn't the day I let them starve.

The pity and disgust I feel for them sits like a hot rock in my gut as I move back through the woods, putting the Wet between them and me once again.

12.

WHAT ON EARTH ARE THOSE KNUCKLEHEADS DOING?

You shouldn't torment them. Lord knows they tolerate you now, but only just.

I tolerate them, more like it. Anyway, they can't see me squirreled away up this tree (standing proud and only slightly bowed, for now), a heavy blanket of water between me and them. The villagers can't see the end of their own noses through the Wet.

Despite my annoyance at dropping off the food, curiosity and boredom has made me slither up a nearby trunk and wedge myself between the forked branches. Through the rain I watch the clearing: empty while they recover from my visit and ensure I am long gone. I want to know about these piles of wood that have magically appeared on their side of the village.

I sigh impatiently, clicking my tongue and picking the grime out from under my nails while I wait. Then slowly, a black head pops out, a craning neck through a doorway, an unsteady hand on a deck. When they are sure I am gone (don't be too sure, little villagers) they slither out, one by one, and form a shaky row near their huts.

I shift my weight on the thick old branch, reach ever so slowly into my reed basket so as not to set off my bell, and start to munch on some berries meant for our dinner, never taking my slitted eyes off them. The steady pounding of water on my back doesn't dislodge me from my perch but I wedge myself closer in the fork of the tree, just in case. Last thing I need is to fall and break my arse in front of these fools.

I shouldn't have let myself be distracted by them, should have kept foraging and gone straight home to Gammy, but entertainment is pretty limited around here. I've been doing this more lately, finding myself drifting toward their side of the clearing, under the shelter of the forest.

They are slipping and sliding through the mud in what looks from my elevated height to be a ragged line: fifteen or so of them. One or two still look almost strong – perhaps they are younger than the rest? – but even they share the same pale wasted skin, hanging wrinkled off skinny arms, and legs that look ready to be washed away at a moment's notice. Their soft, slender feet try to grip deep in the mud slicks, but they can only stand upright for a second or two before sliding and sloshing about, some of them managing to remain upright, some falling arse up in an instant. Slow bursts of activity are paused to allow one at a time to break off and double over, wet coughs shuddering through their bowed bodies. Every breath out here in the rain means a little more mist and liquid inside their already moist lungs.

Some of the villagers have clear white skin, but the rest have straggly beards plastered to their faces; no doubt they are put off by the thought of shaving their already withered, peeling chins to get those mouldy hairs off. Or the remaining flints and razors are too rusty. I can't tell when they wear the black hoods designed, but failing, to keep the rain out of their faces. Some of them have shoved lengths of bark under the rags above their heads to provide some protection from the rain, but the water still streams in torrents over their frantically blinking eyes and running noses.

I pick absent-mindedly at the dark hair sprouting on my own arms and legs, slicked down under the rain but still wiry and wild. Sprouting like the undergrowth wrestling every tree trunk.

I don't know how they can bear to move about like this, constantly teetering on an earth that moves under their very feet. Usually when I see the villagers brave the Wet, I spend my time laughing at those idiots slipping and sliding around with arms outstretched in anticipation of constant falls, but today I am feeling more down than usual, and their fumbling feels me with a kind of sadness.

I focus my eyes through heavy rain that is now slanting sideways in the wind, and keep munching on my berries.

Large branches sit scattered between their huts to help them move from one home to another, dug into the flowing mud as best as they can. If I squint I can see their movements inside the huts through the cracks and holes in the walls: huddled together out of the Wet, drying the reeds I collect, lighting smoky fires with damp wood. They barely talk to each other. Instead they seem to communicate through hacking coughs and nods, and the occasional moaning chant, rocking back and forward on creaking and rotten floorboards. There's never any pattern to their days; they mill around like confused ducks, sometimes sleeping, sometimes drying their clothes over wooden floors, and always looking sullen and exhausted.

They lost their rhythm with the sun.

I know, Gammy. The only time they keep to is the night. If they are scared of the Wet, they are sure as hell scared of the Wet in the dark. The sheer depth of the blackness seems to terrify them, judging by the way they huddle together inside their huts at night, muttering anxiously and peeping out into the midnight roar of the water. I don't know how they sleep, they barely move during the day, so they can't be that tired. I reckon they just sit in their dark huts, staring at the endless wet night outside, waiting for morning to bring the same story it always does. More rain, the rising River, a brief moment of sun.

I haven't seen them all willingly out in the open rain like this for years; back when some of them tried to build better huts, better paths. Before the creeping River and the all-invasive Wet wore down every roof, drilled holes in every floor, and washed away the ground underneath them – and their friends along with it. They used to try longer walks: if I think back far enough I can almost remember movement, building, visitors from afar. But as I have grown, their world has shrunk. Now, it is just this clearing – their huts one end, ours the other – flanked by woods on three sides and the vast expanse of the River at one.

But they are: building again, that is. Not the large slabs of wood they tried to use to join the five villages – I haven't seen anyone from another village in years and they might all be washed away for all I know. Besides, even the large trees are rotten to the core now. No, this is something smaller. Something to bridge the gaps between their huts perhaps, to recreate the spaces they used to share, shielded from the rain? A black robed man standing furthest from the village, the steadiest on his feet, is hacking haphazardly at branches and passing them to his neighbour to pass along the line. Using corroded tools that have probably been sitting discarded in their huts for years.

I lean forward slightly through the dripping green canopy, astonished to see that this mad line is actually working: sure, a villager occasionally wobbles and falls, and it is painfully slow going, but those daft idiots are doing it! Branches are passed down the chain and with a weak throw are deposited into the closest hut.

You should see this, Gammy, you wouldn't believe it. But you can't, of course – they are on the side of their huts furthest from yours – if you peeked out of our door right now, the Wet would mask every sound, and their huts would obscure everything from your sight. Reckon they are doing it away from our view on purpose, Gammy?

I have to resist the mad urge to scamper down my tree and help them. I stand taller and stronger than any of them despite only being twelve (eleven? Gammy can't recall and I have never successfully counted the etches on the time tree), and my feet almost never slip, sure and stable in the mud. I could deliver a hundred piles of wood into that hut in the time it is taking them to deliver one small branch. I chuckle at the thought. They would jump out of their pasty skin if I casually sauntered over there to help. I can count the number of times the villagers have been in close proximity to me on two hands. Usually it is one of them stumbling into my path by accident when they have braved a short walk, and hightailing it away as quickly as their useless feet will take them. Often, it was to move our huts back from the rapidly rising River, and they put aside their fear for a day because of my speed and strength. I hate being close to their rotting black cloaks and watery eyes. They smell like old fish and decay, and their helplessness makes me furious: all fumbling hands and soft skin that cuts so easily. At least Gammy knows how to have a yarn and a laugh: the villagers just reek of desperation and flesh.

Why are you up a tree watching them, if you can't wait for them to clear out of your way? Shut up, Gammy. What else am I meant to do around this place for fun?

I wonder if this is how it is in the other five villages; if it is the same as here. A green-cloaked freak trotted out for emergencies then banished back to their corner when they aren't needed. Maybe in some of the villages they are friends, joining together to eat their fish and sing around steaming campfires. I snort loudly at the thought, the noise thankfully muffled by the water cascading around me. The visitors I have seen from the other villages over the years are the same arseholes we have here: black-cloaked, paranoid, shuffling around the edge of our clearing to avoid being within five body lengths of me, gasping instead of breathing as the water rushes over their hoods. As the years rolled by, they visited less and less. Washed away or suffocated by the water in their lungs or both. Suckers.

My villagers weary as I watch. The constant downpour weighs their black cloaks, which drag in the mud, collecting twigs and leaves and skids of dirt. Their hooded heads become more bowed. Water soaks their hair and dark tendrils splatter across their faces, and they blink more and more as their eyes are rubbed wet and raw. The drops of rain hit their hunched backs like blows.

I usually hack my hair off with a rock sharpened on a wet stone I keep outside the hut. The Wet blunts and rounds and smooths every surface, but the same damp surfaces can be used to fashion my dull grey stone into a long, sharp edge. The short tufts steam at night in the hut, and when we wake up in the morning my hair stinks of smoke, just like the limp strings of white hanging down Gammy's forehead. But the villagers let their long tendrils mat and mould and weigh down on their cold raspy shoulders under their hoods. Maybe they need to feel something between their giant bony heads and the Wet sluicing down from above.

They trudge on as I watch, slender legs wobbling on the ever-moving surface, but it gets harder and harder for them to wade through the mud, to navigate when they can't really see or breathe, to stay upright when the horizon blurs into the grey rain.

Still, good on you, villagers, I think: you're winning at something for a change. My bad mood has lifted like mist, observing their little triumph.

There are leaves in my basket, part-dried by the sun earlier today. I have strung them onto a flimsy stick and made a decoration for Gammy. I know she will love it. I will walk home tonight when I have had enough of watching these losers, and her face will be peering out the door through the rain, searching me out anxiously even though she knows I am always ok. I'll hand it to her and her saggy face will break into a craggy grin, and she will say what she says every time I give her a gift: 'Still a child, after all.' She's a sentimental old git, is Gammy. 'I remember when you were a wee tacker, you never let me cuddle you. Slippery and muscular and full of fight and fury.' Then she will pull me roughly to her and hug me, and I will let her. Not because I need a hug. No, no, it's because you need comforting Gammy. I'll let you hug me, just this once . . .

I'm smiling softly as I slide down the tree, only just remembering to put a hand out to muffle my bell as I descend, and flit back home through the trees.

13.

GAMMY DOES NOT SHARE MY DELIGHT AT THE STORY about the villagers. I can tell by the way she tries to raise her back to sit up stiff and proud and the flash of angry blue in her otherwise pink, watery eyes. She is mighty pissed.

'You risk both of our lives sneaking around like that.'

I mutter something about her being a mad old bird as I turn away to unpack the shells from my basket and arrange them on the empty floor. Suddenly she whacks me across the head before I can dodge out the way. She's bloody fast when she stops pretending to be an old biddy, I'll give her that.

Wounded and sullen, I ignore her raised fist – ready to land another blow on me – and keep unpacking, first the rest of the shells and then snails, reeds, some berries, and lastly a now crackling carpet of moss, in the hope that my spoils will cheer her the hell up. When they are neatly lined on the floor at the edge of our hut, I shuffle around on my bottom and raise the courage to look at her. I could dunk her mad arse in the River in a second if I wanted, but I let her think I am meek and beaten by her. She is an old lady, after all.

She barely glances at my feast before teetering around the edges of our hut, stomping as best as her small body allows. It takes all my effort to stifle a chuckle at the thought of her stomping right through one of those weak old floorboards and dangling into the air below, bowed legs and rotten cloak flailing. Not the time for laughing, probably.

What the hell is she afraid of? Those weak old villagers probably can't even walk their way over the clearing to our hut, let alone best either of us. I thought she would be entertained by the story of their little mission, whatever the hell it is. I thought she might be amused by a tale of something new happening in this dank clearing where nothing changes but the crumbling landscape and the River's girth. Instead, the fury and fear is thick around her like the Wet.

'They fear you enough to kill you.'

They couldn't. I start cleaning the grit off the shells with my rags and place them, one by one, into our old rusting pot, followed by the snails. Gammy is mighty hung up on boiling our food and water. A throwback to the first days of the Wet where everyone's shit and vomit flowed in the streets and thousands of people died drinking from the River. She probably doesn't know I pick those shells right off the rocks every day and eat the insides just like that, juicy and briny and cold. I smack my lips together thinking about the salty taste.

'They killed the rest like you.'

This I have to take Gammy's word for. Holding the pot, I reach out of the hut through our ragged door curtains into the Wet: seconds later, it's full to the brim and I bring it back inside, curtain falling back into place, and set about putting flint to damp twigs in the corner of the hut closest to our entrance. I pull the door rags slightly aside again to let the smoke hiss and twirl its way outside. Snuffed out. Just like 'the rest' of the children like me were apparently.

Gammy coughs dramatically from the steam circling out of the fire, clutching her sagging belly, her bowed legs and floppy tits shaking in rage. 'You arrogant fool; you have no idea what it was like, what we went through!'

I do, Gammy, I've heard it enough bloody times from you. The stories surround you like an extra cloak, never far away, moving as you move, crushing you with their weight.

I look up from the boiling pot long enough to stare coolly at her contorted face, then I keep calmly prodding the fire, and poking the shells that are bobbing furiously in the now boiling water. She tries to remain standing but her manic outburst has sapped all of her energy and she slumps on her wobbly stool (I should find some stronger branches and replace the quickly rotting legs), sobbing quietly, hands now shaking and folded on her lap.

I let her stay there, resigned and whimpering, while I finish up cooking the contents of the pot, then I remove it from the heat, and, using my cloak to protect my hands, shuffle to her side across the slippery wet floor, carefully carrying the hot pot. I feed the broth into her trembling mouth with our one remaining spoon, small dribbles making their way down her wrinkled chin and mingling with her tears to plop onto her peeling white toes below. She eats so little these days. Nothing left of her to fill.

When she closes her lips to more mouthfuls, I use the back of my hand to wipe her prickly chin clean. I set the pot aside and it lets off a little hiss where it sits on the damp wood. I apply liberal amounts of what is left of King Lizard's grease to her mottled legs and arms, looking into her bare, watery eyes as I do, silently letting her know that I will look after her, no matter what. We don't speak. She blinks gratefully and rests her head on my bony shoulder. I know she is still scared; scared of the villagers and scared of my snooping and recklessness, but I know it is easier for her to stop fighting, and to pretend I am in control and keeping us safe.

I don't remember when we started doing this: Gammy cared for me as a child, she must have, but all I remember is caring for her. I hold my back up strong to support her but I am cursing that I let her fall into one of these foul moods again. I am going to spend the rest of the night in silence, with only the pounding water outside to keep me company.

14.

I HAVE STARTED CHASING A TRAIL OF SWIRLING DEBRIS down a slippery hill. It's one of those big piles of brown and dirty black leaves mixed in with churning mud and soft broken sticks, capturing and collecting more undergrowth as it makes its way around tree trunks and over mounds. You know the ones, Gammy; they can get big enough to knock a villager off their feet if they were stupid enough to get in the way. It picks up speed as it swirls back and forth with the constant flow of water, creating a giant eddy of filthy brown and green that spins round and round right past where I was just sitting on my arse and picking my nose, water spurting around me, watching the grey clouds running as one mass across the sky.

I quickly leapt up and now I am bounding after it, laughing as it surprises me with a direction change, trying to predict where the water splashing down the hill will take it next. When it snags on mossy rocks, looking like the bundle will split into a million pieces, I give it a kick with my dirty old toenails and watch it hold together and pick up momentum again. A few times I almost join it rolling down the hill when I lose my footing, but I always manage to right myself again with flailing arms and low-hanging branches – all the branches are low-hanging these days, because the trees bend long and low to the ground, like lanky stick monsters reaching out to catch your fall.

When my mouldy old prize reaches the bottom of the hill it lodges up against an uprooted tree, and the water pressure starts building up behind it, creating a fountain in the air that erupts straight upwards to ricochet off the water crashing down from above. Of course I run down the last part of the hill, bell clanging and green cloak flying through the rain, and leap out of the trees and onto the pile. I bounce furiously in among the spurting water until the bundle breaks apart and separate clumps of dirt and leaves trickle off and make their way around the trunk to join different trails of water flowing through the woods.

That's when I see the villager: frozen like a bloody tree, arms outstretched, bearded mouth open like a big gaping fish, with water plastering his black hood to his face. He is shitting himself: the bell and the green cloak hadn't done him any good as a warning, not with the speed I travel at. He must have seen me launch out of the woods like an enraged duck, bell and all, throwing myself onto a pile of leaves and stomping and grinning like a mad thing. I didn't realise I had made it all the way to the village clearing, and the fool must have braved a small walk on sloppy legs out into the Wet to the forest edge. They haven't done that in such a long time.

I smile at him – you've got to be polite. I smile through the curtain of rain with my jagged little teeth and he turns on his heels, frantically grasping at the trees' outstretched arms and slipping and sliding through the mud back to his hut. More than once he collapses, thick wet black dragging him downward, before hauling himself back up, caked with the ruddy brown and shit green debris, to keep flailing and sliding and crawling his way back home. You should see this idiot, Gammy: it takes him an age to make it less than a few steps, and I just watch and laugh, leaning against a tree.

Gammy hates me laughing at the villagers, but they make it so easy. My feet are hard and scaled and they cut through the moving mud. I can see and hear in the Wet, and the rain just slides right off my back where it seems to push them down a little further each day. Gammy says I shouldn't crow about it so much, but I love the feeling of my heart thumping as I belt through the trees, water and mud spraying around me and knowing no one could catch me even if they tried: the Wet slows their movements and obscures their vision and the mud sucks at their weak feet until they collapse.

I don't love it as much as I love being in the River, but it's a pretty close second.

I turn back into the woods, laughing to myself at the silly old villagers, smacking wet tree branches out of my face as I move further away from the clearing.

15.

GAMMY IS CRACKING THE SEEDPODS ONE BY ONE ONTO our floor, making a bloody mess. We only had two pots left, but a gaping rust-hole opened up in one this morning, so now she has to grind and mix the seeds on the ground, saving the remaining pot for cooking our fish. Our pots used to line the edge of the hut in all shapes and sizes, grey and mottled with rust, but one by one Gammy ditched them, useless, out the window, to slowly make their way into the River. I wonder if they knock frogs on the head on their way downstream.

The pods are huge, the size of my fist, and the insides brown and grainy and sweet. I can smell them from where I sit against a wall, watching her work. She grumbles as she smashes them against the wood, glancing at me occasionally as if to say, *help little old Gammy?* Not a chance, lady. I could pluck a fish right out from the water and eat it then and there. You're the one who insists on cooking, grinding, pounding, boiling. So I stay where I am, naked, long legs splayed out on the floor, grinning to annoy her.

'Are there more of these out there?' She grimaces as the broken shell of a pod splits a thin ribbon of blood on her finger, then wipes it on her rags distractedly.

I frown in surprise. Course there are, Gammy, the forest is full of them. Seeds as big as your fist, as small as your toenail, swaying in the Wet. Above your head, by your knees, brown and black and green. They fall with a *plop!* and hit the water and the mud, swirl around trees, until they smash and split and vomit their insides into the streams and the seeds spray across the forest. More plants, more seeds. I scoff loudly – don't you know anything, Gammy?

I tense excitedly, waiting for the streams of abuse, maybe a seedpod thrown at my face. But instead, Gammy pauses in her pounding and looks confused. Her eyes look foggier than a cold morning and she stares at me with a daft look on her face. The smoke from our newly lit fire circles her head, making her look even less clear, more blurry.

'That's not . . . not what it used to be like,' she says lamely, glancing down at the half-shattered pods like she has forgotten what she was doing.

C'mon, Gammy, I'm starving. I roll forward on to my knees and shuffle over to her, place a seed in her hand, and nudge her shoulder encouragingly. Let's get a bloody move on, Gammy. She just stares at me with a blank face. I'm starting to get irritated now, can smell the raw fish in the pot, and my stomach is grumbling louder than the Wet outside. *Gammy. Come. On.*

'I thought maybe some of the seeds from before would still be out there somewhere, lying in wait, ready to bloom, all this time later.' Old lady has clearly lost the plot so I actually grab her wrinkled arm and start to use it to pound the seeds, showing her what to do. Here, Gammy, keep going or it will be morning again before we eat. I move back a little and watch her expectantly, but her arm just lays there still, limp and useless.

'Funny things, seeds. You can plant a seed and thousands of years later it can still sprout, you know.'

I sigh in defeat and move back to the edge of the hut and stare at her in bewilderment, occasionally raising my eyebrows toward the pile of seedpods in encouragement.

She brushes a strand of straggly hair out from her eyes, finally looking more alert. She peers down at the pile of crushed seeds in front of her. Some of the seed powder has mixed in with the dampness of the floor, already forming the paste she wants to coat onto the fish. They just taste like water, otherwise, she reckons, just like everything else in this joint. They don't though, Gammy – there are thousands of fish in the River and not one tastes the same.

'That's kind of what happened, I guess. It's just Gammy didn't think of it like that until now.'

I've got no bloody idea what you are talking about, Gammy.

She finally frowns in annoyance, flicks an empty pod at my feet. It rolls to a dark corner of the hut with a dull clatter. 'The seeds! Keep up.' She smashes a large pod on the floor and it splinters, shards flying everywhere. 'That's why even the normal ones did what they did. The seed had been planted so long ago. Thousands of years of whispers in their ears, telling them who and how to hate. Even if they thought they were better, even if they didn't think they believed it, the seed was still there. So when it all went to shit, like, *really* to shit, the seed sprouted.

All it took was a new whisper in the ear, saying there was an answer, and the little seed inside them took hold.'

She looks mighty pleased with herself now, sitting in the centre of smoke rings, half a dozen seeds in her manky lap. She grins triumphantly at me across the room, looks to me for my reaction, like she just won a game.

That's nice, Gammy. Now how about some fucking dinner?

16.

SOMETIMES I LIKE TO DANCE. GAMMY SHOWED ME ONE night, back when she wasn't being a miserable old sad sack. Slick moves from when she was young.

So I practice out in the woods by myself. No one is going to see me make a fool of myself out here. Feet shuffling in the mud, in and out, arms raised above my head, I thrust my hips through the Wet and watch the sprays of silver water arc around me. Twirling whirling I go, round and round, heart hammering my own rhythm. No music, just me and my thudding pulse in my ears and the spray falling on my shoulders. Mud splashes out from underneath my stomping feet, and I clap my large hands hard on my thighs as I leap from rocks to logs as fast as my legs will propel me. The Wet pours down my back and I spring harder and higher through the air, arms outstretched, slicing through the dribbling rain like I am a goddamn superhero from Gammy's stories.

The night Gammy showed me how to dance we laughed until our sides ached; the sight of Gammy pottering about with her hands in the air, screeching songs like a strangled duck, bendy old arse wriggling and flaps of skin smacking about her arms. She pretended she was mad at me mocking her but she laughed and laughed as well as we twirled around each other, holding hands in a manic circle, round and round and round until we both collapsed in a heap on the damp floor. She held me tight that night and told me about the dancing before: how she moved under bright lights and between sweating bodies, how she kissed people she did not know, and how the floor stuck to her feet and the music pounded in her ears.

I don't dance with anyone but the Wet out here. In a way, it seems to move with me too: a kiss from a stranger, watery music in my ears, mud between my toes.

'You know you're screwed when they stop the dancing. We should have known then what was coming.'

Yet here I am, dancing still, Gammy. Just the Wet and me.

'First they stop the fun, then hundreds of rules fall down around your ears like the music they won't let you make anymore.'

I am still bobbing my arse up and down under the visiting sun later that morning, the music Gammy sang playing softly in my mind. My green rags lie discarded on a low tree branch to steam and sizzle in the unaccustomed warmth, and I move from rock to rock along the River's edge, brown bum wriggling in the warm breeze, looking for the crabs that burrow narrow holes deep into the muddy bank. The fart I throw in every few beats for good measure sends me into fits of laughter and would scare away any crab within earshot, but I am in a brilliant mood and in no hurry today.

I bob a bit further along, marvelling at the way I can shuffle my feet when there is no water pounding down on them, just squirts of mud squelching out between my scaly toes. Gammy curls her lip in disgust at the rough shell of skin covering my feet, my sharp gnarly toenails, but I look down on them fondly. They help me propel through the mud, but most importantly, they make me different from those soft-footed villagers.

I contort my mouth into a whistle and continue my rhythmic wiggle along the River's bank, bell chiming in unison, prodding the occasional log or reed to see what is beneath, but thinking to myself that I am pretty bored with scavenging for all these lazy villagers, really. Arseholes could come out in these daily moments of sun, and if they stayed far enough away from the River's pull, they could pick a bloody reed or shell themselves.

I pause in my half-hearted fossicking: perhaps they don't come out because they don't want to bump into me? Then I go back to bobbing my head and humming quietly.

People have feared difference since time began, Gammy said. I get that. Except maybe she said *people have feared your kind since time began*. I don't remember. Her rambling stories sometimes wrap themselves up in the pounding of the River in my head and become noise the colour of white, and I forget where her story starts and where the Wet ends it.

It doesn't make a lick of difference to me. Day in and day out, I am out here in the Wet doing whatever the hell I feel like.

The next warm rock I tip over with my toe lets loose a stream of tiny brown cockroaches, running fast away from me like everyone else around here. You too, roaches?

How anyone can be scared of you beats me. You're just a silly little whippersnapper with no manners and a swagger like you own this damn place.

I don't know either Gammy; the Wet has seeped into their very bones and replaced strength with flaccid fear. The folks who once tried to master the murderous, hungry River now hide away from her angry appetite.

The cockroaches scurry along a mossy rock perched precariously on the bank and fall, one by one, into the angry brown water below. Rather fling themselves into the River than hang around here with me. Sometimes I think I'm the only one happy to hang out in this joint.

But that isn't true either, not really; the silvery beige fish that flit through the surging waves love the cold, bitter waters. My friend the old codfish who peers unblinking through the cloudy brown streams – he seems pretty happy with the way things turned out, too. The little critters and the softly loping snails have made their homes with water rushing over them and constantly by their side, just like me.

No, it's just the old folk who hate this world of Wet; the shivering, chafing villagers, the cowed, collapsing trees, the one remaining cockroach or beetle who wonders how the hell he ended up in this waterlogged apocalypse.

Snap – the tiny little sandy-coloured crab with almost translucent grey nippers attaches with quiet fury to the end of my toe, the one I had been rudely prodding his home with. I bend over and look at him squarely in the face, trying to work out where his eyes are so that I can have a truly proper conversation with him, eye to eye, about his role in my world, and more importantly, as my dinner. But with a loud sigh the sun is sucked back behind a swirling mass of grey clouds and the shafts of sunlight are replaced by a heavy cloak of water once again. My crab clings on stubbornly, despite the now torrential streams of water buffeting him from above. Brave little sucker.

Brave, but stupid.

I flick my foot upwards and he flips up toward my outstretched hands, to be placed promptly into my basket with a rock on his back to keep him in place. Bending over in the downpour to inspect my toe, I find that his little nipper hasn't even made an impression on my thick, scaled skin, so different to the villagers and Gammy who wound like softened reeds, easy to tear apart and impossible to stick back together. Gammy often laughs that for all my roaming and climbing and running and swimming in rapids, there isn't a scab or sore on me. I shudder thinking about how their pale bodies split and crack and weep at the slightest pressure.

I move on, past the little crab holes, and pick my way downstream. The roar of water mounts behind me, little trickles escaping from the main River in front of me at its sides, making their own new jagged streams sliding off into the woods. The River's reach spreads every day. It isn't just the angry lapping which threatens to overwhelm our clearing. It is these little trickles that are breaking off and winding their way through every part of the forest and joining to form puddles dimpled by the rain above. In some places the puddles never go away, they spread and seek and search, and before you know it, they fill whole clearings with a deep shimmery blue. Soon, there will be more water than mud, more water than earth. I imagine just being able to see the tops of these sagged trees above a solid mass of water: no clearings, no villages, just water as far as the eye can see. A solid silver disk meeting the angry grey of the sky at the horizon.

I guess that's the problem all the old folk have with this place: even the tiniest marks they can make are quickly washed away, like it had never happened in the first place. Like *they* had never happened. That's what they are really scared of. They know one day, just like their friends, and their houses, their burrows and their trees, that the Wet and the River will wash them away like they never existed.

17.

I CAN'T STOP WATCHING THESE CRAZY SUCKERS AND their painfully slow building line. Sure, I'm pretty low on entertainment out here, but I reckon I'm becoming obsessed. They are still tottering and writhing around on the mud slicks in front of their huts, hacking off chunks of wood from the closest trees surrounding our clearing, and passing them along. The going is tough – more than once, five or more of them go arse-up at the same time, slabs of wood sliding away from them with an awkward skid, just to be fetched all over again. But with more energy than I've seen in years, they slip and slide their way over to the scattered branches, then resume their place in the line, passing the wood back to the huts.

The huts themselves are also a flurry of activity: I have to squint through sheets of rain but I see blurs of black cloaks bobbing around productively, cloaked arms reaching out of a hut door to collect the next piece of wood, and then quickly disappearing back into the hut. Underneath the roar of the Wet, I can hear muffled bangs and yells. They must have a large stockpile of rusty tools, things from before the Wet that haven't been completely destroyed yet.

I shift myself into a comfortable position on my hidden branch, settle back against the wet trunk, and wait to see what they will do next. All around me, the Wet hangs in the air and angry grey clouds thicken the sky. I breathe in the cool moisture.

Gammy tells me their kind were always obsessed with building things, and I wonder if these lethargic old codgers have finally reconnected to some dormant need to clap two pieces of wood together again. *Giant monuments to their own insanity*, as she says. Bigger, brighter, louder. She reckons before the Wet settled in for good, the earth was covered in things they had built. Then, when they thought they had reached their peak, they started to build more things because the things they had built before were killing them, scorching the skies and poisoning their lands. Just when they finally thought they had nailed it – they had constructed the buildings and the machines that would save them all from what they themselves had done – one day it started raining. And then it never stopped.

'And with the Wet went everything we had built – just months it took, for what had taken hundreds of years to grow to be washed away. We could make machines that circled the stars, but we couldn't stop the Wet.'

What's a star, Gammy?

I WAIT UNTIL EVERY ONE OF THE VILLAGERS HAS MADE their slippery way back to their huts. One by one, crawling back through the mud with the evening darkness prowling behind them as they return home. Soon, the village is cloaked in shades of dark grey, and the clearing is empty. I don't know what gets into me, Gammy, but I am not finished with them yet. Heart thudding, I grasp my bell, slip silently from my tree and edge my way around the outside of the clearing. I slink between trees, keeping myself always out of sight behind the sheets of rain, shivering canopies and swinging brown vines. A little thrill rises from my belly as I creep closer, closer than I have been since we last moved the village. I want to look in on their lives, to see what they do behind those rotten walls. Call it boredom, Gammy, call it sick curiosity. Whatever it is draws me in.

As I shuffle carefully around the perimeter of our clearing, the first dark hut looms above me. The mossy stilts bowing under the weight of the dwelling could be mistaken for bending trees in the shadows, and little rays of light from a flickering fire inside the hut light up pools of mud and glistening water swirling below.

I am holding my breath now. *C'mon, just run, you aren't scared of those fools.* So I dart out of the cover of the woods, pulse hammering in my ears and adrenaline pumping through my veins, and rush under the hut. I am excited by my own cockiness, knowing some villagers are less than an arms-length above my head and they don't even know I am there. Imagine how much they would shit themselves if they knew I was lurking just below their stinking hut.

It does stink. The villagers are too scared to venture into the woods to shit so they relieve themselves out of holes in the floors of their huts and into the mud below. Most of it washes away, but a dank scent still clings to the brown-stained stilts.

I twitch my nose in disgust. They really are filthy animals. More than once I have seen a villager curled up in front of a hut, retching in the rain. Not surprising when you slide around in your own shit and piss all day.

I move around under the rotting floor of this hut, trying to find a gap above my head big enough to peer through. Finally, a cavernous hole allows me an unimpeded view up into the centre of the room.

I don't know what I expect, but all I can see is sagging wood, some swirling light and steam, and the occasional cracked and bleeding underside of a villager's foot, shuffling slowly across the floor. I grin despite feeling unsettled; they are completely unaware of my presence. How many are in this hut? Two, perhaps three? Black-robed despite being out of the rain, moving around cooking yesterday's fish over smoking and weak fires. An occasional wet cough wracks through the silence. They move around each other without saying a word, without even glancing at one another. If it were us, Gammy, you would have filled every part of our hut with your gasbagging the minute I set foot inside. But these villagers move in a kind of silent dance against the roar of the Wet and the River outside.

Is this a family? I shake my head in the darkness at such a ridiculous thought. Families don't exist anymore. Gammy and I are the closest thing to family these days, she explains to me, which is a laugh: we look as related as a mouldy old log and a giant brown duck. The villagers live in a pack but seem to be separate; physically close, but I have never seen one touch another on purpose. They barely make noises at one another. They barely look at each other outside, come to think of it. The two or three in this hut maybe huddle for warmth, but the idea of making babies, of affection, are long gone. Washed away when the Wet came.

Good. I could double over and retch myself, thinking about these twisted creatures touching each other.

My heartbeat slows as disappointment seeps in. There isn't anything exciting to see here. The villagers aren't harbouring some secret life behind their collapsing walls, despite their new activity outside. I don't know what I thought I would find, sneaking around like this. They are as scared and sad and dull as ever, hiding from the Wet and the dark. Hiding from the River. Hiding from me. With a small sigh that no one above my head could possibly hear over the torrential rain, I move out from under the hut and slip back into the forest and the thick sheet of Wet, silent and stealthy. From a hut further away, a low and guttural keening starts. The only noise they seem to regularly make, it winds its way around the scattered huts and travels across the clearing to where I am hidden behind the tree line.

They will never know I was there. Any footprints were washed away the moment my scaled feet lifted from the mud. I am just a shadow making my way back around the clearing to Gammy's hut, where her little face peers out looking for me. You were right, Gammy, there is nothing there.

18.

TONIGHT I WANT TO GET GAMMY TALKING AGAIN, ABOUT the building before the Wet, hoping to pry some information out of her and work out what those boring fuckers are up to with their clanging and banging. My anticlimactic adventure to their side of the clearing stings a little and I need a morsel of information to cheer me up again.

I can't ask her outright; she would belt me if she knew how much I was watching them. So I bide my time casually and wait until she is ready to talk. We have finished our dinner, a meagre handful of snails boiled in their own briny juices today, and I am lying on my back on the hut floor while Gammy sits hunched on her stool. Gazing up at our ceiling through the many holes riddling the rotting wood, I can see the swirling black and grey of the night sky punctuated by the silver shards of rain picking up the rare light of the mostly hidden moon. Trickles of water travel down our makeshift beams and meet together to drop down onto the floor. A constant movement of water, even inside. Gammy says the endless dripping drove some of them crazy early on. A few of them even threw themselves into the River to escape the maddening sound. *Drip, drip, drip.* Of course the rest can't throw themselves in, even if they wanted to. They'll miss the dry afterlife if they do that. Have to hang around some more, put up with me a bit longer, eyes on the endgame.

I chuckle to myself, earning a raised eyebrow from Gammy, imagining a crazed black-robed villager rising up and running without warning, arms flailing, toward the River's hungry mouth and throwing themselves in.

You'd think they would be used to noises of the Wet by now, given the water hasn't stopped since I before I was born, but I still catch Gammy wincing sometimes as she sits on her rickety stool, occupying herself with whatever fruitless craft she can find. It's like those tiny drops can pierce her soul and send shivers down her back more than the endless downpours ever could.

When the smoke from our fire escapes outside and the flickering light begins to fade and Gammy is finally cloaked in shadows, she starts to talk. I ask her about boats this time. I like the idea of boats, imagine sharing the River with these big, majestic creatures. I could swim alongside them as they travel the breadth of the land, trailing them upstream to whatever lies that way.

'Like a bloody dolphin!' Gammy laughs sadly. The last of the fire dwindles and we ignore the dirty pot filled with snail shells on the floor. Two seconds placed outside under the rain and the pot will be clean, the shells washed away.

'Boats wouldn't do them any good now,' she says, shifting her weight uncomfortably in the dim light. 'The River is too angry, too fast, too wide, too unpredictable. We don't know where it goes anymore.' She is right; the River in parts is wider than I can see, and always churning, rushing, hiding boulders and waterfalls and steep drops that would swallow a boat whole. Even I don't know the River, not really: so much new water joins her every day that in the mornings when I wake up and leave the hut, her shape and personality is a little different. The markers I place at her side every morning are never there when I next check. She spreads lazily between trees and hills and then before you know it, she has gobbled them all up and there is nothing to separate her and the Wet above. I wonder if she has a plan or if she just wanders aimlessly, taking everything in her path. Does she swallow it all up because she is angry, Gammy?

Maybe she doesn't think about us at all. We are just in her way.

I can tell Gammy is narrowing her eyes at me in the dim light, can feel her mood darkening with the disappearing daylight.

'You wouldn't care if the River took over.' Her voice has a hard edge now, one I don't like. It is the same harshness that flashes in her eyes when she examines my new body, runs her eyes over the tall limbs and strong angles and sprouting hair, and purses her lips.

You're probably right there, Gammy. You are probably right.

I don't offer her the spot next to me on the floor and instead roll onto my side, hands folded under my cheek, and pretend to go to sleep. There is no point talking to her when she gets like this.

It doesn't take long before I hear her grunt softly as she leverages herself off the stool and shuffles her way toward my unwelcoming back. She slides awkwardly down next to me, bones creaking, and sighs; a sad sigh soon taken over by the hacking coughs that rise up and crack her lungs when she lies on her back. I try to ignore her sputtering and shaking frame behind me but soon enough I flip over and put my arms under her bony shoulders, to raise the top of her chest off the floor. When the hacking subsides, she turns her head and smiles weakly at me, before closing her eyes and settling into her breath. Now it is my turn to sigh, knowing I will be propping her up all night, knowing this is the way it will always be.

19.

I WATCH THEM EVERY DAY NOW, THESE FLAILING VILLAGERS, after I have collected our dinner. From my perch in the wobbly nook of a tree, hidden behind a deep wall of water, I see them stagger, slip and slide across the little clearing. I have watched them find surer footing as each day passes. Seven days or more have passed and still I watch, letting the rhythm of their work give shape to my days, which up till now have been dictated only by growing morning light through the rain, and the creeping evening darkness.

I've never looked properly at them before now, not really. It seems crazy, given we have shared a clearing for my entire life. I normally watch the back of them scurrying out of my path when I approach, hiding their long faces behind their black hoods and panting heavily in fear. But now, sitting here with the Wet sliding down my back, I can make out the little differences between them: all cloaked in the same rotten old black cloaks – more faded grey now – hatched together like ours, but here one is taller than the rest, one has lighter hair slicked to their face, there one has stumpy short legs despite being bony and gaunt. Under the bark visor they wear beneath their hoods, protecting their red, irritated eyes from the worst of the downpour, some have narrow faces, some taut, some lined like the hollows of the grounded trees alongside the River.

They must have their own store of rusty needles like Gammy's to hack together their mouldy old rags, but these cloaks are disintegrating and peeling off them. One day soon, surely, they will have to discard them entirely and expose their pale, shrivelled bodies to the Wet. No one is making more fabric around here and these rags deserve to compost in raised heaps like the rotting old leaf litter and flattened shrubs. I can almost smell the scent of fleshy decay that follows them everywhere, even though I am far away, hidden up this tree.

I know it sounds ridiculous, Gammy, but I feel like I am getting to know them, these villagers who have always hovered as black shivering spots on the edge of my vision. But now, seeing them work together, watching them get better at holding themselves up in the mud, watching them exchange knowing looks – I feel like maybe, just maybe, they could be a bit like me. They aren't just blurred black masses any more: they are real villagers with mud-splattered toes, raw, chafed thighs, and tired, worn faces.

My heart stops whenever one teeters on the edge of falling into a mud slick, and I sigh in relief when they avoid the spill and right themselves again. I find myself muttering encouragement under my breath when they get some momentum up and start moving wood quickly along their building line. This afternoon I even pumped a fist in the air when they reached a long, heavy branch and managed to carry it the whole way back to the huts without anyone losing their footing. As they become faster I feel my mood lifting; as they drag themselves out longer every day I stay longer to watch, shifting uncomfortably on the tree branch when my narrow arse cheeks get numb.

No longer rocking and keening behind closed doors all day, they seem braver, surer.

They still gasp in the heavy wet air, mouths opening and closing like Mr Cod. Gammy used to say that they are dry drowning, inhaling the Wet day in and day out. You're not faring much better, Gammy.

But every day they get better at this wonky work line, and every day I silently cheer for them from my tree, before muffling my bell, slipping stealthily down its wet trunk, and wandering home to Gammy, mind full of images of buildings and monuments. When I fall asleep at night with Gammy's tiny body wrapped in my arms, I have started dreaming about what they might be doing the next day, and a little tingle of excitement shoots up my spine.

She called them zombie villagers the other day; moving husks with nothing left inside. The Wet hollowed them out, she says.

But Gammy, didn't we come from them, these zombies? Isn't there a part of them inside of us too?

It's this kind of crazy thinking that draws me to their side of the village in other ways, too. No, I never learn my lesson – you know that already, Gammy. Not just happy to sit in my tree and enjoy the show, I have started inspecting their world up close. Real close. Today, I am breathlessly hiding behind a large trunk, muffling an excited giggle, as they pass less than two body lengths from my hidey-hole. Blind suckers clearly can't see a thing in the Wet, but I can see them as they move back and forward. This close, I can see how pained their movements are, despite looking surer on their feet than when I was watching from afar. Their legs are so weak; tiny, scabby little sticks jutting out from their black robes, with flimsy feet that barely seem to be attached at the ankles slipping this way and that.

Their arms are like Gammy's, peeling and mottled with veins, riddled with angry red chafe. You aren't so different from them, Gammy, not really. My own arm, resting on the trunk that sits between me and the working line of villagers, is so thick and brown it can barely be seen against the rough bark.

The Wet weighs down their every move, and this close I can hear them gasping to breathe, noses running a torrent of green that merges with the rivulets of water dripping into their panting, pained mouths. Despite moving back and forward in an orderly way on their building line, their movement is punctuated by wheezing, laboured breaths that, more often than not, end in painful, chest splitting coughs. Poor fuckers; I gingerly put a large hand up to my own strong chest, take in a deep breath to be sure I still can. The Wet is strangling them, wriggling its way down their throats and grasping their insides and not letting go.

They file past my tree to collect wood and pass it back down the line, none of them with even an inkling that I stand so close.

One villager has caught my attention, and I move my head around the tree a little to get a better look at him as he passes.

95

The strongest one. His breathing is still hoarse, but he doesn't seem to cough as much as the rest. Unlike his friends who stare doggedly forwards all time, blinking in the rain, his eyes beneath his black hood constantly rove and scan the clearing. Right now, he stands directly in line with my tree, surveying the work the other villagers are doing. He is close enough that I can see the sharp edge of his nose, flared nostrils, a slash of purple lips in among the black beard. He isn't loading wood like the others, or trudging through the thick heavy mud. He is staring at what they are doing. It's a look I have seen before, Gammy, like when you look at the spoils I bring home and hatch up a plan for our meal. They used to be like this, didn't they Gammy? Someone in charge? There are images swirling through my head of the days when they moved between villages, left their huts, built things, moved things. When they had tools, some fabric and dye for our cloaks, their own food. Before the Wet stole from them over and over, took houses and friends and supplies. I remember Gammy cowering under those in charge, bowing her head and scuttling around them in fear. Funny how you forget, hey Gammy? Seems like forever it's just been these leftover villagers huddled together without a plan or an idea between them, but perhaps it hasn't been that long, really.

My heart skips a beat: there is something behind this shifty villager's dark stare, I know it. I can't explain it Gammy, but where the other villagers look blankly at the wood they collect and nothing else, he sees. Really sees. Like us, Gammy.

There is a feeling of electricity in the air and I hold my breath as he starts, slowly, to turn his head in my direction. *Shit!* I jump away from the trunk and bound away deeper into the woods, a trail of water arcing behind me and my bell clanging wetly, and I don't stop until I am so far away there is no way they could follow on those wobbly old legs. Laughter bubbles up as I run. I fling aside branches and thick wet hanging vines, sides splitting like those silly old buggers when they are wracked with coughs, but I am bent in two giggling with glee at my close shave. Oh Gammy, imagine if he had seen me there, spying on him like that? Did they hear my bell as I ran off? My heart is hammering in my chest and I am practically spinning in excitement. I have to lean on a collapsed log for support, tears of laughter streaming down my face and mingling with the Wet.

Oh Gammy, best fun I have had in months. It's a shame what we have to do for kicks around here. Gradually my giggles quieten and when I begin to breathe steadily again, I push myself back from the old log, sigh deeply and contentedly, and start to pick my way back across roots and shrubs, back to the clearing, but to our side this time.

GAMMY IS A WHIRLWIND OF ACTIVITY TONIGHT. OLD duffer thinks it's a party in our hut. The elation in the air must be catching.

Her coarse voice is baying out song after song, her creaky hips moving to her own melody as she potters around the fire, stringing lengths of reeds to dry from the curved ceiling. The rain masked the sound of her caterwauling as I approached, but in here, the harsh noises are ricocheting from every wall. I sit, unimpressed and slouchy, naked, against the damp, peeling edges of the opposite wall.

The water has finally addled her brain.

'Shh you, if Gammy can't even sing a song in this hellhole, I might as well throw myself in the River now.'

She ignores my cocked eyebrow and turns her back to me, coughing and spluttering but still wriggling her hips mockingly while she knots the reeds together end to end, the giant rope that is forming looking for all the world like one of the great pythons I used to see knotted through tree branches. Once, many years ago, I tried wrestling one to the ground, thinking we could feast on it for weeks. Instead, I barely made it out of its suffocating grasp alive. I find myself gingerly raising my hand to my throat at the memory.

The idea of Gammy leaving the hut long enough to throw herself in the River is laughable. In among the circling reeds of my memory, I think I see her walking beside me in the Wet when I am small, shielding her eyes with bark and sliding along by the Riverbank, swearing and muttering. She might even have been holding my hand. But in the many years since, Gammy has never ventured further than the makeshift deck in front of our hut, and then only in those brief periods of sun to futilely dry her rags out.

Gammy's coughs are wracking her stooped body now, forcing her to pause her song. I watch her from behind but I don't move a muscle in her direction. Nothing I can do to stop those phlegmy wet barks from escaping her little mouth, and besides, maybe the daft old lady should save her energy for breathing, not singing. I inspect the mud caking beneath my toenails and along the scaly flesh of my feet and wait. Gammy thrusts out a shaking arm to steady herself, her body convulsing violently with each raspy croak. Little spittles of water spurt from her gasping mouth onto the floor. Flecks of green and red shower the wood.

She is getting worse every day, but watching the villagers as I do now, I see the same coughs strangling their chests too. I turn away from her quivering body and focus my eyes on her reed python instead. I don't know why she still tries to dry out the reeds. What's the point? Nothing dries anymore, not really. Not entirely. Even a crispy reed strung up for days will have the smell of moisture on it, and will soon be covered in the black spots of mould. Every day, she throws away her rotten, mottled attempts and starts again, stringing slimy reeds from the roof, only to take them back down again when the Wet has seeped through. Pointless exercise in an already pointless day.

'I have to try. I need something in this goddamn world that isn't Wet.'

Like I said, Gammy, pointless.

When her coughing fit is finally over she raises a shaky hand to wipe her mouth, only glancing for a moment at the smears of blood on her palm, rights herself, and with a look of disdain thrown in my general direction, resumes her humming. She grins gummily at me as the hum rises in volume back to a screeching melody, and she recommences her ridiculous wobbling and hip thrusting.

You're a mad old biddy, Gammy.

I can't help smiling as she nudges my buttock with a flaky foot, prodding me upwards. Alright then, Gammy. If you insist. We both giggle as we dance around the hut, our hands joined across the space of the room, the small fire casting smoky shadows on the damp wall, one tall and strong, one small and bent.

Later that night as she lies next to me, she tells me about the time before. 'We didn't sing and dance as much as we should have.'

You probably would have if you'd known how crook you would be now.

'Perhaps, perhaps.' I can only see her small outline in the dark, can see her laboured chest rising in the shadows. 'But maybe not, maybe not. You can't live like the world is going to end, can you? You have to keep doing what you are doing and hoping you can keep doing it day after day.'

Do you think the world did end, Gammy?

'One did, kid. Do you know what it is like to have the future stripped away? No, you can't possibly understand.' I can only see the glint of the whites of her eyes in the darkness. The rain thunders above our heads, breaking through our roof in spurts and dribbles. 'All the plans you have, the way you thought you would live, suddenly wrenched away from you. Ideas for the future you didn't even realise you relied on, washed away. Staring at a new world full of hardship and pain and chaos and loneliness and always, always the sense of unknown. A feeling of uncertainty and fear so hot and white it burns through your soul. You would never understand.' She sighs in the black.

For once, you are right, Gammy. If Lady River washed away our village tomorrow, what would I care? The Wet would still come and stop for that brief time every day, the sun would rise and set, I would shit and eat and walk and hunt and fish just like every other day.

'*The world is our oyster*, we used to say. I'm so sorry your future was taken away from you, kid.'

You're mad, Gammy. There is no such thing as the future anymore. Or fucking oysters.

20.

THEY HAVEN'T SEEN ME YET. I AM SILENT AND INVISIBLE in the sheets of grey water. I can almost feel my body disappearing into the wall of Wet, becoming part of it as it streams down my back and around my face. I hold my breath, heartbeat thudding in between my ears, and edge a little closer to the edge of the clearing. Three or four villagers stand less than two body lengths away, wrestling with a particularly large branch. Their feet slip and slide together in the mud like a demented water spider, but they work in an eerie silence. They don't even look at each other. Bloody weirdos.

Imagine if they knew I was standing so close, hiding among the trees ready to jump out like a wet boogieman? I raise a hand to stifle the laugh I cannot keep in my belly: they are close enough to hear me. I have already wrapped a rag around my bell to muffle its incessant chiming. My skin is tingling all over with excitement. I inch around my tree again, take a closer look through the rain. I am meant to be collecting food for the day, but the basket sits empty next to me in the downpour.

I was distracted on my way from our hut, distracted and bored and curious.

The tall, strong one is standing still, watching the others work as always. Lazy fucker. Gets his friends to do all the hard stuff and just wanders around, whispering commands. Good job if you can get it, I suppose. His greying black robes seem to sit on his shoulders better than the rest of them, who look like they have hacked up a cloak, eaten it, then vomited the remains back over their heads. A small burp of a laugh escapes my lips and I quickly clamp two hands over my mouth. No one turns in my direction. I breathe deeply in relief, then inch closer again. The mulch and leaves beneath my feet don't make a sound when I step on them; instead they just fold further into the mud below.

Now I am close enough to see the ragged edges of their cloaks flicking mud against their spindly legs. My lips curl in distaste: their skin is peeling off in sheets, revealing red, mottled and raw flesh underneath. Some of them even have a patchwork of green and black swelling up from their ankles. Rotting as they stand there.

They finally haul the log together back to the closest hut and dump it inside. Hands wipe futilely onto mud-soaked cloaks. The three workers look to the tall villager, who is standing still and silent near my tree. If they peered a little closer, they would see my little face peeking out just behind him, but of course they don't; blind as bloody eels and twice as ugly. They look to him, water spraying off their bark visors and down their hunched backs, and then lo and behold, they slide back away from the hut and form a line, ready to keep working.

Without speaking, he seems to command them. He remains with his back to me and I stare at it for a while, eyes boring into his black-robed shoulders. Does part of me want him to turn around, Gammy? To feel my presence in the woods behind him? I shake my head a little and water sprays around me. Why would I want him to know I am here? But my breath catches raggedly in my chest and my heartbeat quickens a bit, all the same.

Soon my interest is waning, though, so I slip silently back into the shelter of the heavy woods, raising my arm to stroke the waterlogged canopies above. I feel a large pool of water that has formed above my head in the crisscross of collapsed debris from the trees, and as I walk under it I tug on a branch, releasing a cascade of liquid that collapses just behind me, between the villagers and me. To them, the release of water would just have sounded like the forest beyond the clearing does every day. Unpredictable and wet and loud and scary. I am too far away for them to hear my bell through the rain when I remove the rag from my ankle.

I don't look back over my shoulder at the villagers. But a little flutter starts in the base of my spine, imagining *him* turning and looking at me as I walk away. Imagine that, Gammy. Just imagine.

I pick my way deeper into the woods, basket on my arm, ready to start work for the day. How long since I have brought them food? Probably too long. I know it's my job, Gammy, but you don't know what it feels like for them to be watching like they do when I walk into that clearing. I'd rather be watching them, hidden behind the trees, behind the Wet. What is one more day without a basket of food, Gammy? They seem to be doing ok – in fact, maybe that's what got them off their arses in the first place. Realised they can't rely on me, need to start doing it themselves again. I've done them all a favour, Gammy, really.

Soon, I have forgotten all about the clearing and the villagers and the log and the mud. It is just me, the water on my back, and the River to my side.

21.

THERE IS A SECRET PLACE I PLAY IN SOMETIMES. EVEN Gammy doesn't know about it, and that old lady tries to stick her beak into all my business.

It's right under our noses, but because I am the only one who knows the River, it is mine and mine alone. If you dive right in just near the village, follow the River round one deep bend, you'll find the place the white people live.

I grin as I make my way there, the cool current of the River tugging at my hair. Round the bend, that's the way. Out of the murky brown waters, they start to lurch out at me. Smiling faces and hollow eyes, long spindly fingers waving at me as the waters rush by.

They aren't real people of course, I'm not stupid. I've seen enough duck and fish bones to know a skeleton when I see one. These bones are tangled in webs of roots and underwater branches like messy nests, some almost whole sets still – faces and arms and legs and tiny little pieces of toes. I swim a little closer to the first cluster of bones, wedged between curling submerged trunks and winding reeds. The bony head spits out a flurry of little white fish and bubbles, the school that usually lives inside, which dart around my horizontal body. Some of the fish nibble at the scaly skin on my toes and I kick them away impatiently. I pull myself in closer with strong strokes and inspect the arms, the ribs. There are spaces where things have gone missing since I was last here – perhaps taken by a greedy River creature? Or maybe just worn away by the endless waves and movement.

The bones weren't always here. They only appeared a few months ago, sailing down the River. No one saw them but me, saw the River rush with new water, flooding and moving and dragging all this shit down from upstream. I have been thinking about it a lot, Gammy, and I think they must have been thrown in the River, then washed ashore somewhere else, long ago. Maybe covered with cold mud for years, rotting away, bugs picking at their flesh, until Lady River scooped them up and carried them downstream until they were caught up in the undergrowth here in this quiet part of the River, so close to our village. Little calm bend, sheltered from the worst of the currents. Maybe they were even from the villages themselves, Gammy, imagine that. There are hundreds of them, these pale white bones. Legs and arms all caught up around each other, spines jutting out of the cold River floor, broken skulls grinning at me from between tree roots.

I talk to them, ask them stories about before. They don't talk back, not like Mr Cod. But they are mine, these secret white people. I don't tell Gammy. I don't think she would like the idea of the white people hanging around so close to our clearing. Old lady is soft. But I like them. The skulls have big smiles; they grin right at me as they sway in the water.

I move deftly around my first white person, and kicking strongly to stay in one place, take the brightly coloured pebbles I have tucked in my cheeks out of my mouth, and start to shove them inside the thick round cavity of the head. Once the head is full of the shining red, brown and green rocks, I rip a handful of reeds from the Riverbed, and wrap them around any bone I can find. Some of the bones break off under the pressure and are whisked away by the water's force, but the thick ones, the ones wedged proper between gnarled wood and tangles of watery weeds, end up with lengths of silky plant wrapped up their entire length. I finish off the last with a firm knot to withstand the soft current, and let the River's force pull me back to admire my handiwork. There you are. You are beautiful. The skull is full to the brim with stones, the colours spilling from its mouth and eye sockets. Brown and blue snaking up the arms and legs, around narrow ribs, between hips, holding these bones secure on branches and roots. What a sight, Gammy. I look around me in satisfaction, taking in the decorations I have laid on the other white people. Some have been snared here long enough to collect little carpets of river moss, and beige, white and silver fish dart in and around their chest bones.

A whole forest of them, filled with stones and shells and reeds of every colour, waving to me from their little perches. It's just like you said, Gammy, weighed down by rocks, bound together at the bottom of the River. I wish you could see this, Gammy, I'll bet it's just like you remember.

My work done, I wave goodbye to the white people, and they wave back. I float happily to the choppy surface, and turn onto my back, letting the Wet run into my open mouth from above.

22.

When you leave kid, you walk into a tidal wave, a tsunami, and my heart throbs in my aching chest. My baby, my baby, my little water baby, disappearing into the wall of rain, swallowed and taken by the sea of grey.

I sit here rotting, decaying; the air is thick and lines my lungs. It's all grey and brown, I can't see, can't breathe, and the Wet takes my baby every day. Can you see that old lady rocking, crying, moaning, my love? That's me, that's me, weeping – like the world needs more liquid. Take all my fucking water, surround me with more, fill me up and flush me out.

Tough Gammy, tough it out, Gammy, but when you leave this house it flows out of me and I am on the floor, flapping fish out of water, flapping old lady, stupid old lady. No one to talk to here, just the drip, drip, drip of water.

Was I ever firm-fleshed and strong, my darling? I'm a different creature, so bent out of shape, so wet, so sad. I see you slip into the sheets of grey like it's nothing, kid, like you belong here. Still I worry, because I know their minds, full of dark thoughts, dark deeds.

Oh you were a squirming thing, restless and full of highs and lows like the crests of the river, always a brat, always a shit, always my love. I thought your screams would anger them, but by then they were broken things, trembling before the anger of something greater, trembling like we all were.

Kid, what you don't know, don't hear, don't see. What I don't know, don't hear, don't see.

You can't wash away the fear, can you, can't get it off. It's all changed, all different, nothing the same, but fear still lines the walls, flows in the river, runs through the mud.

Do you feel it out there? The fear, the madness? The way the Wet speaks to them, whispers in their ears? Can you feel the Unbidden rising? You don't, I know, all cocky and know-it-all. Too big for your boots, if you had boots, no need for them, got those horrid scaled feet. Horrid wonderful beautiful ugly scaled feet, three years old, already dancing on the mud like a little goblin, pointy-toothed grin and greasy skin.

But Gammy remembers. The walls groan and move and shake and the river roars and I am scared, so scared the Unbidden will rise again but more scared of out there. What would I do, where would I go? I've forgotten how to walk, how to run, how to talk except to a teenager, spoiled little brat. Is it all like this? It can't be. This can't be all there is. Because this is nothing.

Stupid Gammy, stupid like the rest of them, thought we could make a dry spot in endless rain, build copies of the old places – so vain, just watery reflections of another world, unstable as the ground beneath us. A few years between leaving lost places and trying to build new ones is nothing, a moment in a lifetime that saw so much change. And copies take even less time than originals to bend and break and wash away. Then they start to stink, kid, of closing minds, of blame. That stink is on the air still, I can smell it, smell it in the mould and the damp. Maybe it had always been there, even in the old places, Gammy just never stopped to smell the rot. Maybe they'd always been there, waiting to tighten clammy hands around a smaller, broken version of before, waiting for the Unbidden to give them permission.

My colours have been taken – do you know what that feels like kid? What's pink, what's violet, what's gold? Nothing, even the flowers are mottled brown and grey. Colours faded like rags after too many washes. It's all grey and brown and blue and black and death death death. Wet, watery death, leeching the colours, softening my bones.

And I had nothing, but when they gave you to me my heart wrapped around yours. It was horrible, awful then, and nothing since but icy panic and fear.

I'm scared of these walls closing in but I fear how big it is out there. Nothing remains that I know. And I'm scared of you and I can't follow or protect you or shelter you. And what if one day you don't come back? Would I throw myself in to join my friends and family? Did they even exist?

There aren't noises outside. Ever noticed that, kid? There aren't noises, aren't birds, the cackling of crickets, it's just the sound of water and the things being dragged down by it. The noise of mud moving fills my ears and fills my nightmares fills my mouth until I choke and cough and blood splatters the walls.

Brave face, brave heart, Gammy, what's the plan, there is no plan.

Is that you kid? Have you come back? Did you come back for me?

23.

THE TIME I WASTE NOW, WATCHING THESE STUPID villagers and their insane project. I used to spend my days wandering to the edge of the forest, finding new clearings and rocks and lakes and flying through the water. Now, I waste my time up a tree, rivulets of water streaming around my face while I stare transfixed at their handiwork.

I still can't tell what they are playing at: no structures have been built, no boats, none of those planes Gammy drew for me in the mud when I was little. If I am honest, Gammy, I am a little disappointed. I think I had hoped there was some of the old blood pounding through the veins of these remaining humans. Something to tell me that they weren't done for just yet. A grand monument perhaps, a work of art, just like you told me about. I've always wanted to see one for real.

But instead, all their hard work seems to have resulted in messy piles of wood floating in the mud, nothing more. Even my tall villager is boring and dull today; nothing but lazy orders and milling around. I sigh and pick my teeth with a hard stick, my eyes wandering away from the clearing to where the horizon would be if it wasn't cloaked in a thick grey cloud. Sometimes, gaps in the rain forge a long grey tunnel and you can see for miles, the periphery a shimmery silver haze of water but a clear line of sight nonetheless. Sometimes, if you catch yourself in one of these gaps in the rain and look upwards, you find yourself looking up a dark grey column toward the angry clouds hanging heavy and low above. A gap to the heavens, Gammy used to say. Except they only said that in the old days when the sun shone through. And the villagers don't believe in that kind of heaven anyway. They believe they will only be saved when the world ends – when the final rains come – scooped up by someone or other, and taken to the driest place they can imagine. It's why they have to hang on in this joint.

I am getting ready to descend from my tree when out of the corner of my eye, I see one particularly bow-legged villager collapse onto a mud slick and skid away from the building line.

The others don't react. Not one raised head to look at the poor idiot. He just sits there, cowed under the buffeting rain, mud swirling around his arse, hands above his head in a futile attempt to fend off the water cascading over his black hood. On they go, passing branch after branch back to the huts, not even glancing his way. I grip the slimy branch closest to me in my tall tree and crane my neck forward to see better, wondering if he is going to get up.

There isn't even a flicker of concern from the line of villagers. Cold bastards.

I squint my eyes in disbelief, because while the villagers are ignoring his plight, their mate seems to be decreasing in size every second, like he is melting into the ground and eroding on all sides, becoming a smaller and smaller hump of black nestled into the swirling debris. He is now just the shape of a man blurring into the mud.

My heart starts to hammer harder in my chest. Surely someone will move to help him. Reach a branch out in the rain, help him slip and slide his way back to the huts?

I don't know how long I am up there, watching and waiting for someone to approach him, to lift him up, to look at him, but my arm cramps where I am clinging to my branch, and my arse cheeks go numb on the thin branch I am precariously sat upon. Still no one moves toward him. A sense of dread is bubbling up from the pit of my stomach, and I inhale deeply to push down the hot sick rising up my throat.

Still he lies there, sinking further, flattening to the ground, entirely motionless now. My heart is thudding loudly in my ears, stomach churning. I am going to crap myself on this branch, I just know it.

Their work done for the day, one by one the villagers squelch their way back to their huts, black cloaks dragging and dripping around their shaky pale legs. Not one of them moves their eyes toward their battered friend. The murky grey around us gets dimmer, the heavy sky sinks even lower above our heads, and still I sit in my tree, staring at the small, lifeless black mound in the clearing that the rest of the villagers refuse to look at.

Only one of the villagers remains now in addition to the fallen man. The one in charge. He at least pauses as he picks his way carefully back to his hut, moving slowly through the

Wet which is now dappled with night shadows, sliding across the mud slicks with less difficulty than the ones who had left before him. He will be the one who helps his fallen friend. Their leader, their helper.

A warm flood of relief flushes my cheeks and I loosen my hand on the branch, marvelling at the indent my panicked grip has left on my calloused palm.

The upright villager stops as he walks across the clearing, and gives the briefest of glances at what now looks like a small bundle of black rags buffeted under the Wet.

Then he turns away from the crumpled and motionless body without approaching it, and starts to walk back toward the huts, leaving the broken villager behind as darkness falls.

Then my heart jumps right into my mouth, because I could swear to god, through the grey wall of the Wet and the dark shadows of tree canopies, he just turned around and looked right at me.

TONIGHT IT'S ME WHO ISN'T SAYING ANYTHING WHILE Gammy keeps prattling away. There's a heavy feeling in the pit of my stomach and I sit in the corner of the hut, bare arse on rough floor, with my legs curled as tightly to my body as I can, trying to warm myself up. My blood feels icier than the coldest part of the River. The Wet moves in great noisy gusts outside, banging and crashing around the edges of the clearing with a roar.

'I wasn't nothing fancy, you know, but I worked hard, all the same.' She forgets sometimes, when she talks, how fragile her bones are; how they bend like saplings under her slight weight. She scurries around the four edges of our dark hut like her back is still straight and strong like mine, yammering away, boiling water in the rusty old pot, steam twirling up through the gaps in the ceiling to be snuffed out by the trails of water dripping in. A lone brown crab rests on the floor next to our fire. But I can see Gammy's bones creaking and flexing beneath her, shoulders bent out of shape like the nippers of the crab she has now flung into the bubbling broth. She bends to meet the ground just like the weary waterlogged trees.

Just like the abandoned villager. The image of a flattened and mulching pile of rags returns unbidden in my mind, and I shake my head angrily to dislodge it.

'I wanted to be a teacher at first – can you imagine? A room full of arrogant turds like you?' She searches my face briefly for a reaction before returning her focus to the hissing pot. I haven't laughed. 'But I didn't speak or write properly. Not in the way they wanted. Christ knows what I've taught you, only hearing my voice all day every day. I was smart, but I wasn't book smart.' She pulls the pot off the small smoky fire and throws the water quickly outside – between our door rags – the boiling contents disappearing into the larger wall of the Wet.

'Oh shit!' Stupid git has thrown the crab outside with the pot water. Furrowing my brows at her so she knows how unimpressed I am, I slowly unwind my bare legs and lethargically saunter outside past our door rags, and jump to the oozing mud below. The rain hits me like a smack and surrounds me with its cool darkness. It's pitch black, the only light coming from our hut behind me, and the smattering of lights dancing across the clearing through the sheets of water: individual fires in individual huts fighting against the constant damp. Maybe I could stay out here forever, where the air is moist and heady, unlike the stuffy, damp hut filled with mould and smoke. Stay out here with the weight of the water washing all the fear and ugliness and motionless bodies away.

The airborne crab has landed next to one of the mud-encrusted stilts barely keeping our hut upright. Adventure over, crab. I pick him up by a pincer and reluctantly turn back to our home, dragging a trail of water behind my naked body back inside the hut like I am clothed in a grey, murky cape.

Gammy's feeling pretty stupid about ditching our dinner outside so she talks even faster as we eat our unlucky crab; me, crouched on the floor, water still dripping down my bare arms and through the cracks in the floor, Gammy sitting on her stool, her white and purple legs – trembling ever so slightly – jutting out from under her ragged cloak.

Through a mouthful of steaming white meat she continues. 'That was a real thing you know: the looking down on us. Not smart enough, not reading enough fancy books, not knowing everything going on in the world. But we worked hard, not that we had anything to show for it.'

She wipes a dribble of pink juice from her mottled, hairy chin. 'And in the end, the Wet didn't care. I watched them all get washed away, smart or fucking idiots, young or old, slackers and workers. The Wet did not give a shit.'

She's got that look in her eye, that faraway bloody dreamy look, and I can't bear it tonight, not with the image of that huddle of black rags in the clearing still flickering in my mind. She doesn't even notice that I'm caving in on myself like that poor bloody villager, knees hugged to my chest, trying to shrink into the manky floorboards so that I can slide, drop by drop, back out into the dark Wet.

'The Wet didn't give a shit. Not in those early days in the old places, and not when it overpowered us again here. They didn't give a shit either in the end, not really. They lost their fucking minds trying to blame someone, anyone. They practically stank of fear and hatred when they came for us. They didn't care about book smarts or street smarts either for that matter . . . they just wanted the whole goddamn world to burn, but it was too wet to light even a cinder.' She rises shakily from her stool, soft peeling hands only just managing to grasp the rounded sides, and wobbles slowly across the few feet of floor between us. I'm surprised to find salty hot tears streaming down my face and she strokes my short hair, the nape of my neck, my cheek. She bends over precariously, long tits waving under her cloak, and looks me straight in my eyes, so close I can see the whiskers above her lip and on her chin. 'And then look at you. My little water baby. The Wet tried to get us, then *they* tried to get us, and when we thought there was nothing left, we got our own little water babies. So fuck them. Fuck them all.'

That night, as we lie tangled together, Gammy's tiny body wracked with wet coughs, I let the image of the dead man melt away, because if Gammy can forget hundreds of thousands of people, I can forget this one. The little bundle of black cloth washes away in the roar of the Wet and the River, and I trail off to sleep.

I dream of the eels that night. Soulless eyes and slimy bodies snaking out of the River's darkest places. In my dream, I am trying to swim upstream, and their hard brown heads dart at my legs, over and over from their holes, sinking their tiny teeth into my calves. Hundreds of them trying to hold me back from the way forward. Just as I am about to be pulled into the depths, I wake trembling. The dark clearing is silent except for the rush of the Wet, and the occasional hacking cough travelling through the rain from the far-flung huts.

24.

WATER BABIES. I'M LYING IN THE WATER RIGHT NOW, spread-eagled on my back just below the surface, arms and legs slowly but strongly fighting the energetic current. If I kick out with all my strength, I can keep hovering right here, angry grey water splashing above my head, swirling brown water below. Suspended between water in the sky and water in the River.

I'm not hunting for food, not right now, anyway. I just need the cool pressure to wash over and around me and clear away all my thoughts.

Water babies. That's a strange one, Gammy. Real strange. You've said it yourself, many times before: they don't allow babies to be born into this world, not since the Wet. You also told me every village was only allowed one of my kind: *They feared you enough to kill you, and they feared you so much they still kept some of you. Too chicken-shit to go the whole way.*

I reach out and flip over to face downward, hands barely visible in the murky torrents, and kick myself steadily toward the River's floor. That's where I sit for a bit, clutching a buried root to keep me anchored, watching spinning shafts of dim daylight splicing through the expanse of water above my head. My hair is buffeted by the current's force, and without my green cloak, discarded messily on the bank, my bare skin almost hums along with the River's movement. My bell glints among wet shadows.

Water babies. She talks about it like it was some bloody gift, being allowed to live while they killed the rest of us. A gift for who? Not the villagers, surely, who would cave my head in with a rock tomorrow if they weren't so scared of what that would mean for them. I know they think they need to hold on to me to get to the dry afterlife, but do any of the ones left really still believe that? I can't be a gift for Gammy, either. I think she would have given herself to the River years ago if she hadn't had to raise me from a baby. I don't mean that in a good way, either – she would have been better off if I hadn't arrived, better off leaving this place for good. Wouldn't have wasted years and years decaying slowly in her shithole hut, with only her water baby for company.

A pod of tiny fish dart past my resting place, unperturbed except for having to divert their school slightly to the left to avoid my nose protruding from the shadows.

I exhale slowly, bubbles rising that are almost as big as the delicate little fish.

Not a gift for this place, surely. This place rages and storms and fights without a care for the little people clinging desperately to their past, whatever the villagers think. This place couldn't give a shit about the villagers or Gammy or me or anyone else left alive. This place barely tolerates us.

Water babies. That's a strange one, Gammy.

25.

HEY THERE, LITTLE FROGS. I HAVE CREPT UP ON THE suckers, two of them, cowering below a large leaf at the edge of the River. Their skin is a dull mottled brown, matching the dirty leaf-streaked mud beneath their little webbed feet. The rain seems to loll about their slimy bodies; they sit perfectly still, unblinking, while the water forms streams around their lanky brown legs. Their eyes are big discs of emptiness.

I lean down closer to look one right in the face, but he has nothing for me. I'm alone in a world of empty faces, and one mad old lady.

Still, could be worse. I could have been thrown in the River when the Unbidden came. With a swift movement I reach and out grab the stupid frog by its thick neck, and watch its vacant eyes bulge as I squeeze. His mate doesn't even react, just sits calm and still while I choke his friend. Either a callous bastard, or a stupid one. I grin at him while I tighten my grip on his partner, but he doesn't even seem to see me. Some survival skills, there, buddy.

Later that afternoon the lazy frogs roll limply at the bottom of my basket and I pick my way down the River. It's one of those days where the clouds sit in layers in the sky, grey and fluffy, and the rain comes in trickles rather than the usual heavy blanket filling the air. The time of sun has come and gone, and there is no noise to bother me but my own prattle in my head. I try out my whistles, long and low, and they travel farther downstream without the usual suffocating Wet in the air.

I am moving toward what I know is a large bend in the River, where it starts snaking its way down to the other villages. It's been an age since I went this far – who would want to accidentally bump into the other villagers? – but it's been so long since I saw one, I reckon I am safe.

But lo and behold, Gammy, that bloody River has gone and changed on me. No longer just a narrow bend, she stretches out in front of me as far as the eye can see, angry and dark and swollen and restless. I pause my whistling, lips still pursed, and take in the sheer size of her. Gammy, if only you could see this. You'd either laugh or croak it on the spot. I used to be able to follow her winding path for a whole day, snaking swiftly through the woods and clearings, but now I see no way through her immense body.

This must be why we haven't seen any other villagers for so long. She's gone and eaten the bloody world out from underneath them. Sneaky bastard probably did it silently too, gurgling and writhing and creeping under cover of darkness until, too late, they felt her cold grip on their gnarly old toenails. Bit like me, a little shadow in the night sneaking up on their huts.

She's a massive old body of water now, never still, always raging. I can't see where she ends. Could this be what the ocean

Gammy speaks of looked like? I creep my way to the edge of the riverbank and peer over. Touched by only a pattering of rain, I can see my blurred reflection. Ears too big for my head, short-slicked brown hair, narrow eyes and pointy teeth behind thin lips. Thick neck meeting the ragged green cloak.

Scattered throughout the River close to the banks, bare white tree trunks jut out of the water, their leafless branches reaching up in a silent scream toward the sky above. Flooded midway through their already hard lives, the trees are now stripped and dying. Too much water for their little roots to handle.

I turn and put my basket well above the water's hungry edge on a slimy, jagged branch, and fling my green cloak next to it. One last glance to make sure the rain trickling down on the flopping heads of my frogs won't dislodge the basket from the branch, and then I leap into the icy water, ready to meet this new stretch of River.

Below the choppy black surface, she is misty and blue. She has expanded so quickly that hundreds of little trails of reeds and plants and tree roots still twirl around frantically, suspended between the floor below and the dim light above. Dislodged from their homes and now lost. I wonder if that is how my white people felt, as they were carried off in her frothy embrace.

I can feel her immense weight crushing the air out my lungs. Like a big old hug. Better than Gammy's hugs, which have always been spindly and sharp and a little bit uncomfortable. Old River's hugs feel like a friend's.

I kick out and roam about the riverbed, exploring this new underwater world. She hasn't ripped all the vegetation away yet, so lone plants still cling desperately to what would have been the riverbank before it disappeared ten feet under. They'll either wilt and die, be pulled from their homes, or adjust to live down there, never spying their sun again. Bit like us, really, all the people who live in the Wet: only three ways to go around here.

I pass some craggy burrows hollowed out by the new currents, and pick my way along the rocky floor, marvelling that this surface might have been mud in the moist air just a few months ago. The layers of mulch and slime and roots and collapsed trees have been smoothed away and I can now make out the hard lines of what might have been the earth years ago. It tickles my fancy to swim along an old path, flat belly scraping the bottom, imagining thousands of feet treading there before. What would they make of me now, I wonder? Giant tadpole in the dark waters, winding my way without a care in the world. Would they be terrified? Haul me out of the water, take one look at my scaly feet and oily skin and throw me right back in?

I know, Gammy; I know, that's exactly what they did. But that was the others, the ones who were too young to know how to swim, the ones who drowned. If they threw me in now, I would flit away like a baby fish, laughing at their stupid old faces.

In front of me along the grey earth, looming out of the wet shadows, is a white, rounded thing. I kick out with more urgency, trying to see what it is. The currents are strong here and try to drag me away and to the left, but I work my way back, arms straining, and manage to reach out and grasp it in both my hands.

Tiny bubbles escape my mouth as I gape, wide open. It is made of rock, solid, but clearly one of the structures from before. Until now, it would have been hidden under piles of mud. Here it is, finally free and exposed, and no one can see it except me and the dopey fish. It must go down deep below the riverbed. All I can see is the top, jutting out white and round. The mud slicks were so strong when the Wet first came that giant cities disappeared underneath them, sinking and sliding into the collapsing beneath the earth below. Trees and bushes then shot up in the rain, so quickly that Gammy says it felt like they were mocking the cities for having ever tried to claim that soil. Gammy reckons our little clearing could be on top of hundreds of buildings just like this and we wouldn't ever know it. It wasn't just our River; floods, rains, breaking dams, mud slicks, they all converged at different places and washed away the world they once knew.

Curious, I try to stroke the smooth edges of the structure, make out its corners, imagine what this world was like before I was born, but the strength of the River is too strong. She wrenches me away and off I go, propelled along with her buffeting my limbs, until finally she throws me against a hard and rocky wall.

Disgruntled and sore, I clamber up and out of the water by grasping roots and branches, then when I am finally free, I stick my middle finger up at her, the way Gammy showed me once. Gammy regrets it now because she sees that finger reappear whenever she tells me what to do. But you have to give me a break, Gammy, I am sick of you all bossing me around. You with your fucking keeping the hut clean and trying to keep me tethered to our side of the clearing, the bloody villagers with their bells and their cloaks, and now this arsehole River, telling me where to go and tossing me around like I am nothing more than a leaf on her waves.

Bossy River, bossy Gammy, bossy villagers.

I have ended up on the same side of the River as my basket again, and the Wet is now flooding down, sluicing the mud off my legs as I stamp angrily back to the tree. My cloak is sodden and difficult to pull back over my head in the rain, and I rip it down roughly, feeling newly mended seams split soggily. Fuck, Gammy will be pissed.

As I stride away from that smart-arse River, the sound of my bell clanging softly adds insult to injury. Fuck the lot of you.

Behind me, I swear to god the River chuckles a bit.

26.

GAMMY IS NONE TOO IMPRESSED WHEN I COME HOME with rips through my cloak and a scowl on my face. I toss my basket on the hut floor next to the rapidly pooling puddles of mud and water I have dragged in and point grumpily at the frogs, hoping to get her off my back.

'Teenagers. The whole world ends and teenagers are still a bloody pain in the arse.' She scans me up and down, covered in mud and twigs and shredded green rags, and tuts angrily.

'I never signed up for a teenager. Not then, not now. I wasn't going to have kids, you know. Wasn't going to bring them into the kind of future I thought we were in for.' She snorts to herself and moves shakily around the hut cleaning, completely ignoring me standing in the middle of the room, drenched, arms outstretched to show off the delicacies in my basket.

'And right I was. Any kids I had would have ended up at the bottom of that bloody River. But then I got you.' She finally stops her fussing and looks at me appraisingly. 'An apocalypse teenager, for all my sins.'

I don't understand a thing that comes out of your trap sometimes, Gammy.

I know I have gone too far, made her furious, but I stand defiantly in the middle of the room, glaring back at her now angry little eyes. She doesn't respond, but instead yanks the basket out from in front of me and peers in at my little amphibian friends. They've shrivelled a little on my journey home despite the flood of water rushing down outside. Maybe they curled up in fright and disgust as we got closer to the village. *Please don't take us to that sad, musty old shithole!* they squealed.

Gammy pulls both frogs out in one fist and examines them sadly, their little heads rolling about on limp bodies. She places them gently on the damp floor, then starts our nightly ritual of lighting a fire from stubborn wet wood and leaves. The familiar smell of smoke, slightly tangy from the burning greenery, makes me curl my nostrils in disgust.

It's only when we are seated side by side munching on our dinner, my stupid cloak discarded in the corner of the now smoke-filled hut, that I work up the courage to ask her about before. I hate bringing it up, hate seeing the flash of old anguish in her yellowing eyes, but I need to tell her about the expanding River and the lost villages. Although it didn't scare me exactly, I feel what I have seen weighing me down despite sitting naked and unencumbered.

She stares at the opposite wall of the hut dreamily and at first I don't think she has even heard me. Finally gone deaf, hey Gammy? Bound to happen one of these days, old lady. The shadows from the sputtering fire shrink and grow as we watch, telling a little story I am sure I can make out if I stare long enough.

She munches slowly on a skinny frog leg. 'It was going to happen eventually, I suppose.' She pauses to cough a little: even slimy frogs seem to stick to her dry little throat when she eats. 'The Wet will come for all of us, in time. I don't even know why she let some of us stay here as long as we did.'

Shits and giggles, Gammy?

Hearing her favourite phrase come out of my mouth makes her chuckle a little, and she moves closer to my cross-legged body. My frog has long legs and a tiny, hard little bum. Bit like me. I can only get a few nibbles of good meat from his buttocks before I throw away the rest, dissatisfied and scanning the hut for anything else to eat. Oh fine, Gammy – she has shot me a look that could kill – so I stand up with as much drama as I can muster, sighing and heaving, and pick up the frog corpse and throw it out our door, before sitting back down and rolling my eyes. Gammy narrows hers before continuing.

'Do you know why they built the five villages?' I shake my head, suddenly more interested. 'I think there was a time, the briefest of times, when they thought they had mastered it. Thought they had found a new kind of normal after the Wet. God knows what kind of world we thought we could make, but the ones who survived wondered if we could somehow live in this new place. We had been fleeing to higher ground for so long, dodging mud slicks and floods with nothing but what we could carry, and finally they said, *we are high enough. We need to stop, need to try to make something of this.*'

The last of the fire sizzles then snuffs out, always too weak to leave embers for next time. Gammy is still staring vacantly ahead, her half-eaten frog resting in her clenched palm on the floor. His little head peeks out from her fist, but I don't want to point it out and risk that she stops talking. I realise I am holding my breath; I so want to hear what she has to say next. Perhaps I want to understand what the villagers are doing now on their side of the clearing. Perhaps I am feeling a little sad, unnerved even, by the swift and silent takeover of the five villages by old Lady River. Perhaps – and I scold myself internally for even thinking it – I want to know more about them. The reason doesn't matter; I just want to hear more. I don't dare to breathe out until she continues.

'And of course by then, we didn't even know where we were or what had happened to everyone else. The shape of the earth had changed so much from the Wet. So the villages sprang up. Little shanty versions of what they had before. I think some of them even dreamed of trade and travel, grand pathways between all five villages. A new world, rising from the mud!' She splutters violently this time, the moisture and smoke in the air filling her frail lungs. I can almost hear her bones crack with each hoarse cough. A little shudder of disgust runs down my back but I still don't speak.

'But there wasn't a plan. No way of adjusting to the Wet and the River. There was just a pale imitation of a world that was never coming back. Buried under mud and mulch and water. It was only a matter of time before they found themselves twenty feet under again.'

Are you sad, Gammy? About the other villages, I mean?

She is struggling to speak now, her throat constricted by her own spittle. But she still lets out a raspy little laugh. 'Sad? I am sad all the time, kid. Sadness is like a stone I carry around in my belly, hard and cold and useless. Did you know they put stones in their pockets, and in their mouths? The ones they threw in the River? Tied them together, four or five at a time, weighed them down, bound their mouths, then threw them in. Old, young, children, babies. No, I am not sad about the other villages.'

She has let her frog fall from her now open fist and it lays spreadeagled in the shadows. A little leg is bent awkwardly at right angles. The Wet is coming down even harder outside, so heavy I glance up warily at our poor excuse for a roof, wondering if it will make it through the night.

Gammy inhales deeply; her forehead creases into a small frown. 'I am confused, I think. I don't know why they lived when so many died, why the Wet let some people survive and stole everyone else. I don't know why we built the villages, what we thought would happen, how we thought we would live. And I don't know why what came next happened, not really. And after those bastards lost it, after the Unbidden arrived, after you arrived, I just sat in my hut and watched it all, and watched you grow, and I still don't have any answers.

It isn't all bad, Gammy. We are still here, after all.

I can tell she isn't smiling, despite the dark that has stolen over the hut since we started talking.

'That confuses me the most and the least in all of this, kid. You make complete sense. You are made for this world, can swim through both the Wet in the air and the water below. But there was no reason other than fear for letting you live. After the new waves of Wet came through the villages, after doing everything the Unbidden told them to, someone – someone completely undeserving and unknowing as usual – reared their ugly head up from the mud and sludge and said we had angered the River too much now. Can you believe it, kid? After all they had done, *now* they decided they had gone too far? And the only way to stop it was to save the last of you and plonk one of you in each village with a damned nursemaid. A down payment on eternal life, I guess – save one, pay up at the gate of your dry place. And when there is no order, no sense, then any idea sounds like a bloody good one. So here we are.' She is swaying a little and I shuffle closer to her across cold floor, let her rest her slight weight against my straight, naked torso. 'So here we are.' I breathe in her dusty scent; slightly acidic like rotting leaves. I am grateful she has spoken for this long. Told me more about before.

I open my mouth to tell her about the villager I have been watching, feel suddenly compelled to share it with her, but something in her dreamy face stops me, and I bite my bottom lip.

I wonder if they get pissed off, Gammy?

'What do you mean, kid?'

Like if the plan was just to hold on long enough, if the Unbidden told them to do what they did, and they just had to wait and put up with one of us in every village and they'd be rescued and taken to a better place, a dry place, didn't they start to wonder after years and years why it hadn't happened yet?

'Huh,' she laughs grimly. 'Bloody hell, it's a plan for eternal salvation, kid, it doesn't need to be watertight.' I can imagine her grin at her pathetic joke, but I can barely hear her tremulous voice through the roar of the rain outside. The sheer strength of it is rattling every corner of the hut.

'I don't even know why I am here anymore. You stopped

needing me when you were a toddler. Stubborn, headstrong little shit that you were.'

I turn my head into her shoulder and hide my face, and she pets my short hair affectionately, tutting and fussing.

But I am not sad, not like she thinks I am. An unexpected rage is bubbling up deep from inside me, so strong and mean I need to hide it from Gammy, hide it from everybody. I bury my face deeper into her arm to stop it flooding out of me, clench my teeth in anger so hard I think I might have chipped a tooth. I am trembling all over and have to sit on my own hands; I am terrified I could reach out and strangle her just like that stupid frog.

Gammy thinks I am sad, thinks her little sob story upset me, and is petting me and fussing over me like I am a little child again.

But the anger is white-hot and clear inside me, Gammy. I am angry at all of you. Angry at your weakness and fear and fucking stupid villages and huts. Angry with your remembering. I can almost smell the sadness on you and it makes me want to punch a fist through one of these rotting walls and run outside into the Wet as far away from this graveyard of a clearing you have made for yourselves as I can.

'Shhhh, it's ok, it's ok.' She hugs me closer, and I breathe in and out, long and low, long and low, and try to let the dull roar of the Wet and the River wash over me.

27.

I CAN'T SLEEP LATER, RESTLESS AND AGITATED AND STILL irritable, so once Gammy is asleep, complete with nose whistles and gurgles and the occasional hacking coughs, I slide out from under her bony embrace. Not bothering to put on my half-dried raspy green cloak, I sneak silently out of the hut and into the dense hug of the Wet. It's so heavy it's like a tree trunk across my bare shoulders, pushing me into the soft mud below. Even my scaled feet struggle to grip as the water and muck and debris rushes by. At the edge of the clearing, the trees in the forest are bent and heaving in the dark, struggling to remain upright as the sky pummels them from above. The dark black clouds feel like if they dropped a little lower, they would hang around my ears in great midnight swathes. There is no sign of the marker I left this morning – already whisked away in the relentless Wet. I can move through the deluge but just barely, snaking my way across the clearing. I don't bother to hide my approach; the villagers are so scared of the dark they wouldn't even peep out of a door hole, in case they saw their worst fears realised.

Control. It's all about control in the end. Gammy had continued talking late into the night, not sensing my anger or disinterest. I sat there stewing, chewing my inner lip so hard it almost bled, waiting until she was tired enough to stop her incessant yapping. My whole body now aches with the strength it took me to keep from lashing out, yelling and screaming and kicking and telling her I don't care.

There are little lights shimmering in the smattering of huts, only just visible through the heavy sheets of the Wet. It's almost like a solid grey wall, but I still move through it. They are too shit-scared to let the fires go out. I snort derisively, but move toward the huts all the same.

Control. The clothes, my bell, the structures, the villages, their stories: it didn't really mean anything or serve a purpose, it was all to try and control something.

I'm almost at the closest hut, can see its ramshackle walls shaking and heaving like the trees.

How's this working out for you all then? Feeling in control, tiny villagers, cowering in your shitty homes? I've got news for you. Your mates downstream probably thought they were in control too, had some green-cloaked freak with a bell they thought they were in charge of.

They are all fish food by now.

I'm right next to the hut wall now, a malicious shadow just outside their safe haven. I could burst in, naked and terrifying, scare the crap out of them all while they sleep. Imagine how they would scream, probably curl up into balls like little millipedes. I'd kick them and scream and then run back into the dark Wet and they would think it was all their bloody nightmares come true.

Instead, I stay just outside, breathing in the smell of rotting wood and decay that winds its way out of the cracks in their home. One gap in the wall is as big as my fist and through it I can see their black forms huddled together, shaking in their sleep with coughs that could be identical to Gammy's rattles.

Their hut is in worse shape than ours. Silvery black water streams down the inside walls and splashes across their splintered and peeling floor. The shadowy outlines of objects are strewn across the ground haphazardly. I curl my upper lip in disgust, imagining Gammy's fury if I left our hut in this state. You think I'm a grot, Gammy. These people are fucking animals.

I start suddenly as one of the black forms inside rises up slowly, waking from a deep slumber and looking about sleepily. A thrill runs through me: could the villager see me out here, my eyes glistening in the dark?

A pause, then the head goes creakily back to the floor, asleep again.

The disappointment floods through me like cold water, snuffing out the fire of my anger. I turn away from their room and trundle slowly back to our side of the clearing, head down, watching my feet move through pools of water and mud slicks. Old Lady River is laughing at me again. *What did you think you would find?*

That's why I am so mad, Gammy, so mad I can barely stand it. The rage threatens to rumble up from deep inside me and I don't know what it will make me do. This little pile of piss-weak villagers in their huts tell us what to wear and where to go, make you sit in your dank hut alone, tell me to wear a bell and green cloak and fetch their food: stay in sight but stay away.

It makes no sense to me Gammy. And I don't mean the question of why they are here or why they do what they do. That part means nothing to me.

Anyone watching would barely make out my naked body weaving through the rain to our hut. Maybe I am a figment of everyone's imagination. A little night terror, here to keep them on their toes. Weariness weighs me down as I slip back into the hut and crouch next to Gammy as she sleeps. A piece of dried snot hangs at the edge of her nostril, floating up and down with her laboured breaths.

It's not that they are here, or that they do what they do.

It's that we let them, Gammy.

28.

I AM RESTLESS AFTER COLLECTING THE DAY'S FOOD, AND I don't want to go watch the villagers. It isn't that I am scared of them now, Gammy, after seeing them leave their mate to die, I am just a little . . . unsettled, I think the word is. As I shuffled from the hut after dawn, the doors across the clearing watched me like half a dozen giant black eyes. I felt their presence at my back long after I slipped into the forest, and the prickly feeling along my spine took the whole morning to wash away.

The reeds were easily accessible today and slipped smoothly from the wet soil, the fish practically jumped into my basket to sleep alongside them, and I found a whole submerged boulder coated with juicy molluscs. I searched for a while for the origin of a croaky frog's call, but gave up in frustration after fossicking without satisfaction under a few rocks and bushes. Now the grey morning seems to drag on and on, the water pounding on my back and weighing down my green cloak as I roam aimlessly through the woods. Even my bell chimes half-heartedly, bored with the scenery as well.

I should drop off more food to the villagers, but my mind keeps wandering to that mound of black rags on the clearing floor, and I don't know how I would walk past it. They'll last another few days without me.

I run for a bit to see how far I can go, long and low, dipping in and out of trees, loving the feeling of skimming above the earth's surface. Any mark I leave is instantly washed away by the rain. I run back the way I came, re-staking my path, swinging around trees and branches.

I stop for a while, panting from exertion, to throw rocks at an old rotting tree corpse, hoping to make it collapse and career down into the raging River at my side. Each rock caves in through rotting flesh instead of breaking up the whole trunk; my catapults just pepper the old wood with gaping wet holes. Dissatisfied, I give up and move back through the dark woods, hands out to catch the Wet.

I wonder if that's what would happen to the villagers if I threw a rock at them. Or Gammy. They look soft and wet enough that their skin would just cave in on impact, gaping holes in their arms and legs.

I find an upright tree, still unusually strong and straight, that's weeping golden sap from every shard of bark. Its branches reach out to the sky seeking out a sun that will only show its face once a day. Sorry tree, the pale rays that shine down in that one time every morning won't be enough. You will start shooting dark green leaves but they will soon be stripped off one by one to form mulchy litter below. Your arms will become coated in furry brown lichen, weighed down by ropy fat vines, and slowly bend closer to the trails of water running below you.

Your bark will peel off in great sheets like Gammy's skin. Then one day, when you least expect it, you will bow too low and your desperate roots will slide out of the soil and you will heave to the side. Then, your once tough wood will soften and peel and break down until you are just a heaped pile of compost.

I stare at the doomed tree and imagine a face on its mottled brown and green trunk. Pale, sharp nose, chafed skin. A black beard. I put down my reed basket cloak and circle around, picturing *his* face peering in the shadows.

Bang! I punch him in the nose. My knobbly knuckles split with warm red blood on impact but I hop backwards on my feet then circle the tree again, fists up and ready. The rain washes the blood away. *Bang!* Another hit, another burst of pain in my arm. I shake off the blood and water and smooth my wet hair off my forehead. Rain streams over my face and down the sides of my neck. I steady myself, focus through the Wet, and move forward. Dislodged bark reveals streams of sap now appearing more red than gold, like my blood, but harder and immovable. *Bang.* The still-strong trunk resists my force and this time the pain in my fist is agonising. I grip my punching hand with the other and wince, the dull red marks I have left on the tree bark slowly washing away. I shake my head in frustration, drops of liquid showering off me in a semicircle, then pick up my basket and cloak and move away.

Stupid tree won't last more than a few months anyway.

I take a few steps into the forest, then pause and circle back to the tree, inspect it more closely. Congealed sap oozes from every exposed crack in its trunk. The reddish-golden trickles look alive in the faint light of the Wet. The tree is skinny and tall, but it has taken on a nightmarish appearance of human decay. A monster, defiant while weeping blood from every orifice, looks back at me. I rub my eyes and peer again, see it is just a raspy old tree, covered in honeyed liquid. A little shudder still runs down my spine, but I put my basket back down and pick up a rock, then start to mark the tree's trunk with small etchings no wider than my little finger, just like the ones on my time tree. Sheets of bark strip away, showing new, unexposed timber below and I start again. I mark line after line on the new white flesh, then step back to admire my work – a series of tiny lines on top of each other reaching as far as I could above my head. It makes me feel better, seeing my own mark on a bloody tree that had given me the horrors only moments before.

Just a tree.

I walk away slowly after that, picking my way carefully over piles of debris and overturned trees, jumping over puddles and meandering trails of water. The Wet is heavy around me and my thoughts are heavy in me. I pretend it was just the villager's face I saw on that tree. A black cloak and manic eyes, punched again and again by my aching fist. And if I saw your face for a second as well, Gammy, well, so what?

My aimless wandering leads me back to the woods closest to our clearing.

I don't know when I decide to go and spy on the villagers again, but the day is dragging without any sign of dimming light, and I feel a strange urge to seek out other people. Even traitorous bastards like the villagers.

This isn't like me. It used to be that I would rather stuff my eyeballs full of rounded pebbles than be within sight of these folk. Starting to lose the plot out here by myself, I reckon.

My fist is still smarting, but blood never sticks to anything out in the open rain.

Craning my neck through the dripping green leaves, I can just make out the busy circle of villagers through the thick sheets of rain. I have put more distance between me and them today: the callous look on *his* face as he peered across the clearing at his dying mate has faded into the Wet, but I'm still on edge. So this time my little nook on a high branch is far enough away that I know none of them can possibly reach me without a struggle. I absent-mindedly munch on silky reeds from my basket, the brackish water that coats them tickling my throat as they slide down, and squint to make out the smudged black shapes in the distance.

They are behaving much the same as every other time I have watched them, but they seem more orderly, more coordinated. I try not to let my eyes wander over the patch of mud where the last villager fell: in any event his friends don't seem too bothered, heads down, passing wood back and forward. The dead villager could be a pile of leftover snail shells for all they seem to care.

One hooded shape, standing straighter and taller than the rest, is barking instructions – I can hear his gruff orders sliding through the fog and rain, but can't make out what he is saying.

Who knows what I have taught you, Gammy says. It occurs to me, perched on my branch with water streaming down my cloaked back, that I might not understand anything they say even if I was close enough to hear. The only person I ever talk to is Gammy: I can't recall ever hearing more than a muffled grunt from a villager when they are busy splashing out of my way. I pick some slimy green reeds out of a crack in my front teeth and spit out the remains. We could be speaking another language for all I know. We certainly live in different worlds within our little clearing. Wouldn't that be a thing – we finally get to talking and we can't understand one word to each other.

Gammy has probably been teaching me all my words wrong just for kicks, for entertainment. She would do something like that, the bored old biddy. Given the distance the villagers and I keep between us, we are unlikely to ever find out.

They are moving with more purpose than I have ever seen. Much steadier on their feet than last week, last month, last year. Instead of a line, they are now in groups, two or three at a time huddled together, a flurry of arms and movement obscuring whatever they are doing with what looks like piles of wood. The tall man appears to be organising them again: he walks up and down their side of the clearing, dripping with rain, inspecting what they are doing, disappearing into the nearest hut and out again, barking orders. The rain weighs down his black cloak like the rest of them but he remains upright and straight-backed. Is that banging I hear travelling through the Wet? It is just the faintest sound reaching my ears now and then; clangs and bangs and more deep commands floating up to my nest above the branches.

He is all but ignoring the water rushing down around his hooded head. Less light on his toes than me, he still plods with a bit of hesitation, but all the same, he hasn't slipped in the mud once. A little thrill starts to flutter in my belly.

It's then that I notice his feet. In the place of the usual black, muddy rags the villagers wrap around the soles of their feet and up their calves, he has a neat wooden slat. A perfect rectangle strapped to his feet and resting on top of the mud. I crane my neck through the canopy in surprise, peering intently at his legs to be sure I am not seeing things. There has to be something under that slat: my scaled feet and toes dig through the fluid surface of the ground and keep me from going arse up, so there must be sharp prongs or jagged blocks underneath the wood that I can't quite make out from my vantage point.

I breathe out slowly through my mouth, whistling in reluctant admiration. They all have them, these rough-hewn shoes, which is why they are holding themselves with more strength than I have ever seen. The mud swirls around them with the same random urgency, the Wet continues to fill the air, but for the first time, the villagers are moving through it rather than being beaten down by it. Floating on the mud instead of being sucked down into its slippery depths.

What a thing.

Could they possibly walk long distances with these things? Watching them now, working in tandem, I still don't think they would make it. The mud slicks are unpredictable and most of the food is by the River: and the River is greedy when villagers come close. I can't see from my hiding spot, but I am sure they still gasp through the Wet like beached fish, wheezing and flapping their gums and coughing up moisture.

No, they are probably still prisoners to this tiny clearing (the thought flashes through my mind: still prisoners to me and my food). Still, I thought they were sure to be wiped out in the next year or so, with most of their numbers depleted anyway, the villages downstream already lost and the River rising so fast.

But maybe I underestimated them.

One of your kind in every village. Just enough to appease the Gods after wiping out the rest of us. Too scared to keep us alive, but too scared to kill us all.

Maybe you bought yourself a bit more time on this planet, little villagers. Good for you, I guess.

I am about to swing my leg over the bough and plop down onto the swirling mud below, when I see out of the corner of my eye the other project they have been working on. Crudely fashioned instruments placed neatly under a shelter outside one hut door. Long, jagged and angry looking pieces of wood. Ends sharper than anything I have seen for a long time.

For hunting, perhaps. Maybe the idiots think they can pierce the bubbling waters and skewer their own fish for food. Hah, unlikely. Fools.

I slide silently down my branch, silencing my bell with two pinched fingers, and wander back into the woods, whistling through the Wet. I only turn back once, to check that the villagers are still moving industriously, and that the black-cloaked heads are still turned away from me as I leave.

29.

I SNEAK BACK LATER THAT NIGHT. OF COURSE I DO, Gammy. I dart out from the woods under a cloak of Wet and hug my chest to a stilt under the first hut, feeling my invasion of their space like a charge through my body. They are worn out by the day's activities, and through gaps in the floor I watch them all fall into a restless slumber. I move from hut to hut slowly, weaving this way and that, creeping underneath and peering up and in where I can. The dark, heavy feeling that weighed me down after the villager died has evaporated like the Wet in the sun, replaced by the nervous hum of energy I feel whenever I get this close to them.

This close to *him*.

I stop before the hut I now know to be his and reach up to touch the damp outer wall. For a second I wonder if he is awake on the other side. For a crazy moment I wonder if he can feel my presence, a looming ghost out here in the Wet.

A strangled cough from inside breaks my thought and I shake that feeling away in surprise. Can't let myself get as soft as Gammy out here.

I turn away from the hut, satisfied without looking in, and lope back through the cool rain to our side of the clearing. Sleep well, little villagers. Let's see what you get up to tomorrow.

30.

MY PISS IS THUNDERING DOWN ON THE LEAVES TODAY.
With the annoyingly warm sun on my back, the minute one
mottled leaf swirls into view I am firing my hot stream at it so
that it plunges back into the murky water, bobbing up again
only when it has reached the edge of my sight.

Down, down, down, one by one, those suckers go down.
I whoop loudly and beat my bare chest: I am king of this fucking damp world and the leaves are my loyal subjects, swirling
around my brown rock entirely under my goddam control. No
needy eyes, no shit-scared scurrying, no whispers and sobs
and coughs and groans, just me and my brown mulchy minions
dancing at my feet.

I'll piss on the lot of you. I could be a bloody god out here
and no one would know it but the leaves.

My piss dries up and I yell and push but only a tiny gold
dribble comes out. I sigh in disappointment and hop off the rock
with a splash, rolling lazily onto my back in the water and letting the current take me for a while, gazing at the eerily pale

blue sky; ears submerged, arms flung out to my side. I know I am drifting away from my cloak and my basket, but the water pressure around my ears is soothing and the River vibrates through my body like a gentle hum.

My eyes, able to see miles through the Wet, are unused to the glaring sun and I close them against its orange heat, thinking about the kings and gods and warriors in the stories Gammy tells me, thinking it's strange that in this world there are none of those things, despite what the villagers believe. Not so strange, I guess – there's almost nothing that wasn't washed away by the Wet. But, while the sun still fights through the clouds to show its face, even just for a time every day, not one of those kings or gods or warriors is anywhere to be seen.

Maybe I am the closest this place has to a god. Me and my hairy brown arms and bony ankles and scaly feet. I chuckle softly at the thought, imagining Gammy's sideways eyes flashing at me when I tell her my grand thoughts.

I drift further down the River, the rumbling of rapids rocking below me but my body moving with the waters. Up and down I bob, side to side, always remaining straight and long like a stiff wooden branch. Maybe I could float this way past the village. Imagine their shock seeing my rigid, naked body shoot past their huts. I could wave nonchalantly from the water as they scurry back to their homes, leaving a trail of mud and fear behind them.

Maybe I could travel to the end of the world, wherever that is these days. The villagers might be locked into their tiny little clearing perched on the edge of the woods, but not me. Free as a fish. Freer, even.

The smack of the rock into the side of my head sends shooting pain from my temple down my neck in a sharp eruption and I momentarily plunge under the water. God or no god, I don't know up from down right now and I frantically grab at my head, realising too late I wouldn't know if there was blood pouring out from my smarting temple with all the gurgling brown water swirling around me. Trying desperately to calm my hammering heart and hold my panicked breath under the waves, I let the current suck me backwards. Finally I begin to float upwards, the River naturally righting my still body until I burst out from the dirty surface and, feeling foolish, hold my head with one hand while the other strikes out unevenly to what looks like the least slippery part of the bank. I am annoyed to discover there is thick red blood congealing on my face and trickling down my neck. The lack of rain means it is thickening fast and drying in the sun rather than washing straight away. It instantly feels dirty and sore.

I sit for a moment on the bank, clumps of wet mud dropping beneath my weight, contemplating my own stupidity. Bloody god, alright. God of the idiots.

In a place full of them, that's a pretty big call.

When my heart has slowed and my hands have stopped trembling, I gingerly lift myself up off the crumbling bank before it collapses under me entirely, and start to wander back alongside the River, picking and weaving my way through caved-in trees and overhanging vines, sheepishly this time – carefully.

No gods and kings and warriors out here, that's for sure.

As I move from rock to rock, aggressively ripping out any reed or shrub that gets in my way, the rhythmic pulse of the

River and the tinny chiming of my bell work to soften my mood. A cheeky thought takes me and without missing a beat, I reach up to cover my fingers in the warm blood still forming a wet crust at my left temple. I dab it down my bare chest, make a giant rust-brown cross. I dab some on my taught thighs, on my nose, my cheeks. I can still be a king and lord and god and warrior around here. God of the bloody dance, I am.

I shake my legs as I duck and weave through the low-hanging canopies, my bell ringing loudly. I start to whoop in unison, leaping from rock to bank to log. The blood has caked onto my body in the sunshine and gives off a slightly rusty, metallic scent.

A sense of release floods through me and I think this is how they must have felt, those powerful men from the past – like they'd had their heads smashed open by a goddamn rock but the place was still theirs and theirs alone. I raise my gaze to the sun and laugh out loud at my ridiculousness but I keep dancing and prancing down the bank, mud and water and debris flying in my wake, my arms pumping above my head and my blood-streaked body slicing through the clear air like a red bird: like a fiery red fish.

I burst from the thick undergrowth alongside the River into a clearing and leap onto a large craggy boulder. Standing tall and proud I thump my chest in the sunshine and dance and stomp my feet until I can barely lift my arms anymore and then I collapse, laughing, tears streaming down my face, naked arse on my warm rock, bell finally silent.

I see the face as I am letting out a long exhausted exhale. With a jolt I register the pale white features, ragged black beard and torn black cloak, partly obscured by a crisscross of fallen branches and cobwebbing vines but still there, watching me in my clearing. So far from the village.

I am so shocked I can't even rise to my feet. My heart restarts its thumping but more irregular this time, an intense pain searing through my injured left temple as I clench my teeth in horror. In an instant he is gone, and at that moment a shadow falls over the clearing and the air is heavy with moisture and the crashing noise of the Wet once again.

I don't move from my perch on the rock, ignoring the rising water lapping around my dangling feet, the caked blood on my chest and limbs washing away as quickly as I had put it there, my eyes never leaving the point where he had been.

The villagers can't walk out of the clearing without sliding over into mud slicks or getting bogged or worse, slipping into the raging River. They can't see through the Wet, they can't move, they can barely breathe.

But there he was, watching me.

31.

'LORD OF THE BLOODY DANCE,' GAMMY SAYS WITH A shriek of laughter, whacking her skinny thigh loudly in amusement. I am crouched over our fire in a futile effort to get the still damp logs to do anything but hiss and steam and splutter. Gammy laughs so much she ends up doubled over, wracked with wet coughs, flecks of green spittle flying sideways onto the kindling. I give her a sharp look so that she is in no doubt about how unhelpful I am finding her contribution, and turn back to my pile of wet branches and mulch, flashing my flint to try and make something – anything – catch for more than a few seconds.

Gammy pulls herself upright herself and continues to chuckle, still not doing anything useful, just watching my frustration grow.

'If you looked anything like you do now, your little kingdom is in a hell of a lot of trouble,' she says, with another shriek of laughter. Thinks she's bloody hilarious, does Gammy. I snort in anger and turn my bare back to her, violently swiping my flint on the small knife we keep in the hut.

I haven't told her about the villager, of course. She would just worry, would give me one of those panicked looks she always flashes me, like she doesn't trust me to handle the situation. I can handle it just fine.

Anyway, I am already starting to wonder if the knock on the head was making me thick, foggy in the brain, making me see things. The idea that one of those idiots could travel through the woods and up the River on their own without becoming bloody leaf litter is absurd, impossible.

But I told her about my little performance, marked up and bloody, showing the world all the dances she had so carefully performed for me. She is still giggling to herself, silly fool that she is, while dark shadows streak across the hut. I am no closer to lighting this goddamn fire.

Gammy grins at me across the room, all gums and spittle, and watches me try to set some damp twigs alight. 'The kings and warriors and gods always thought they owned the bloody fires, too,' she chuckles to herself. It's one of the many jokes from Gammy I don't understand. 'Always thought if they could tame the flames and cook the meat that they owned the joint.'

She looks at me accusingly, like I am somehow responsible for the idiots who came before me, and rises creakily from her stool to snatch the flint out of my hands. With one swift flick of her wrists she has a spark sitting in the centre of the pile of leaves, and in another second a tiny orange flame is licking at the sides of a twig and creeping slowly to the larger branches. She flashes me a smug look and wobbles back to her stool, sitting down with a clumsy crash, her whole body seeming to sigh with the effort it had taken to show me up.

I move away and sulk on the other side of the hut at the door cavity, only a few body lengths between me and Gammy, face turned to the darkness outside. My temple is tender and my pride more than a little wounded.

Gammy is still chuckling. I can imagine her leaning back against the rough wooden wall and rolling her eyes upwards, like she is plucking memories out of the sky.

'Lord of the bloody dance. Lord of the Flies, more like it.' I look around to meet her gaze across the small room. She has stopped laughing.

A silence stretches out between us, me sitting cross-legged on one side of the hut near the open door, her slumped at the other end. A few feet of rotting wood floor and our smoking fire between us.

'You know, these people, some of them were the greatest scientists history had ever known. They predicted everything – all the droughts and the heat and the fires and the disappearing animals and insects and water. They knew it all. Some of them even predicted the Wet coming. They made graphs and machines, they talked to some of your kings, reasoned with them. They made plans – detailed plans – to prepare us all for what was coming. They were so scared but they were still so proud of their science, and they laughed at the ones who believed in the gods.'

She hasn't lowered her gaze across the room, her eyes glinting in the quickly dwindling light, the shadows from the now crackling fire making her soft face seem sharper, harder. I'm uncomfortable under her stare, like she is somehow including me as a bad guy in this story. I finally drop my eyes and stare through a hole in the floor, watching black water puddling on the mud far below. The rain patters against our slatted, cracked roof.

'And these scientists. The smart ones. The smartest ones anyone could find. When the Wet came proper and whole cities went under water, and people started to drown or rot from the inside out, and the water washed through our sewerage and started to poison anyone who was left; those scientists still thought they had answers. But by the time the second waves came and washed over the new villages, those scientists? The ones who were still alive blamed the gods just like all the crackpots they used to laugh at. The crackpots and the scientists and every other bloody person who had never visited a church in their goddamn life started to talk to the gods and that's when they started the killing. Because,' she shifts her weight from one sore arse cheek to the other and I realise I am holding my breath, waiting for her to continue, 'because there is nothing like a good religious conversion to convince you that someone needs to be sacrificed.'

I don't know when she stopped being funny but now it feels like the air is heavy enough with her anger to snuff out our already flickering fire. 'And it doesn't matter if it's the end of the fucking world, there is always someone who looks like a sacrificial lamb to the shit-scared.' She pauses, looks away from me to the struggling fire, and starts to rise shakily to her feet again. She potters over to the flames, floorboards creaking threateningly with every step, reaches past my shoulder to grab a stick from next to the door, and starts to poke the embers, slowly pushing the flames back to life. So gentle sometimes, my Gammy.

The air feels a bit lighter now and I realise I am still hold-ing my breath, so I exhale deeply as she starts to fossick in my baskets and place reeds messily into the pot. The tense moment has passed and my belly is rumbling, so I spring up to join her and squat at the basket, foraging around for the hard shells of snails and molluscs to start preparing on the rough damp floor. Gammy grins at me from where she is stirring her pot, close enough to the fire that the light is softening the crags of her face. She only has two teeth now – the rest have fallen out of her soft gums.

'So you may as well be lord of the dance out here, kid. They believed in every and any god by the end, and still none of it saved them. So we may as well have fucking Lord of the dance running the joint.'

She's chuckling again in between muffled coughs, and even I can't help giggling at her craggy, nearly toothless smile as she swishes around the pot, humming a long-forgotten song. I step away from the food and lean back against the wet wall and close my eyes, her humming mingling sweetly with the crashing of the Wet and River outside, and think it's not the worst place in the world to be a god. Not really.

The image of the villager's face peering out of the woods fades along with the remaining light radiating from behind dark clouds.

32.

I CAN SURVEY MY ENTIRE KINGDOM FROM THE TALL TREE closest to our clearing. It's really only twice my height, and already bowing to the ground like its broken neighbours, but because it is clinging to the top of a small hill, I can see further from up in its branches than any other vantage point. I don't fancy its chances of lasting more than another year; the hill on which my tree currently perches is shifting ominously below me and tiny channels of water wind all around its base, but the roots are still submerged deep enough below the moving mud that I have taken the risk and scrambled up its solid girth.

The Wet cloaks everything in thick, endless grey, but in lighter periods, if I strain my eyes, I can see through the mist and water and make out the curling path of the River as it winds upstream. I know every inch of what is in sight from travelling it by foot, but up here, I can also make out the moving bodies of water to either side: trickling streams and rushing waterfalls, flowing mud slicks and falling trees spinning down hillsides to be buried in mud and rotting debris below.

This place never stops bloody moving, Gammy complains. *Not one inch of it*. She hates the constant flow of liquid and mud, the shivering of leaves under droplets, the always-present patter of water on every surface. Even the air above swirls and whirls, filled with heavy dark clouds without spaces between them, but moving around each other just the same in a churning frenzy.

That's the way I like it, Gammy. The world around me heaves and churns, throbs and crashes, and I move with it. I feel the waters in my belly rolling as clearly as the water cascading off my back. If the Wet stopped and the movement stopped with it, I think I would collapse, dizzy with the stillness. A sight for sore eyes that would be; me, disoriented and clumsy for once, bell silenced, the rest of them sure on their feet.

The idea makes me chuckle, but an odd feeling also starts bubbling low in my belly, the same feeling I get whenever I think of that black mound of a villager being pummelled into the soft sludge by the rain. His body is still there, rotting away in the rain right near where they eat, shit and sleep, little bits of him floating off as each day passes. I shift uncomfortably on my arse and will my stomach to be calm. I am annoyed at these new feelings of doubt that rise suddenly without warning: images I'd rather forget. Soon I will be a basket case like the villagers and Gammy, jumping at shadows and memories.

I have walked even further upstream than I can see, from where I sit perched in this tree, no matter how hard I crane my neck. But I reckon I can see further upstream than the villagers have ever set foot. They never head that way, even when they could. Upstream is where the River begins, and in their tiny little minds that's where the Wet comes from too. All their troubles are upstream, all their friends downstream. At least, that's where they used to be.

The bubbling in my stomach becomes hotter and heavier. *They don't think the Wet comes from upstream. They think the Wet comes from you.*

Right now, there's nothing coming from me except long, claggy shits from all the reeds we have eaten recently, Gammy. My bell chimes tinnily as I jump from my slender bough into the slippery mud below, and as if to prove it to her, I squat right next to my tall tree to relieve myself, watching my tapered black crap join the busy movement of water, slop and leaves down the hillside.

The heavy feeling in my stomach is probably the piss poor dinners we have been having. Might be time to focus more on foraging, less on the idiot villagers. Rising quickly, I turn in the direction of the River, and take a running start down the hillside and through the undergrowth before leaping into the frothy waters. I spend the afternoon submerged in the cool brown water, collecting flapping beige fish we will sizzle on our smoking fire that night.

'DO YOU EVER THINK ABOUT THE OTHERS?' HER FACE IS gentle, but prying all the same. She knows better than to press me – I would as soon as walk out into the midnight Wet than talk about things I don't want to talk about – so she asks casually, glancing up through red-rimmed eyes while she mends my ragged cloak. The rusty needles are snagging on the coarse, damp cloth, so she is bent almost double in the flickering firelight, carefully pushing and prodding through the rotten material. She's using old threads pulled from her own rags, trying desperately to keep mine together, make the shape of clothing. Waste of time, Gammy.

Do I think about the others? Of course not. I have too much on my mind, looking after you lot.

Her face remains still, almost featureless in the dim glow. Her gnarled fingers are peeling, always peeling, where they meet her soft nails. Sometimes I think Gammy will peel back layer by layer, whittled down like my little stick, until there is nothing left.

I would never tell Gammy, but I used to wonder, sometimes, when I hopped along the banks of the River: is someone else like me doing this downstream? Green-cloaked, bell chiming, jumping along identical banks of the River in a different place? Do we look the same, scaly feet and all? Do they have huts too? Are they allowed to live near the villagers? Have they grown like me, can they hold their breath and swim down to meet the fish too? Do their villagers scurry out of their path, fearful and suspicious?

Do they have their own Gammy, or are they completely alone?

You've told me enough, Gammy. I don't need to waste my time thinking about them. One in every village. Water babies. Born as the Wet took over new homes just like it took the old ones. Born in the Wet, of the Wet. The only ones spared when the deaths didn't appease the River. Saved to stem the tide. For a while.

Do I think about the others? Of course not, Gammy. They are probably washed away like everyone else. No sense thinking about others, Gammy.

She doesn't say a word, just sits silent and still on her stool, shoulders hunched, peering at me through the shadows.

Do I think about the past? What is this Gammy, why all the questions? She doesn't crack a smile, doesn't laugh at my tone. I ignore her watery pink eyes seeking out mine, and turn my back to her, pretending to inspect the long lean muscles of my arms and legs instead.

You and all the villagers wallow in the past, Gammy. You wallow in your stories like the sticky mud. Your history leeches strength from your soft bones and sucks at your weak ankles and drags at your cloaks. I don't want to wallow with you lot. I want to fly through the Wet.

33.

A bee landed outside the door today, kid, when the sun came to visit. Not sun, not really, weak, pathetic thing, doesn't dry my heart out, doesn't dry my lungs out.

Pack your bags and go. Move to higher ground. We'll see you there. But when we get there, how will we know how to find you? Where will you be?

Camp here, little makeshift camps. Move again, keep going, the waters are rising. Here, let's stay here. Build wobbly replicas of a time that doesn't exist anymore. Why didn't they tell us that you can't get back if the shape of the world changes, bends, moves, floods, washes away?

What's that, my love? It's the Unbidden, whispering in their ears. Truth or dare? You can't have both. Truth gets in the way when you need answers, kid. Bunker down, stay calm, it will pass, it will never pass.

The bee was black and brown, not gold, a watered-down version of everything I have known, have remembered, have seen. Different looking, different shape, shiny hard coat instead of fuzz, buzzing through the rain like a yellow submarine, like a brown submarine. No fur, course not, nothing with fur survived, weighed down, waterlogged. Only slimy, scaly, oily things remain. Maybe that's what it was always like. Do you remember, kid? Course you don't.

Do you know where the bee goes? What do you see out there, kid, where do you go? It's a topsy-turvy world, topsy-turvy, like me. Do you walk upside down, outside these walls?

I can't keep the wet out, clog up the cracks and holes with rags and bark and feel the wobbling below and pray that we stay upright, stay safe another night, stay safe. The words swirl in my mind when you are gone, kid, like a whirlpool, rapids, a churning river. They only come out right with you, for you, I take a deep breath when you come home, and make the words come out right.

You don't care, though, do you kid? Should slap you, should draw you close, never let you go. Stupid kid, only one, all I have, all you have, oh god, my sweetheart, my water baby.

Are you coming back today?

34.

IT'S TRUE TO SAY THE CODFISH IS MY ONLY FRIEND. You're not a friend, not really, Gammy. You looked after me when I was little, now I look after you. It's a fair deal and one we are both happy with. I put up with your prattling because you teach me about the time before the Wet, you put up with my . . . well, nothing, Gammy, you love me and my dirty feet and puddles of water and rancid farts. I chuckle in the murky brown depths of the River, imagining her raising an eyebrow at my cockiness.

But the codfish, he is different. He is the only living thing I talk to who doesn't need me, doesn't rely on me. I reckon Mr Cod was here before all of us, before the Wet came, lurking in the deepest parts of this place. I kick my legs downward and fight the currents to his lair, coaxing him out to meet me face-to-face. His wide copper head always appears slowly out of the shadows. I love the way his rimless white mouth opens and closes as if he is talking to me. I know Gammy, I must look like a crackpot, talking to a fish, but at least he isn't scared of me like the villagers. In fact, sometimes I swear he is trying to tell me something, and if I hover down there long enough, he might give me the answers no one else can give.

He hangs around in the darkest part of the River near our clearing, and it takes all my strength to steady myself in the swirling torrents and speak with him. I started visiting Mr Cod when I first began exploring the River as a little tacker, long skinny legs struggling against the River's rage, bobbing around madly below the surface until I learned to keep myself steady. I could barely hold my breath back then, rushing up to gasp the air then duck diving back down below. Day by day, I held my breath longer, used the gnarled roots to pull myself down, built strength in my shoulders to propel myself through the water. Soon, I could travel thirty body lengths with one held breath. My skin threw off the water, my eyes could stay open and scan the murky depths, and I learned to love the weight of the River crushing my lungs.

When did I first meet him? I was scavenging for reeds and fish. My memories of that time are tangled like the murky grass swirling in the water; I don't know what is my recollection, what you've told me since, Gammy, and what is a dream, so I don't remember how I learned to find the safe foods, how I knew to deliver them to the villagers. I think they were once less helpless, less cowed, more connected to the other five villages. They weren't happy, exactly – those miserable fuckers could never be happy – but they weren't so defeated back then. Then day by day, the Wet made it harder to walk, harder to build, harder to get between the villages, and the coughs started hacking away at their already weak bodies, until one day they were helpless. The visits from other villagers went from months to years apart and then stopped altogether. By then, they were already relying on me – a baby to save them, then a kid to nourish them.

The first time Mr Cod made an appearance on my swim, I nearly shat myself. I had been showing off (*To who? The fish?* Shut up Gammy, maybe I just wanted to prove it to myself), trying to see just how deep I could get. The force of the River was tearing at my little arms, almost ripping the hair from my head. I was hauling myself along a craggy bank, grasping buried stones and slippery sticks and kicking frantically, barely able to see a metre in front of my eyes. Suddenly his big brown whiskers appeared. I swear, Gammy, I almost peed myself right there and then. He could have been a monster of the deep for all I knew, lurking in the shadows.

But I knew he wasn't. He looked at me kindly, his mouth gaping open and closed, and seemed to tell me not to be scared. His eyes were sad, and after what he had seen – the floods and the death – I didn't blame him.

He looks at me today from his dark hole, big whiskery mouth gaping. I swim forward even closer, putting my face to his. Bubbles from both our mouths join together before rising up to the surface, far above.

What did you think, Mr Cod, when the bodies started floating past you in the night? Did you hide and watch from your burrow deep behind the rocks? Did you know what was happening up top, far above your cold murky home? Did you hear the madness and the screams and the crying and the fear? Were you scared, these strange figures plunging into your world from nowhere? Or did you see those bodies float past, clothes splayed in the eddies, and think – *good riddance?*

Then when the bodies stopped, and the water kept rising, I wonder if he cared, or if it was just another day at the bottom of the River.

He does understand me when I speak, Gammy. He knows more than the lot of you combined.

35.

I KNOW I GAVE YOU SHIT, GAMMY, ABOUT GETTING BOGGED down in the past. And I don't want to talk more about it, not really. You know I get sick of all the yapping and whingeing. But I do wonder, sometimes, why you never ask me about what I think is to come. Is it because I am a child, and you think I don't know?

Because I have to say, Gammy, you guys didn't quite nail the whole predicting the future stuff yourselves.

I am sitting on a small hill watching the world move around me, trying to resist the temptation to spy on the villagers again. Wasting my life watching those losers, Gammy. Rivulets run down the slopes in front of my filthy feet and meet to form large puddles and streams, each one weaving and winding its way, gaining width and strength before finding the edge of the River and adding to her expansive belly. It's like she has thousands of tiny arms now, all spreading out and exploring and devouring more ground for her. An army of miniature rivers doing her bidding. Trees sway and groan and crack as water gushes down their sides. Mud moves in waves around their roots. If I follow one of the surges of liquid black, filled with rotting reeds and shrubs and leaves, I can never tell which way it will flow. This way, that way, everything meanders. The only sure thing is that they all end up in the River eventually.

The Wet hangs heavy in the sky, sometimes in visible streaks of rain, sometimes just a lighter mist that settles on the hairs of my arm.

Today the Wet has flowed strongly, washing my muddy calves and soothing my tense neck. Days like this are my favourite: when the Wet and the River and I seem to move as one. I gave up on hunting and searching for food and instead decided to sit here and watch the earth through a cool grey wall. Everyone deserves a break once in a while, Gammy.

Looking at the woods and water dancing like this, I do wonder what is next, Gammy. The River fills up the edges of my sight now, the forest roof is lowering, the sky seems darker. Only the world of the old codfish remains unchanged, cool, dark and brown in his burrow.

I think that's why you don't ask me. Because you couldn't have imagined this world, let alone the next one.

I stretch my arms up lazily, letting the Wet soak through the holes in my cloak, and reluctantly rise to my feet. I walk slowly down the hill toward the River, one foot forward in the flowing mud and then the other, ignoring the temptation to run alongside the collection of dirt and leaves rushing down beside me. When I reach the River, throw off my cloak and plunge in, I feel like I am now properly joined up too. In the right place.

I'm not interested in finding fish today. Instead, I spend time hovering close to the rocky riverbed below, little rising bubbles tickling my nose. Except for my discovery in the River downstream, I have rarely found any relics of the past down here. I used to think if I explored far enough, inspected every twist and turn of the great River's edges, I would find the shells of buildings or monuments. Old material, rubbish, objects. Anything from the time before the Wet. But the water is so fast moving and the rain so relentless that it all must have been washed away years ago. Washed away and beaten or smothered or worn down into pieces so small that they can't be seen or felt or heard. It's like the world now refuses to remember. Even your footprints wash away before you can glance back. The only relics of the past are the villagers, stubbornly clinging to their old lives.

I kick out and propel myself long and low, the weight of crushing water above my head sitting with a pleasant pressure on my bare back. As I pass a rocky outcrop, five little heads snake out of dark holes and stare at me with sinister eyes. Eels. Another relic from the past. I don't stop to watch them but instead pause a few body lengths away and wade my way around to look behind me back at the eel nest. They still sit half-writhing out of their respective caverns, swaying gently in the current. A shiver runs up my spine and I swim away quickly. I fucking hate eels.

The clouds are fast darkening by the time I emerge from the River, pull my scratchy rags over my head, and turn back toward the village. Gammy will be waiting patiently for me. I smile thinking of her gummy grin peering through the water, out of our hut like a strange little frog poking its head out from under the leaves. She'll be wondering where our dinner is and desperately wanting someone to yap to after a day with nothing but the spattering of the Wet for company.

I trudge slowly back through the woods, picking my way over debris and through pools of mud, arms outstretched to catch as much rain on my skin as possible before I move indoors for the night. This is the best time, when the Wet still moves like a living thing down my back. When I move inside with Gammy, I feel the absence of its weight and the lightness makes me feel unhinged, anxious, giddy. Like I could float away into the sky, and no one would be able to tether me down. Maybe that's the way Gammy and the villagers feel all the time – like they could float away on the mud slicks at any moment.

I feel a crackling in the air, and wonder suddenly if a storm is coming.

The dark hairs on my forearm stand up as the sky above deepens. My heartbeat picks up when I see the angry dark clouds rolling in from upstream, filling the already shadowy grey sky with an even heavier presence. The rain has tailed off a little, as though in anticipation of what is coming next.

I let out a gleeful yelp and run excitedly all the way back to the village, letting scraggly branches and long vines whip my body as I fly past. A storm *is* coming.

Gammy's face is peering anxiously out of our hut across the clearing when I fly into the open in a spray of water and leaves. There isn't a villager in sight – there is no way they'd be out with a storm brewing. She frantically motions me inside but there is no way, Gammy, you know I love a good storm. I ignore her pleading eyes and instead stand just in front of our hut, mouth dry in anticipation, scanning the horizon above the trees for the chaos I know is coming.

Then it does – with a crackle and a whoosh – it comes.

Colours I never see on an ordinary day roll across the sky. Mottled purples the colour of Gammy's bruises, midnight blues, angry flashes of silver. The sky is alive, electrified. I bounce from one leg to another, eyes wide and hands clasped in sheer delight in front of my green-cloaked chest.

Suddenly the sky is alight, fingers of white-hot lightning reaching above my head. The flash lights up the whole clearing and for a moment time is suspended and I can see our whole world clearly: scared villagers peering from their huts, white faces lit up like haggard ghosts. Gammy behind me, equally scared, trembling behind our door. The clearing, small and sad, filled with tiny, rickety huts, dwarfed by the surrounding River and forest and sky and Wet.

Trailing the lightning like a shadow is the thunder, a clap that reverberates through the whole clearing and shakes me to my core. I laugh and throw my hands up in the rain, feel the rumble from my fingers to my toes. Each new flash of lightning reveals the wild eyes of the villagers across the clearing but I am not looking at them now, I am looking at the angry, churning purple clouds, the Wet lit up like shards of silver, the snaking, crackling electricity streaking across the sky. The crashes of thunder that rumble through the clearing feel like a rhythm my own heartbeat is matching and as I stand there, arms and face flung upwards with the rain crashing down, my chest feels like it could burst with scalding hot energy. I feel electrified, exhilarated. The noise is a wonderful rush in my ears, overpowering and spine-tingling.

A snap right behind me startles me and I turn to see Gammy sliding out of the hut. Horror is etched on her face. Gammy would never usually leave the hut in the Wet, let alone a storm like this, but her grasping white hands are leading her down the outside steps and toward me. Flashes of lightning light up a disjointed, ragged dance as she slips and slides her way along the side of the hut, bare feet barely gripping in the mud and hands doing all the work.

Her eyes are pleading for me to come back inside with her, but I stand where I am, hands still raised to the sky. She can't walk further than the hut as her clumsy feet won't take her forward in the Wet without her hands gripping something. Her cloak is flattened wet against her bony head, white tendrils of hair plastered along her face, mouth gasping in the rain. I turn back to the clearing, ignoring her frail form behind me, and raise my face to the stream of cold water rushing from the sky.

Oh, for fuck's sake, Gammy.

Without looking behind me, I can tell she has fallen to the ground. I want to ignore her but her presence is like a stick in my back, ruining the moment. The rush in my ears lessens to a dull roar, the crackling through my insides fades.

One last flash of lightning shows a dozen or so little white faces peering across the clearing.

When I finally turn back to her, Gammy is collapsed next to the hut in the rain, a panicked grip on a wooden stilt and mud slicks piling around her crumbled form. She sobs. I hear the whimper, and with a long exhale, I lower my arms.

The rushing quietens to a low hum. I turn in the rain and stride back to her, picking her up gently from where she lies sprawled in the mud. She gazes up at me through the heavy Wet with terror in her eyes, iridescent snot running down her face.

C'mon then, Gammy. Carrying her sodden, muddy form back across our threshold, I glance at the sky one last time, now a muted grey. The thunder is more distant, and the rain is easing to a trickle.

I don't know when we will see another storm like that again. My chest constricts as I step over the gap in our door and into our hut. Smoke and dampness and a rotting smell overcome me. An irritating ringing fills the space between my temples and my eyes begin to sting.

I place Gammy gently on the floor, water still streaming from her wet cloak, and move to the opposite corner to peer back out the door. The clearing is now dark; the only noise the roar of the River and the patter of the Wet on our roof.

For a moment I think the breath has been sucked right out from my lungs. I feel suffocated, itchy and stuffy.

I glance back at Gammy where she rests on the floor. She looks so relieved. Trembling like a leaf in the rain.

36.

I SNEAK OUT OF THE HUT BEFORE DAWN TODAY.
Emptiness sat on my chest all night like a sad old codfish, staring me in the eyes and refusing to let me sleep.

I know, Gammy, it is just a storm.

But I feel intense disappointment that it ended. For a moment, Gammy, I felt like I was a part of that angry, raging sky; that I could snake and fork my tongue across this land and taste every part of it. I know that won't make sense to you.

I wander aimlessly away from the clearing and through the woods, feet hopping lightly but my thoughts heavy and black like the clouds hanging just above the forest canopy. I haven't bothered to put down another marker, but I don't need one to tell me the River is swollen and grasping, flooding the edges of our clearing even closer to the huts.

It sounds mad, Gammy, to be so disappointed, I know. But you lot have your stories and your memories, I have nothing but the rhythm of the Wet and River and sky. I feel like I lost that rhythm last night.

A strange thought sneaks into my little head and I try a whistle, a clap of the hands, just to see if the beat really has been stolen from me in the night.

Idiot. I better watch out, or I will end up as crazy as those villagers. Crazy as Gammy. I shake my head and concentrate on walking, one foot in front of the other, trying to drown out the irritating voices in my mind. The Wet hangs solid and even in the air around me, and the mud slicks swirl slowly and steadily in circles around my filthy feet. I glance down at my bell, muddy and rusted on my bony ankle. I bend down briefly, think of yanking it off for good. Does it really make you feel safer, tiny villagers, being able to hear me coming?

I didn't think so.

A deep inhale reminds me that the air out here is clear and moist and refreshing, unlike the mouldy old hut. The steady patter of rain hitting wet trunks and puddles starts to relax my tense shoulders.

We'll be ok, Gammy.

I don't fetch food today, can't even remember where I left my basket. I just walk and walk, inspecting the forest floor full of bracken and moss and mulch and mud and little trickles from the River. The whole day I walk, circling our clearing, weaving my way up and down the River's bank. I see again the full expanse of the River downstream of our valley, peer across her body stretching further than my eyes can reach. She has gobbled up more of the land. I imagine the riverbanks collapsing as she reaches up hungrily, trees shrieking as they fall sideways and are whipped away by her currents.

I sit for a while at her edge, rain pounding on my back,

watching her dark raging waters barge their way forcefully downstream.

I follow thick horizontal roots rising from the earth like serpents before they burrow down deep into the mud. I memorise each rock and log on the way back home, smiling in the knowledge that by tomorrow they might have moved again, washed away or covered or obscured. The constantly changing shape of the world finally soothes and calms me.

I think back on Gammy's little body slipping and sliding and clinging desperately to the side of the hut in the storm.

What the hell am I going to do with you, Gammy? I know – we all know – that Lady River is coming. You might not see her approach, but I reckon you can all feel it. It's why the villagers have been in a flurry of activity in recent months, why they are desperately trying to learn to move again. Shaking off the decay and the rot, looking for a little sap in those rotten old legs.

There is a feeling hanging in the air among the Wet, something knocking them all even more off balance than normal, scaring the crap out of them. I could feel it in the space between the flashes of lighting and the roar of thunder last night: a great gaping fear sucking the air out of our clearing.

Why is he following me, Gammy? I don't know. Maybe he thinks I have the answers. Hah. I am still a kid, after all, you lot are meant to be in charge. What good are your rules and colours and bells and boundaries if you aren't really in control? If you don't have any answers?

I have been gone all day. I am sure Gammy is freaking out, thinks something happened to me last night in the storm, but frankly, Gammy, I don't give a shit. I take my time picking my way back through the undergrowth, letting my hand trail through long wet grass and across mossy trunks. I stop occasionally and lift my face to the Wet and let it roll down the front of my neck and into my green cloak. The itchy material chafes where it meets the skin on my collarbone, and the cool rain calms the angry pink burn.

I am close to the clearing now but in no hurry to enter it, even with the dimming light. Fuck them all; let them go find their own food in the rain, let them move the village. They've got their fancy shoes and weapons now, let them try. See how far they get without me.

My whistle plays out, long and low, through the dim light, the Wet sucking the sounds out of my mouth and snuffing them in front of my face. I try louder, face contorting with the effort, and bloody hell: maybe the Wet has finally soaked through and addled my brain but I could swear the woods just whistled back.

I stop in my tracks, ears pricked.

Long and low, long and low, a foreign noise winds its way through the broken trees. A strange wail, sometimes snatched away by the rain, sometimes reaching my ears in full. It isn't an echo of my whistle. It isn't like anything I have ever heard.

The noise moves and creeps through the Wet toward where I have paused mid-step.

It's getting louder.

Anxious now, a strange heat bubbling and rising from deep in my belly, I start to run toward the village; head down through the wall of water, flailing arms moving aside curtains of vines and branches, a trail of destruction behind me. As I round a large log I can tell the noise is coming from our clearing and getting louder as I approach: a noise full of fear and hysteria, circling like moving tendrils through the trees. The noise is alive and terrible.

I skid to a stop just outside the edge of the clearing, mud splattering my drenched cloak, and crane my neck nervously toward our hut, terrified of what I might see. It only takes me an instant to make out her pale face at the door, seeking me out, terror etched on her craggy features in the fading light. Her fear is an echo of my own, an echo of the noise.

At first I think the noise is coming from her hut and that she is hurt, but soon I realise the keening is circling from back behind our hut: it isn't coming from her at all. It starts much deeper in the clearing, coming from the other huts. I squint through the grey toward the other villagers' dwellings and hear unnerving wails rise out of every craggy opening. Long and low, these wails echo around the rainy clearing, joining together in a strange song of misery and fear.

I turn back to where Gammy stands at her door, still desperately seeking out my face in the Wet. I begin to understand that although I can see her, she can't see me through the rain. She is looking at a solid wall of water and trying to find my green.

It's then I realise with a jolt: the Wet never stopped today. There was no sun, no light, no respite from the rain.

I sink shakily back against the soft wet bark of a tree and listen to the fear circle around the clearing, growing louder as the darkness sets in.

37.

GAMMY IS UNHINGED. COMPLETELY AND UTTERLY unhinged. She's pacing about the hut in hysterics, not even noticing the pools of water I have dripped across the floor, fire unlit, loose skin of her arms flapping in the shadows. I can barely make out what she is saying; she is muttering in a high-pitched garble, her soft, wrinkled cheeks actually trembling in fear, her words drowned out by the rush of the Wet and the mad wailing still circling the clearing. I can't think with all this fucking noise and I sit in the corner, hands over my ears.

Her hysteria makes me want to shake her: it makes me angry that she is as weak as the villagers, as shit-scared as they are. The sun didn't appear today, but it will tomorrow, as sure as anything. The sun has appeared every day since I was born, every morning. I lower my hands from my ears and start to pick my teeth with a dried reed, trying to feign nonchalance while watching Gammy's frenetic pacing from rotting wall to the door and back again. The reed is rotten and I spit on the floor in surprised disgust.

The revulsion on my face seems to stop her in her tracks and she turns to me, face gaunt in the shadows. 'You have no idea. No idea. No idea.'

I do. I do have an idea. I know you are all fucking hysterical and the sun will come again tomorrow. Maybe the Wet was heavier today. Maybe you missed it while you were all staring at your bellybuttons. Maybe this will be what happens now: a day or two without sun but radiant warmth the next. This place has never stayed still, Gammy, not once, why should the sun be any different? And after you stop having a fit you can go sit in the golden light with the scared little villagers and complain about the Wet together while you try to dry out your chafing armpits and mouldy arses, just like every other day.

Quick as a flash she is in my face, spit splattering over my forehead, her concave chest heaving from the effort of her anger and her fear. 'They killed you all, don't you see? Wipe that fucking blank look off your face – don't you understand? They will blame you for this. Little water baby to sacrifice if the River became too hungry. Appease her again, like they did last time. They will kill you and they will kill me. They are terrified and they will come after you, I know it, just like they did before.' She moves away from my face and flops weakly against the wall, bowed legs shaking. 'I watched them throw children in, don't you understand?'

I am still wearing my wet green cloak so the arm I throw around her is damp and scratchy, but she doesn't seem to notice or care. She leans weakly on me, sobbing now, her tears mingling with the water dripping down my still wet legs in murky puddles on the ground.

'I thought the Unbidden had gone,' she mutters quietly.

It has, Gammy. We are still here, aren't we? The little water baby and the old lady. You'll see. These idiots can barely hold themselves upright, what hope do they have of coming after us, even if they wanted to? You'll see, you'll see.

She rests heavily on my side but her frail body is still tense and taut, like a sharp little stick.

We don't eat that night, or light the fire. We lie down on the floor where I take her in my embrace, Gammy still shaking with fear, my arm still around her bony shoulders, the keening from the villagers gradually getting softer but somehow also shriller at the same time. I'm not worried about those fuckers, but the noise sends shudders up my spine all the same.

When Gammy seems to have fallen into a restless sleep, I carefully untangle myself from her musty body, drag off my mouldy old cloak and throw it into a shadowy corner of the hut. Without the usual smoke from our fire, the hut stinks of rotting wood and old fish. A bit of old lady scent in the mix too – a sharp, pungent smell with a hint of sweet decay, like overripe berries.

Thinking about what Gammy said, I walk to the door and pull the curtain rags aside, looking out at the clearing and the black woods beyond. The moon, obscured as always, casts a pale light through heavy grey clouds and makes the falling sheets of rain between us and the wooden structures across the clearing appear almost silvery, like tiny little specks of light falling softly to the ground. For a moment, I think I could put my hand out and capture the sparkle in my palm. A little light for our dark, empty home.

I peer out into the night sky. The keening continues longer than I expected and I try not to think about what Gammy said about the babies. It wasn't the first time she has told me about the Unbidden or what they did to the children, but the muffled moans emanating from the rickety walls of the villagers' huts are making it hard to push the images from my mind. Tiny bodies being sucked down by the River. My old friend Mr Codfish watching and weeping silently on the dark River floor as babies plunged like drops of rain through the raging surface.

Unsettled, I shake my head violently, like I can knock the image out of my mind with brute force. I wish the bloody noise would stop – a knot is forming in the pit of my stomach and I feel uneasy, so uneasy. Maybe this is what the Unbidden sounded like, too. There is no movement outside, nothing I can see through the rain, but I am still unsettled.

I am nervously chewing the inside of my mouth and a sour brackish taste is rising in my dry throat. If only they would stop screaming, then I could think. Instead, their mad cries have me imagining people running, of them captured, bound and thrown into the River. Bodies suspended in murky green and brown. Floating hair like halos, waving clothes becoming heavier with liquid. The greedy River opening her mouth and swallowing them all, before swallowing their hunters too. Swallowing everything.

I stand at the door, scanning the clearing one more time in the dim grey light with Gammy snoring and spluttering behind me. My naked body is now dry under the ramshackle roof, my breath rising like a shadowy mist out from under the raised curtain. The clearing is lit with an ominous purple-grey.

When the villager catches my eye I don't move away from the door. I breathe in slowly, a fist of fear replacing the acid in my belly. He stands quite still in the clearing, away from the other huts, and I stand equally still, framed by the door. My naked body trembles slightly but I don't take my eyes off that arsehole, not even for a second. I puff my chest out and stand a little taller, hoping I look strong and invincible in the moonlight. Stronger than I feel. His features are obscured by his black hood and the rain but I know somehow it's him. The one from the clearing: the strong one. The one barking orders. The one in charge. And the only one not wailing miserably in his hut. He just stands there, rain pouring down his black-cloaked form, motionless in the near dark.

In the end, it's me who drops the curtain and turns back to Gammy's twitching body on the damp floor. When I peek nervously out of the door again, the clearing is empty.

The wailing has stopped. In its place is the steady rush of the Wet and behind it, eerie silence.

38.

'THEY WILL COME FOR US,' SHE MOANS SOFTLY, CROUCHED in shadows in the centre of the hut. Her sobs are punctuated by the steady dripping from a hole above and just to the side of her bowed head. I watch as the drops skim past her white, scab-covered knee where it juts out from her cloak and splatter on the rotten floor, disappearing into the damp wood.

I am exhausted and angry. The brief respite when Gammy fell asleep ended the moment I turned away from the door and the clearing outside. Her warbling cries have been relentless since. Not loud enough to wander through the mist and Wet outside and travel to the ears of anyone listening in the village, but loud enough to send shudders down my spine and force me to pace back and forth in the hut, my scaled feet tracing the route Gammy was taking across the room just hours earlier. I watch her from above as I pass – her weak white arms hugging bony knees, ragged cloak falling to the floor, matted white hair plastered to her scalp with wet and rot – and I feel a surge of rage rise up through my throat.

Her sobs stop suddenly, and she lifts her head weakly to look at me as I stride past.

I need to tell her everything I have seen. In response to her pleading eyes, honesty falls out of me instead of the bile I have felt churning in my stomach. Yes Gammy, I'll tell you everything. They saw me. One of them did. He has been watching me. He's seen me piss and shit and dance and sing. Covered in blood. Lord of the dance. He sees it all. He has been watching me. Stalking me in the woods. He was outside. He has been watching me. He sees everything.

And I have been watching him.

I tell her about the stockpile of wood, about the strange tools and the shoes they made, about their growing steadiness. She closes her eyes while I talk about his barked orders, wincing when I speak about his motionless gaze. Every word I throw at her hits her like a physical blow. Now that I have started talking the stories spill out of me, the words chasing each other around the hut and landing squarely on her soft jaw. Tremors reverberate through her body.

Her eyes, so recently glassy and scared, flash in the darkness, and she rises slowly, creakily to her feet. She takes the arm I stretch out and leans on me as she walks uncertainly to her stool. Once seated, she surveys our small bare hut, like she is making some kind of assessment, then rests her wobbly head on a bony hand, staring at the door and shadows beyond. My words have all tumbled out of me with flooding relief, and now the roar of the Wet outside hangs heavy in our ears.

'They will come for us,' she repeats, but slowly, softly this time. No panic, just stillness. 'Yes, they will come. When the

Unbidden came last time, it didn't take long. No one saw it coming. We were all as scared as each other and thought we were all in it together. But as the waters rose and our new villages fell, they made gods and demons – gods to pray to and demons to blame – faster than even the Wet could come.' Despite the pillowy darkness around us, I know she is looking at me intently. 'You will be their demon this time, sure as I know anything. Their demon and their sacrifice.'

We both stare at the door, listening to the rushing rain outside and the echoing crash of the River. The keening may have subsided on the other side of the clearing, but the silence makes the hairs on the back of my neck prickle even more. I am feeling light-headed from no food, no Wet, but at the same time I feel a thrumming start in my chest. Rhythmic and calm. The birth of a new kind of steadiness after the madness and chaos of the lost sun. A new plan.

Gammy is finished speaking and with a loud sigh, I walk to the corner of the hut and pick up my basket, tossing in a knife, a flint and some dried reeds, and fling it over my shoulder. I turn in the dim light and reach a hand out to Gammy's. One large and calloused, one soft and pale. We don't speak, but we understand what has to come next. She takes my palm gingerly in hers and as she rises unsteadily, I turn away and kneel in front of her in the damp, my head bowed low this time. Her body is frail and unnervingly light on my back as she wraps her spindly arms around my naked shoulders and neck. I tuck her tiny legs around my waist and under my arms, and lift us both off the floor. She weighs almost nothing, like a tiny damp frog clinging to my back.

Off we go, Gammy.

She has to duck her head as soon as we leave the hut to block out the rain pouring down, and that is how she stays as I wade through the clearing, her head nestled into the bristles on the back of my neck, her hood pulled forward, raspy breath tickling my bare shoulders. My ripped old cloak lies discarded on the hut floor. A pile of rags to compost like the leaves.

I only glance at the village for a second; enough time to see the clamour of motion, and to know that they were coming, the villagers, just like Gammy said, but we beat them to it. They are incapable of speed; I can outrun them fifty times over.

The River alongside us is silver in the darkness and fast flowing. Her sides are swollen and she has edged even further up the clearing. My eyes might be playing tricks on me in the night, but she seems to breathe out even as I stare at her: an exhale that never comes back in. She is expanding toward the huts with a dull rumble. I close my eyes and wonder how long it will be before she is lapping silently at the stilts of our own house, wonder if she had planned to steal us away quietly in the night like she did to the other villages.

I open my eyes.

Off we go Gammy. Into the Wet. Guess you were right, after all. Know-it-all.

She chuckles softly into my wet back, and I turn into the woods, ankle bell chiming softly.

39.

SHE'S NOT HEAVY, GAMMY, BUT SHE'S SCARED, AND I CAN feel her fear like a jagged hot rock on my back. Her breathing is laboured and she clings tightly; so tight I can barely breathe as I walk. It's a good thing, too – her bunched cloak sticks to my naked back and is the only thing stopping her sliding down in the rain. My basket bangs awkwardly against my thigh as I move. I'm not in any hurry, despite her clinging arms and pounding heart: the villagers won't be able to catch us, even in their fancy new shoes. They probably didn't even outrun Lady River.

Gammy's frantic looks back over her shoulder tell me she doesn't agree. I keep my eyes fixed straight ahead.

The Wet is a thick black blanket in the middle of the night, its roar even louder than during the day, and the silver rays coming from behind the carpet of clouds in the sky only just light up the odd drop of rain as we slice slowly through the grey sheets of water. The dark, bowed trees seem to lurch out at us from the shadows, branches slapping my face and making me jump like a jittery villager.

Gammy is shivering now, cold from the constant stream of water down her back. I don't know what to do, Gammy, there isn't anywhere dry to stop. There's nowhere dry anymore, not now that we have left the village. Ahead it is just mud slicks and Wet and crumbling riverbanks and broken, mossy trees.

Almost all the other villages were downstream, and there is no way we will head that way.

But we sure as hell aren't hanging around here, not with our own villagers losing their minds like this. Losing their minds over me – fucking lord of the dance, with my painted body and scaly feet.

I don't get it Gammy; there's only one of me, and I just want to be left alone. Not lord of the dance, just lord of the cod-fish or something. That sounds nice, really, nice and warm at the bottom of the River, quiet and dark with nothing but the rush of water in my ears.

Gammy is asleep on my back now, her ragged breathing getting shallower, arms still wrapped tightly around my neck. I hoist her a little higher on my hips to relieve a dull aching in my lower back. She shudders with a wet cough then relaxes back into my neck. Nice for some, Gammy. Nice for some.

My feet sink into the muddy ground more than usual, pulled downward by Gammy's slight weight, and I concentrate on putting one scaled foot in front of the other, watching the rain poke pattering holes into the moist earth around my foot, then wash the footprints away the moment I raise my foot again. Despite myself I keep jumping at the looming trees, imagining shadowy faces behind every cracking branch or collapsing canopy. Gammy's wet breath is right in my ear and muddles my hearing, and I struggle to make out anything over the noise of the Wet and the River.

Gammy. Of course I left this place with her on my bloody back. Gammy, the only person I really know. Her and the people in her stories, that is, who are more real to me than the villagers.

Gammy, who sent me out when I could barely walk, knowing she couldn't follow me anymore. How did she know I would stay afloat on the mud slicks, could swim in the River like a fish? She probably didn't, come to think of it. What else could she do? Little kid in a collapsing wet hut, scraps of food collected by the villagers as they slipped and slid across the riverbanks, anyone who survived the floods and the Unbidden coughing and sputtering in their damp houses. She probably sent me out thinking I would surely be taken by a mud slick and swallowed by the noisy River. Just a little kid. Savage, Gammy, savage.

And what do you get for your treachery, Gammy? Food and shelter and someone to tend to your shedding skin, and a royal ride out of here when the going gets tough.

She coughs again, almost losing her grip, and whimpers a little, hunching further into my back as if she could get herself out of the rain if she just dug deep enough.

Gammy, who tells me stories about the time before and dances like a lunatic, and holds me close at night. A lump rises in my throat and I clasp her frail legs a little tighter around my hips, ignoring the pain stretching from my lower back to my abdomen and through my chest. My body has never hurt like this. Not even when I was first sent out from the hut, cracking my ankles on hidden rocks and scratching my face on craggy trees. This pain hangs like a dull ache, pulling me downwards.

Where to Gammy?

My body is screaming and my eyes bleary by the time I notice the sky changing shades of grey. I have kept the River to my right as I head upstream and I start to make out the colours of the riverbank: crumbling black mud and blue-brown reeds, green moss and lichen, ragged grey logs. I know somehow Gammy is awake now, her breathing lighter and clearer, but she stays quietly nestled in the nape of my neck, hooded head shielded from the constant downpour. I know she isn't looking at the world outside. She will be studying the back of my head, focussing on breathing through the Wet, nothing but a wall of blurred wet movement outside of my presence.

I'm going to have to stop soon, Gammy. I know. I know.

Her despair makes me feel sick in the pit of my stomach, gives rise to a hot liquid that burns my throat. There is no way those idiots could track us this far, but still her terror seeps from her like a rancid smell.

Irritated, I look around for somewhere – anywhere – where Gammy can be sheltered from the rain. She's no bloody help, can't see through the Wet, and I'm starting to get real shitty as I scan past mangled trees and water-soaked canopies. I'm exhausted, Gammy. But she doesn't care.

When I finally get to a small, damp patch sheltered by a trailing canopy, far enough from the River that a mud slick won't send Gammy sliding and slipping straight in the River's mouth, I drop her roughly on the ground. Giant brown seed-pods sway in the rain around her head. She stares up at me like some wounded animal and I storm off away from her before I really lose it, reed basket on my shoulder, angrily parting vines and branches with a wet spray to stomp through the undergrowth.

I'm furious at her fear, angry at the villagers, angry that we have no plan.

I'm not gone for long, but I can tell she is terrified when I return with my basket bulging with reeds and some tiny sweet snails I found on a rotting tree corpse. I have already popped a few in my mouth and crunched them between my pointy teeth, shells and all. Their warm insides relieve my light-headedness, and my crankiness.

She raises her head at the sound of my bell – for some reason, I can't bring myself to cut it off for good, not yet – and so I chime a warning to her as I return. Her red eyes are wide and watery, her bony arms wrapped around her cloaked legs, trembling violently. She looks small and rounded like a rock, a little bubble just sheltered from the wall of rain outside her resting place. The grey mottled clouds hang so low above the canopies it looks like they are reaching down to smother her. I try not to feel too bad as I slowly approach and lower myself next to her. I'm in pain. Even without Gammy riding me, my lower back throbs and vibrates. Small droplets of water still seep from the canopy overhead, pattering down with a dull thud on her soaking wet back. Yeah, I know, you won't take the stupid rags off. You're all as bad as each other.

She sends me a dark look and hugs her legs tighter.

'I am nothing like those sadists.'

You know that's not what I meant, Gammy. I sigh loudly as I reach for the flint and knife in my basket and try half-heartedly to light some wet twigs in between where we sit together. We both know we will be eating raw food today, and that if the sun doesn't come out for a second time, we have no way of drying Gammy's cloak or keeping her warm. Still, it's important to keep the old lady's spirits up and so I keep flicking the flint, over and over, while Gammy stares out at the moving grey of the Wet.

'No one was ever like those sadists,' she continues. Her nose is dripping bright green mucus. She absentmindedly wipes away the snot with the back of a dirty palm, and fiddles with the edge of the cloak hanging next to her mud-spattered feet. 'It's like they rose up when the waters did. Normal people – once bankers, musicians, doctors, parents – who rose up with the floodwaters and became something we had never seen before. The Unbidden and the fear went through them, just like the Wet, and they turned into monsters, and then they turned on us. Some people said, right at the beginning, when it all started, that we should have seen it coming. That it had been hiding in them all along, a darkness inside our neighbours and friends, itching for an excuse to get out.' A bony hand snakes out and snatches one of the reeds from my basket. Gammy has all but given up on the fire too. 'I didn't agree. Those monsters were shells of the people we had known. Nothing left but fear and hysteria and hate and water-addled brains. We never could have seen them coming.'

Shells are exactly right, Gammy. The villagers are hollow. Nothing but basic emotions like fear and hunger, huddled together, just barely surviving. A tremor moves up my spine and I try to push aside the image of the villager's face staring at me from the clearing. His searing eyes.

'When they came to find their sacrifices, I looked right into the eyes of one of them and saw nothing in there but anger and fear. That's when I knew we were done for. These weren't the people we had known before the floods, or even the people who tried to set up the new villages after we fled to higher ground. They were a new type of monster born out of the chaos and loss, convinced that they could kill their way to something better. I knew then that this was how the world ended. Not the way the scientists said, not through the weather or the floods. The world was going to end because people emptied their minds and souls and saw imaginary demons in the destruction.'

The limp reed hangs from her fingers, barely a nibble taken from the end. There is a gnawing fear in the pit of my belly. She has spoken like this before, but always in the confines of our hut, with the villagers nothing but a trembling mass across a clearing. Out here, knowing I'm all she's got, it feels different. Sharper, like nothing in this place of smooth edges usually feels. The fear is swelling up and vibrating through me like the sound of the crashing River.

'So many people fought back. More than you would expect. They came out of the woodwork too; surprising little heroes where we least expected them, standing up to them, trying to stand in between them and their prey. But in the end the fear was like an infection, and the only people left were the diseased.' She places her uneaten reed onto the mud and I watch it gently slip away in a stream of oozing sludge. Gammy hasn't noticed.

Look where it got them, Gammy, all the madness and killing. They couldn't keep their own kids alive, or their oldies. Lost the lot of them. Now, there's just a smattering of crappy villages, a hungry River, a green-cloaked freak to fetch them food. Some prize for surviving.

She can't control the shivers anymore. Her body is in constant reverberation, droplets spraying off her hood, her tremors broken only by her ragged coughs.

My flint catches and we have fire, small and low though it is. Steam rises off her cloak. The coughs don't stop.

40.

WE HAVE TO KEEP MOVING, GAMMY. HER FACE IS BLANK.
She's been ignoring my pleas, her hunched back pressed to
the wet tree trunk, refusing to move. For someone who was in
such a bloody hurry to get out of the village, she is in no rush
to keep going. Her legs are locked in place, bony arse making
a hole in the mud, immovable and motionless. Like a fucking
tree stump.

Her expressionless stare is making me nervous and irritable. I violently kick out at a collapsed log near her leg, watch it
crumble and start to travel away from us in a claggy black mud
slick. She doesn't even flinch.

See Gammy, everything is on the move here. We have to
keep going.

I don't believe the villagers could follow us, not really, but
the memory of that pale face keeps rising up unwelcome in my
mind alongside visions of the expanding River, and I can't bear
to stay still any longer. My feet dance on the moving mud with
nervous energy. I don't really know if there is anything better

upstream, but we sure as hell can't stay here under this tree, just swapping one desolate clearing for another.

This is the first time you have been away from the hut in how long, Gammy? Since it was built? Since they gave you me, your little water baby, to care for? You should be enjoying the scenery! Not staring into space, all empty-eyed and remorseful. Sure, it's the same mud and water and shit as back there, but look around you. We are away from those idiots once and for all. Let's kick ourselves in the arse and get a move on.

Her lifeless eyes scare me more than the thought of every villager on Earth coming for us.

Come on Gammy. Please.

WE SIT SIDE-BY-SIDE AND WATCH ANOTHER DAY CONTINUE, the Wet unrelenting. I sit outside of the canopy, naked and shrouded in water. She huddles under the sparse shelter of the trees, cloak still wrapped stubbornly around her narrow chest. Neither of us speaks, but we both know when the pause in the Wet should come, and we both stay silent as the time passes and the water rushes down uninterrupted.

The villagers will be losing their minds. If they have survived.

Gammy stays mostly motionless, only occasionally shifting in the thick mud to relieve the pressure on a bony buttock. She grimaces with the movement. The silence that seems to hang like a curtain in front of the roar of the River only lifts when she releases a stream of hacking coughs.

Her breathing is deep and gurgling, the Wet lining her lungs and rising up her throat in phlegmy specks.

'The sun isn't coming today,' she rasps.

Of course it is Gammy. As sure as the River flows.

But it won't. I know that now. I feel the rhythm deep inside me and something that had been erratic before now feels calm, circular, constant. The Wet won't stop ever again. It floods me with relief even as it fills me with fear for Gammy.

We sit in silence, watching the endless sheets of grey melt the rough edges of the woods.

I HOLD HER TIGHT THAT NIGHT, HER SHUDDERS GRADU-ally weakening as my body warms her through her coarse damp cloak, I wonder if she cowered when they came for her, when the Unbidden rose up and the killing first started. Did she tremble like this, a small, powerless, weak old lady, helpless against the forces around her? Did they look at her and know, like I do now, that she would be utterly reliant on them, utterly in their power? Or did she fight: were her pink-rimmed eyes once sharp and clear and violent? Did she stand tall and proud, daring them to do their worst?

She probably spat in their fucking faces, old Gammy. Spat in their faces and kicked and screamed and tore at their hair until they shut her up by handing her an unwanted baby – a baby they all believed had destroyed the world. Some victory.

Her bony little ribcage barely rises with each breath now. I watch it shudder and fall until the darkest of the grey lifts, holding my own breath nervously, waiting each time until I see her inhale.

41.

'SPAT IN THEIR FUCKING FACES?' SHE MANAGES A LOPSIDED toothless grin.

I knew it.

Her eyes, more alert today, are roaming nervously through the mist, plotting and scheming and planning our next move.

I can barely wipe the smile off my face; the relief at her sudden animation is so strong in my gut. I still ache like crazy, but the anxious jitteriness I felt while she was doing her empty vessel trick of yesterday has lifted.

'I watched them throw people into the River, first an example here, a scapegoat there, but they didn't come for me at the start. They picked off the ones they said were trouble-makers, the ones who hadn't played by the new rules that had multiplied by the day until we were swimming in them, until no one could remember what the rules were, or who was making them up. I heard rumours of missing friends, people I had grown to love in the other villages, going for a walk and never coming back. Of course I was scared, but some part of me was convinced

I wouldn't suffer the same fate: that they would be satisfied with a just few sacrifices, and that if I played by the rules I would be ok. But the River kept rising and the Unbidden told them to feed her more, and then they were tossing in any one of us they could find. Most of us were locked up by then anyway, strapped and roped to trees and crumbling walls. Others ran and were hunted down, back when we could still move between the five villages and through the forests. They were hunted and bound to their friends and children and thrown into the waters wherever they were caught. But it was strange. I watched so many huts swallowed up by that arsehole River during that time, and still they didn't come for me. The walls they had shackled me to collapsed and fell downstream too, and still they didn't come. I thought, for a while, they were punishing me by making me watch it all.' Her eyes wander the whole time she is speaking, scanning the horizon intently.

'But they weren't that organised – who needs a plan when you have mass hysteria? They'd just forgotten about me. When they finally did come, there wasn't even a roof over my head. The rain felt like it burned, it had been wearing down my skin for so long. I thought it was my turn in the River. Part of me was relieved, but mostly I was angry that they had let me suffer for so long just to throw me in at the end. I didn't know, when they finally did come, that I was one of the only ones left.'

Her voice sharpens with a new steeliness. 'I fought and spat and kicked with the strength I had left but that's when I saw that the wildness had left their eyes. These monsters had nothing left, not fear or even anger. They had thrown their future into the River to appease their crazed gods and still the rains came, still the waters rose. They were broken. So they turned to me in the Wet, with their tired eyes, and gave me you. A baby born in the Wet that they were too exhausted and broken and scared to kill, and they convinced themselves that it meant something, that saving you could save them.'

She rises stiffly from the ground and I reach out a hand to steady her as she stumbles awkwardly before righting herself and standing straight. A musty smell rises from her cloaked legs. Her eyes flash brightly as she looks down at me and grins. She's a tough old bird, Gammy.

'You coming or what?'

I give an exaggerated sigh and haul myself up on a nearby branch, my bell chiming weakly.

On you get, Gammy, you mad old thing.

GAMMY DOESN'T SAY MUCH ON MY BACK AS WE WALK, but I can tell she is peering around reluctantly, looking at the heavily wooded forest rising around us. I know right, Gammy? It's starting to look different.

Not the Wet of course, which hangs in the air like a welcome friend. It's the trees. They stand taller, prouder. Instead of groaning under the weight of the constant deluge, they seem to reach up and embrace it. They stand with their faces turned up to the sky, laughing at the weight of water on their boughs. Their roots seem deeper, and I realise that instead of clambering over collapsed, rotting logs, we can carve a path just by parting long, multi-stranded grass and bushes covered in fine, dewy droplets. The forest almost sways in the Wet, sighs in relief instead of cowering and groaning in defeat. Fine, Gammy, I know I sound like a fool, talking about the forest like this. But it does feel different, sound different, doesn't it?

The River, bloated and angry downstream, here winds its way with purpose through the proud trees.

Gammy doesn't respond, just clings to my neck in silence as the water beats down on her back. I keep having to heave her up on my back to stop her arse skimming the water I am wading through. More water than land now. It moves under crisscrossed hatches of wooden branches, through nests of reeds.

We both start when we hear a squawk above our heads.

'What the hell is that?' Gammy can't look upwards into the Wet, but I crane my neck this way and that until I see it: a flock of birds. I let out a low whistle. Well, I'll be Gammy. When was the last time you saw a bird? A flock of birds, at that, creating a ruckus in the sky, darting through the rain like little fish. Little red flying fish. They spin around above our heads, snatching the swarming insects I have noticed fanning above the wet tree canopies and around swaying seed pods. I jump in surprise whenever one of the insects lands on my face. Cheeky buggers. I'm not used to having visitors like that on my skin. Gammy swats them away, annoyed, with one hand, never loosening her other hand's grip on my neck.

'Only blessing I ever had in this place, that the fucking mozzies and flies went away' she grumbles. 'Now look. Lose my hut, gain the bloody insects. This goddamn place . . .'

We haven't walked much further when we stumble across the village. Or what is left of it. We have been picking our way awkwardly through some thick wet undergrowth, my usual sprightliness hampered by Gammy's extra weight. Tangles of wet grass snag my ankles as I walk. Instead of moving black mud, the earth here is covered in thick, matted green undergrowth.

We first spot something different as we crest a bare hill, scrambly vine-covered shrubs barely clinging to its muddy sides, and start to descend into a deep valley. Gammy is as surprised as I am – time has warped her sense of direction and memory so that when the blurry outline of huts appears through the Wet, the shallow breathing on my neck stops and I feel her heart begin hammering in shock. Neither of us knew there was a village further upstream than us.

I keep to the trees, taller than the ones near our village, craning my neck for signs of black-clothed life. A green cloak, even. My fingertips are tingling and I am ready, ready to fight.

But through the roar of the River I can't make out a sound.

As we pass the outermost tree before entering the clearing Gammy is still trembling violently, and her grip has tightened on my neck so that I almost feel like one of the bloody villagers, gasping to breathe.

We tread forward slowly, approaching the edge of the first hut. Its moss and mud-covered stilts slant precariously in a rickety crisscross fashion, and the wall closest to us is peppered with holes big enough to fit my whole head through.

It's ok, Gammy, the suckers have all been washed away. I sigh in relief and drop my tense shoulders. Gammy doesn't loosen her hold around my neck.

They have been washed away. The hut that loomed out of the rain-filled air before us only has one side; the rest of its rotting bulk has collapsed and disappeared into the churn of the River. What looks like a makeshift wall has been breached and the River is lapping right up to the middle of the clearing. It must have risen before they could move the village back, risen by feet rather than fingers like it sometimes does. Here and there, shattered wooden logs appear trapped in the swirling mud, but by and large, the remains of the village have been washed away entirely. There must have been five or so huts before the River rose, and the clearing is small. I wonder if they started out this small, huddled together, or if that is all that was left before the end.

I reach a hand out to touch the mud-caked sides of a stilt. So similar to the ones we had in our village. I feel a small pang remembering our shitty little home. You said I didn't know what it was like to have the future washed away, Gammy. But I do feel a little untethered out here with you, away from the clearing. I grew up in that home. I was a baby, born in the Wet, not even a year old when they handed me to you.

The four walls of our hut and Gammy placed squarely inside is my only real memory. Now we are out here, out in the open, I feel those memories sliding out from underneath me like a mud slick. Washed away. Blurring into the grey horizon and the Wet filling the air around us.

It's hard to know what Gammy is thinking: something tells me not to turf her off my back, but to keep wading my way past the collapsed hut, and move quickly through the abandoned village. We both know where the villagers are; they wouldn't last one day out in the open and would have been swallowed up by Lady River.

Good riddance.

The waterlogged clearing makes way for creaking forest canopies and peeling trunks as we move forward. The ruined village disappears behind us and neither of us looks back.

We cross the threshold of the woods and find ourselves back in shaded darkness, the Wet finding its way past branches and down lanky vines to trickle onto our heads as we bob through the undergrowth.

'How many times will we go back to the beginning, kid?'

You mean back to the villages, Gammy?

Her voice is a whisper tickling my neck. 'No, kid, I mean back to the beginning of it all. We know how the story ends, why do we keep rereading it? We built the villages thinking it would be different. But the ideas, the memories, they come with you wherever you go. Same mistakes, same old fears, same ideas, the end.'

Lucky for us I don't have your memories, then, Gammy.

'Hmph, you might be right there, kid.'

She doesn't mention anyone else. Is there a green cloak among the black rags, cascading downstream, snagging on rocks before shredding into a thousand pieces? A flash of green weighed down on the River's cold floor perhaps. A rusty bell caught on a submerged branch, tarnishing slowly as the waters rush past.

I only listen out for a chiming for a second before turning my head forward. The River has taken the village, and everyone in it as well. Old Lady River doesn't leave anyone behind when she is hungry. Her waters would have risen quickly, maybe in the murky darkness of the night, her silent creeping masked by the thundering of the Wet. They probably went while they were sleeping, waking up to find themselves afloat on their floorboards swirling down a part of the River that hadn't existed the day before, before slipping under and meeting the flitting fish below. Green and black circling and dancing under the waves together.

Gammy is still on my back, and I know the Wet is seeping through her sodden cloak and piercing her skin. She must be freezing, and her tired arms feel clammy around my sore neck. I can feel her lying flatter against me with every step, like the water is slowly wearing her down. Her crushed body is like the broken trees and bushes from where we came, bowing down to touch the angry, swollen River. I can tell she is still scared, but the rhythm of my slow plod through the mud, over fallen branches and slimy stones, and the constant onslaught of the heavy sheets of rain, has lulled her into an unusual silence. She doesn't even swat away the buzzing insects anymore; resigned to them crawling along her dragging wet cloak.

We move like that away from the abandoned village, Gammy pressing into my back, the Wet flattening her rags and hair.

No worries, Gammy, I didn't need the company anyway.

She sniffs indignantly into my neck but still doesn't say a word.

I wonder silently at how much scenery has changed. Same River, same trees of course, but here the undergrowth is thicker and a darker green. The leaves shimmer in the Wet. They reach upwards to drink greedily, instead of closing in on themselves until they collapse in defeat and drop into the swirling eddies of litter below. The mud still moves and sways beneath our feet, but the pools of water running off from the River are stiller and larger. Every way I turn my head I can see dark blue puddles deep enough for my body to disappear into, and twice as wide as our old clearing. In some places, the puddles have merged and there are no gaps showing on the forest floor. Some of these lakes are covered in swaying blankets of pink flowers, shaking under drops of rain, and tangles of green floating stems. Some of the clearings are marshy flats, covered with pale green grass that vibrates in the Wet. I have to make my way carefully so Gammy and I don't find ourselves plunging unexpectedly into a deep dark pool. Rising from these surprise lakes are upright green and purple reeds, swaying happily, and long trains of algae circling around submerged trees and boulders. We pass a valley entirely filled with water, not a single tree branch breaking a surface dimpled only by fat droplets of rain. Even where I spy trees at the water's edge, they have remained strong and thick, though gnarled and bent. Long, ropy blue vines swing from canopies withstanding the weight of water piling across their tops.

The forest here feels calm, not cowed. What's the word, Gammy? Flourishing.

I'M USED TO MY OWN COMPANY, BUT GAMMY'S QUIET presence is giving me the creeps. We have been walking another day without her saying a word. Not even a grunt or mutter or scolding. C'mon Gammy, where are the stories? Where is the incessant chatter, the yabbering filling the air? In our hut,

Gammy filled the entire space with her noise. As cold and wet and dark as it was, warmth had radiated from her creaky old body as she moved around inside its four draughty walls. Out here, though, it's like she has shrunk, like she is disappearing into the Wet like that poor old villager left in the clearing. Now, she is flattening and dissipating into a pile of old rags, soon to become mulch beneath my feet. Out here, I realise, she is slowly fading into the grey sheets of water. The bigger the pools we pass, the wider the River, the smaller Gammy becomes.

Which is strange, Gammy, because with each step we move from the clearing, I am feeling stronger. Sure, I have a slippery old lady on my back, which is throbbing and pounding, but as we leave the villages behind us I feel lighter inside, like that knot of hot dread is escaping from my body like steam. I even find myself humming, little bursts of song that leave my lips in spurts before being swallowed by the Wet. The song wells from deep in my chest and reverberates through the rush of the rain, and I pick up speed. I hear Gammy's raspy breathing, punctuated by short coughs, in my right ear, and she leans her head against me, her hood only partially protecting her nose and mouth from the onslaught of water as we speed forward.

My breathing is getting deeper, stronger. I hum louder, gleefully, and I realise Gammy has let out a chuckle.

Well I'll be. There's life in these wet rags yet.

42.

'STOP,' SHE SAYS, WITH A WET SPLUTTER.

I take a few more steps, just to spite her. Since she perked up, she has been annoying the crap out of me, telling winding, swirling stories with no end. Delirious ranting streaming into my ear as I try to focus on putting one step in front of the other. We have just climbed up a tortuously sloped hill and my calves are screaming in pain. You're the one who wanted to leave the River's path and go up the hill, Gammy. Shortcut, you said. Shortcut to what, Gammy? We have no fucking idea where we are heading.

'*Stop!*' She raps me across the side of the head and I swear loudly before dumping her behind me with a dull thud in the mud. She leaps up – I see you can use your bloody legs when you want to, Gammy – and stares behind us down into the valley we just came from. She's lost it. She's a fucking madwoman. I am going to have to leave her out here with only the forest and frogs for company. I cross my arms grumpily across my chest and wait.

She looks like a little water spider hunting in the rain, her cloak flattened against her bony torso and her neck craning as she peers around.

That's when I start to feel it too; a buzzing traveling toward us in the rain. It is simmering at the edge of the valley and across the forest. The hairs on the back of my neck stand up and electricity starts to thrum between my temples. In the distance, I see angry mountains of clouds roll up from the horizon and rush our way like a purple and black mud slick.

A storm, Gammy. I am bouncing from one leg to the other and shoot her a toothy grin.

She isn't smiling, though. Looks like a stunned codfish in the grey rain, pale face all trembly, mouth gaping in horror.

I'm still grinning like a fool as I fling an arm around her tiny shoulders and smack a kiss on her wet-cloaked head. C'mon, old bird. As I manoeuvre away from the peak of the hill and toward a short tree, she looks at me like I am insane. Trust me Gammy: it's the safest place we can be. The lightning has started to snake toward us, but it won't strike the forest down. I've seen enough of these storms in my time to know that.

She doesn't look convinced but a distant flash of white makes her jump out of her skin and so she lets me half-push, half-carry her toward the tree. Its sparse canopy doesn't provide much protection from the rain but we don't have time to seek out a better shelter. Gammy looks so bedraggled and scared that I almost laugh. She doesn't feel what I feel: a great wave of vibrant energy washing over the valley and up the hill, filling my lungs with elation and white-hot fire. My heart is pounding so fast I keep trying to crouch next to Gammy, but bounce up again with excitement to watch the storm roll in.

Those bloody birds rise up from a tree canopy below – a great, screeching mess of colour and noise in the pre-storm calm.

Gammy folds in on herself, peeking anxiously through clasped white hands as the Wet, lit up in flashes, cascades around her.

The first flash of lightning lights up the leafy canopy below with a violent flash. I yip in delight, hands outstretched, trying to draw the white light to me. The crash of thunder rumbles moments later and the Wet seems to ride behind it, settling around us in a heavy flood. Gammy begins to cower under its force, head bent as the rain pelts down.

Soon the thunder rolls all around us without pause and the whole sky is a spectacle of crisscrossing white lines and angry black clouds. Despite the torrential rain and thick grey in the air, the sky is lit up brighter than when the sun used to come. I can see for miles in every direction. The mighty River looks like a giant glistening black serpent snaking her way around the valley. Wild tendrils curl off her and charge away to form the deep, shining puddles of lakes that have swamped over trees and rocks.

Oh Gammy, how can you be scared of this? I feel like my whole body is alight.

She stays perfectly still behind me, head bowed, water streaming down her crooked bent back. 'Get back here, you stupid idiot, or you'll electrocute yourself.' Her words don't have their usual bite, though, they are more a panicked mutter, so I just shrug and turn back to survey the valley, arms outstretched, the water pounding my bare shoulders. Even breathing in the sharp tang of the rain is a pleasure, and when I stick out my tongue to catch some, I swear I can feel the tingle of lightning on the tip.

A startled squawk from behind me breaks my reverie. I turn back to see Gammy staring at a point in the valley where the largest part of the River cuts its course. I try to follow her frightened gaze but the flashes of lightning make the trees dance in front of my vision, change the shape of the landscape so that I can't make out a fixed point. The next flash of lightning is so intense it almost blinds me and I start backwards, losing my footing in the swirling mud below. I smack onto my arse just when the thunder cracks, so loud it feels like it breaks something inside my chest. For a moment I am winded and I am gasping for breath in the Wet just like Gammy.

I turn my head to look over my shoulder, and stare straight at her white, drawn face.

I saw it too.

Without standing I scramble on my haunches through the mud back to her and crouch in next to her soaking wet body.

I saw him too.

The rain is fast easing and growls of thunder echo quietly after the now distant cracks of white light on the horizon. A calm seeps slowly into the valley with a little murmur, and the colours begin to mute to the usual shades of grey. Gammy and I don't move. We watch the tiny lone figure struggling along the River's edge below in the valley, buffeted by new streams of water and piles of slow-moving mud. He can barely put one foot in front of the other because the storm has up-ended even more of the wet earth underneath his wobbly legs. His hands are wildly grasping for tree branches, vines, anything to keep him upright as he stakes his way out alongside the River.

He is at least a day behind us and I can tell he is weak. He seems to move in agonising slow motion. Like he is imitating movement, mocking it.

Gammy seems to be transfixed, not even trying to shield her face from the Wet as it runs over her narrow nose.

The figure is barely more than an ant from this distance, but I know who it is. I feel his presence as bile in my stomach and I swallow nervously to push the salty acid down. How did this arsehole make it this far? How did he know we would follow the River?

We scramble to our feet at the same time with a splatter of mud and water. Gammy has to use my arm for balance, clasping it tightly as her little feet slip and slide through the sludge and puddles. I don't want to turn my back on that bastard so, heart hammering so loudly I am sure the villager can hear it way down the valley, we start our skidding descent down the far side of the hill with our eyes locked on him. I think we can still cut around above him and beat him to the River's edge, far ahead of where he is. It's too precarious to put Gammy back on my back so I yank her alongside me as I stumble my way down, bell chiming loudly on my ankle, stopping only for panicked looks down the valley to be sure he is still there. He is struggling with the great tide of water and sticky mud oozing its way toward the River between the trees, and I don't think he has noticed us crashing our way down the side of the hill above his head, but I feel sick imagining his head turning and glimpsing my naked arse flashing on the hillside. C'mon, Gammy.

Her gasped breaths are louder than the now distant peals of thunder. She is wheezing up the entire storm.

I feel Gammy's grip on my arm loosen as I stride forward and then she has slipped, skimming through overgrown tangles of thickets and shrubs to land a few feet below our path. When I scramble down to meet her, she lies limply across a small rock. The twigs and branches she fell through have opened tiny slits down her arms and legs like a gutted fish. I fall next to her with a clumsy splash and shield her face from the rain with my body, willing her eyes open.

They flutter quietly and stare vacantly at me. Fine, Gammy is fine. Panicked, I leap to my feet and turn back to where I last saw the villager.

'You should leave old Gammy,' she chokes, weakly raising her upper body from the mud. Long streaks of black mud cling to her cloak.

Fuck off, Gammy, not a chance in hell.

I lean over, ignoring her protesting, and haul her up from under her narrow armpits into a sitting position. She turns to face the point in the valley I am staring at. Small coughs rattle her frame, but seem to stop short of her normal, bone breaking splutters. Like she is keeping quiet to hide from the villager, I think wildly, although of course she can't do that on purpose.

As we watch in silence with only the splashing of the Wet around us for noise, we spot his tiny figure in the distance. The villager is still weakly fighting the mud slicks and Gammy gasps quietly as loses his footing another, final, time. Despite wildly grabbing for support, he spills over in a splash of mud and water and debris. I hold my ragged breath as I watch the mud slicks envelope his body in a slow wave and push him further into the valley. He disappears, almost without fighting, in a slow-moving mound of dark brown.

I exhale the breath I have been holding and look up to the sky in relief, the Wet cooling my hot and prickly face. The valley is silent except for the roar of the River and the steady patter of water.

Gammy and I turn to each other in the rain and her grin echoes mine like a reflection on the River's surface. He's gone. He's finally gone.

I feel a great weight lift off my wet shoulders. He must have been the last one: there's no way those pathetic fuckers could have come this far as a group. He was the strongest, and now he is a pile of wet mulch like the rest of them. A small laugh, more like a hoarse bark, breaks through my lips.

I stand up and offer an outstretched hand to Gammy in the rain. After a pause, she takes it and rises creakily. I crouch down again next to her bloodied and scratched legs to let her climb onto my back.

See, Gammy, all that bloody fuss about storms. They aren't so bad!

'Shut up, you cocky bastard,' she says as she nestles in against me. But I can tell from her voice that she is hiding a smile against the back of my neck as well. We start to walk down the other side of the hill toward the continued path of the River. I can't wipe the bloody grin off my face.

43.

HALF A DAY LATER WE ARE STILL WALKING. GAMMY HAS slept off the storm, lulled by my steady stride. She snored like a strangled bird as she napped, shrill and scratchy and punctuated by deep rattling coughs. She is awake now though, her quiet breath tickling the back of my neck. Her bunched-up rags scratch the small of my back and I move her around my torso, irritated and itchy.

The trees in this part of the forest are lined with vibrant green vines, twisting their way strongly toward the sky and brushing my face with silky tendrils as I walk past. Under the tangle of vines, carpets of moss peek out; some green, some vibrant blue, even some shades of pink. When I reach out to brush them with a fingertip, they flake off in great velvety chunks. My feet move through water that splashes as high as my knees, winding about the strong trunks of the trees. The Wet dimples the puddles lightly, spraying like fine mist around our bobbing heads. Can you see it, Gammy? The River spreads out everywhere here. Touching all corners, lapping at all edges.

She grunts into my back, hawks up some juicy phlegm and spits it to the side as we move.

I'm baffled that he came after us, Gammy. Perhaps, without any options, he thought he could follow us for food? Desperation, like a parasite, hoping to suck a little bit off us everywhere we went, maybe. His whole world washed away and we were all he knew.

Of course you don't agree, Gammy. Full of smart-arse opinions and wanting to put me in my place, as usual. I can barely hear her voice in my ear as we walk, she speaks so quietly. The Wet tries to steal her words before they reach me, despite our closeness.

She clears her throat, a rattle in the quiet. 'Nah, use your brain, kid. It was the Unbidden.'

Still think it's a fucking stupid name, Gammy.

'Still think you're a bloody know-it-all.' She sniffs. 'It's just what we named it, kid. You think I had a dictionary at the end of the world, had time to run some names by you to see if they worked?'

You probably should have, Gammy. Seems you didn't make the best decisions back then. I hoist her a little higher on my hips, and duck to dodge some low hanging vines. I grin mischievously when I hear Gammy swear as they slap her across the top of the head.

She stays silent for a while. Probably watching the passing trees in panic, trying to work out where the hell we are.

Was it like this, last time you were on the move, Gammy?

'A bit, I guess. We didn't know where we were going either. Just had what we could take when the waters came, totally unprepared despite the weather changing for years. Should have known. It'll pass, they said. Bunker down, it will pass.' She shakes her head vigorously and I have to jerk sideways to stop us both teetering off our path.

She's told me these stories before, but I still like to imagine the great lines of people snaking their way to higher ground like giant twirling serpents, leaving behind crumbling cities and poisoned waters and death.

'We just found what shelter we could, scrambled together for support. Little communities forming around wet steaming fires in the ruins of buildings, under tarps and corrugated iron and any scraps we could find. There was fear, of course, but we were all united in wanting to survive. Those instincts are strong and kicked in after the initial terror and chaos.'

Little villages in the rain, Gammy?

'That's right, kid. Like ours. I don't know what we were thinking, building those villages. It was the same old problem, different place. The Wet was still there, the River still creeping our way. Although, where else would we have gone?'

Moudas, Gammy. You were a bunch of moudas.

She reaches around my head and pinches me hard on the cheek. Ow Gammy, for fuck's sake. It's hard enough to carry your dead weight around.

'What the hell is a mouda?'

A mouda, Gammy. Those eyeless fish digging at the bottom of the River. Big useless brown things. Can't see a thing, just wallow in the mud all day. Taste like shit. Good for nothing.

I grin as I walk, satisfied that I have flummoxed her.

It's my name for them, Gammy. And you – you and the

villagers – are a bunch of moudas, no purpose, can't see what is right in front of you, good for nothing. What, you think you had all the words, Gammy? You don't have the words for the new things in this place.

She sighs unhappily and rests her head on my back again. Bet you're sick of the bloody rain up your nose, Gammy. We've been out here for hours.

'Always sick of the rain, kid. All the rain, always the rain. Our new villages, drifting in the mud. People started chucking and shitting as the river soaked up the poisons from the world before. I watched them heaving their insides out when the waters turned bad, and then saw the waters run clean again when there were no more people to be sick. Every day, more and more people were washed away. The very young and the very old died first. We all grieved that together, at the start.'

Then the Unbidden came. I know this story already, Gammy. She keeps on regardless. On a roll now. She won't shut up for hours.

'That's right. The Unbidden. A whisper of death arose, unbidden and swirling around like its own living thing. No one knew where these whispers came from, but they snuck around and spoke madness into sleeping ears.'

Never sounded too bad to me, Gammy. Just a bunch of stupid thoughts. How scary can it get?

For a while I don't hear anything but the splash of my shins wading through murky puddles and the buzz of little flies in my ears.

'You'd be surprised, kid.' My back is screaming in discomfort now, between Gammy's raspy arse rags and her weight, and all this walking. I peer through the heavy woods looking for a canopy with decent shelter. The least wet patch in the forest.

'I imagined all different kinds of dangers around that time, always slept with one eye open expecting other horrors. Then the Unbidden came, and I never worried about those dangers again. It drove out the light and logic and made them the shells they are today.'

Not so fast, Gammy, I correct her. The last of those shells is at the bottom of the River's bed by now. *They* don't exist anymore, Gammy.

'Hmmm,' she murmurs softly. 'He was possessed by the Unbidden too I reckon – it's what drove him to follow us for miles and miles without food or water or reason. Pure pursuit. One foot after the other, driven only by a lust for blood.'

My blood, Gammy?

'For sure. The Unbidden made them think they could kill their way out of the destruction. It whispered to them of a target, a demon in the mist that had to be purged. The cause of everything. Destroy it all but in doing so, destroy the future. An ultimate sacrifice. Destroy the cause of the floods and rains and your time in the sun will come. That's you, kid. Well – the others like you, at least. Then they had to save a couple, just in case things went pear-shaped later.'

How can you tell that was the Unbidden, though, Gammy? Could have been anything making him crazy like that. It's been more than ten years. He probably just went bonkers.

'You could tell someone was possessed by the Unbidden because they would look at us suddenly with new eyes. Empty eyes.'

I shudder, then, remembering the dead black eyes of the villagers.

'We started calling it the Unbidden. Even marvelled at the first few who listened to its whispers. Crackpots, we thought. We should have noticed how things were closing in – the distrust, people getting high and mighty and moralistic, needing so desperately to believe in something that gave them reasons for their pain. All the things they were starting to hate, the new laws to rid us of what they thought was to blame for the floods ... they weren't *things*. In reality, they were remembering who to hate, who to blame. Echoes of ideas a thousand years old. Pretty damn unoriginal.'

She coughs raspily, and a speck of warm phlegm lands on my cheek. I curl my lip in disgust; focus on putting one step in front of each other in what is now thick, sludgy mud.

'Until it was all of them,' she says, clearing her throat again. 'We went off scavenging among the piles of muddy rubbish one day and came back to the village and we saw the look in their eyes, and realised the Unbidden had taken over us too, carried from other villages maybe, or perhaps it had always been sleeping among us, just waiting for a chance to get out. And then we ran, those who could; tried to run on an earth that moved under our feet.'

I know the rest of the story. She doesn't have to tell me. Those black-eyed shells roamed around hunting and killing hundreds. Threw them in the River: even the littlest. Bound them with ropes and chucked them in screaming and crying. They went back, scoured and roamed through the Wet to find more, always more to throw in. They threw in anyone trying to help or stop it too, hundreds in the end. But months of hunting and killing didn't stop the rain, and the mud slicks started carrying away great swathes of the new world they were trying to make. The entire surface of their world changed and moved and swirled and disappeared. The killings hadn't worked, the River was still angry. Gammy always chuckles sadly when she tells me this part: *from the smartest species in the world to withering idiots believing in nature's revenge in the space of a year*, she would say. So when they found a few of us who had survived, little water babies, they chucked our parents into the River too, but kept us. Little offerings to Lady River. Trying to appease her in this new world, trying to appease her in the next world.

Gammy sighs deeply where she clings to my back, and I can tell she is shaking her bobbly head, urging me to shut up and keep walking. Little sprays of water flick off her cloak. The rain is coming down with more force and threatens to dislodge her, but an idea is ticking away in my mind and I need to ask her something.

Is the Unbidden like the anger of the River and the Wet, then, the way it eats up everything in its path?

'Keep moving, kid. Gammy can't stay out here much longer.'

I reluctantly trudge on, passing trees that reach higher than I have ever seen. They reach into the thick blankets of grey cloud, their branches long scraggly villager arms lurching out of the Wet.

I guess it isn't quite the same, is it Gammy? The River is cool and dark and full of a deeper force. She never seems angry; she just takes what is hers. Not a bitch, just in charge.

226

I hum quietly to myself and the River, moving like a coiled snake, hisses in unison by my side. I try to imagine the way the Unbidden felt – believe I almost felt it when we sat in the storm watching the villager come our way. It was like the keening in the clearing had sounded when the sun didn't arrive that day. Like hot shards of pain piercing your skull in the spot between your ears, blistering down into the deepest parts of you. A fear and rage and emptiness that isn't tethered to anything here in the world; not the forest or the sky or the streams or the mulch. A rotting, decaying, erratic and fearful thing.

A thing that doesn't live here anymore, I realise with relief.

44.

'HERE.'

I dunno, Gammy. Looking around, there are only knotted canopies as far as the eye can see. Not the best place for a stop.

Don't give me that look. I sigh in mock despair, the retort fading from my lips when I look at Gammy's furrowed brows. We will stop.

I squint through the ricocheting grey water and see a squat, wide tree, which stands about four times my height, atop a muddy hill with an alarming slope toward the River. It's the only real shelter I have seen for the entire day. The mud swirls down past the tree but underneath its thick broad canopy, the earth looks only damp, not fluid. This will have to do. A scan around me confirms that we are surrounded by pools of rising water, babbling brooks, and swampy, treacherous marsh. A ragged path leads along the River's edge away from us further upstream, but around here the land has been taken by the Wet.

Want to play explorers, Gammy, like the ones in your stories? This hill can be our little island.

No reply.

I grunt as I clamber the few steps upward required to get us to the top, Gammy tightening her weak grasp around my neck as I climb. Fuck, Gammy, get your claws out of my skin. She manages to raise a weak hand and rap me across the ears, causing a loud howl of pain. I could dump you on your arse right now, Gammy, and you would slide straight down into that raging River over there. But when I start to lower her down to the earth and look at her closely, I see how her chest is shuddering, how her stomach caves in below her rib cage, and how her throat gurgles with every cough, and I feel like a right arsehole.

I am startled to realise the tree on the top of the hill is split in two, its great trunk forking about halfway down from its middle into the mud below. I lean forward and peer inside and let out a low whistle. The entire trunk is hollow and dark and mostly dry. Except for the entrance at the front made by the giant split, the round wall of the trunk remains intact.

Furry pink and green moss covers the outside of the trunk in iridescent swirls.

I help Gammy carefully onto the damp earth next to the tree, avoiding the mulch piles surrounding us that could collapse under the weight of a leaf, and lean her gingerly back against the slimy outer tree surface. Another unlucky tree lies sideways right next to us, its large, unearthed roots flailing in the air. A swarm of beetles in its cavernous opening are disturbed by our presence and scurry out from the mouldy base of the trunk, only to be caught in an eddy of mud and swirled around and around down the hill, plunging into the River below. Sorry, little critters.

Where the hell are we going to go, Gammy? Nothing out here but the Wet and the River and the things they are taking from you.

'Upstream,' she whispers, sliding herself up against the slimy pink and green tree trunk. She lifts her head in the rain and looks around. Little dribbles of water run down the trunk and join the rivulets of water dripping from her cloak. Her hood, so faded from the Wet it is almost indistinguishable from her hair now, is plastered across her white-lined cheek along with specks of mud. Her skin, away from the flickering golden fire-light of the hut, looks grey and translucent. Funny how I never noticed how much Gammy looks like the see-through-skinned tadpoles that roam the stiller pools around the River. If I squint, maybe I could see her addled brain in there, rotting away.

Little purple veins pulse at her temples and down her nose, like a veiny old leaf.

She slowly shuffles her creaky arse backwards across the damp ground to wedge herself right into the hollow of the tree. It is just big enough to fit her tiny body and she folds her knees to her chest and crams herself inside. You look a sight, Gammy, little stick woman wedged in her colourful tree trunk.

'Downstream is the other villages. Downstream is death and destruction. You need to go upstream.' Her voice, coming from inside the tree now, is muffled.

Same, same to me, Gammy. The River runs the same wher-ever I am. I lower myself next to her tree and we stare across the valley through the heavy mist and spray. Gammy's eyes are slits in the dark of the hollow, trying to make out shapes in the murky grey. I can see further than she can, can see the path we left behind and the winding River in front. The undergrowth is thicker and lusher here than back home, but the skyline is still bowing down, great trees bending and swaying under the constant downpour. Is it possible that the horizon dips lower every day? The broken branches are hazy black silhouettes against the grey, appearing in and out of the rain, never completely visible. The River's breadth, down below us, must be more than three hundred times the length of my body now, and its choppy edges melt into the Wet as it pummels down. Soon there will be more water than earth. Soon, maybe, there will be nothing but horizon.

'You'll like that.'

You're pretty cluey when you want to be, Gammy.

She looks anxious as I move away from her but her tummy is grumbling as loud as mine and it's time to fetch some food. My hard feet cut a path down the hill toward the River and without a glance below, I throw myself into the frothy brown waves.

I swear I hear the River give a happy sigh as I plunge into the dark.

I DON'T KNOW THE RIVER THROUGH THESE PARTS BUT MY eyes adjust to the dim light and I soon find my way through the murky dark. I stay close to the surface, where the rain up top makes a pattern above my head, sharp drops of water slicing through the waves one by one. Tiny little dribbles all adding to the greedy River's girth. Her cool waters envelope me like an old friend and I let out a yip of glee that is eaten up in her thick, churning waves.

The tension and tightness I have been feeling all over my body releases into the depths and I kick hard to spin around while the rough currents tug at my arms. The River here is deep and fast, having carved its way through the bowels of the earth, the dark craggy sides are free of the gnarled roots and reeds that pepper the banks further downstream. It sounds silly, but she feels stronger and more permanent up here. I let her buffet my body and feel the hair on my head being whipped round and round.

Gammy would laugh out loud at me talking about the River this way. But a sharp pang, deep down inside my chest, reminds me of the time before we left the clearing, when my days were just like this, fighting upstream, diving, dancing – whatever the hell I felt like until it was time to go home to the hut. Something tells me, Gammy, that those days are long behind me now.

When I let out a small exhale, tiny bubbles twirl before my eyes toward the dim light of the surface.

I move through the currents toward the rocky bottom and spot the silvery fish that I need for dinner flitting past. Steadying myself with long and low kicks, my hand darts out twice to clasp a slippery, wiggling body tightly. Got you, suckers.

I launch backwards with a wild paddle as a giant creature appears out of the murky depths right near my face. Four slowly wading webbed feet at the end of reptile arms, all sticking out from a large, glossy green shell. A friendly green face, wrinkled and beaked. When a fish darts too close to his face, his thick neck hauls his head back into the shell, only to pop it back out again moments later. Neat trick, friend. Gammy needs a little shell like that on her back, a travelling home to hide in when the going gets too tough. I wave at him with a fistful of fish as he moves slowly past me in the current. The last I see of him is his dark shell disappearing into the swirling brown depths downstream.

I turn reluctantly to look up at the surface, wondering if I can stay down here a little longer. Forever even, with the comforting weight of water on my back.

But I am mighty proud of my foraging when I haul myself onto the crumbling wet banks with one arm, my two prizes gasping in my fist like the villagers do in the wet, foggy air. It's weird, Gammy: the sky is filled with the water their tiny flapping bodies need, and yet here the fish are suffocating just like the rest of you. Their misty eyes still stare at me even after I have smacked their round heads over a moss-covered rock. Maybe asking me why I survive better out here than they do, especially when they had the first claim over the old River.

Fuck knows, little fishies, fuck knows.

As I clamber up the bank grasping my fish, something catches my eye in the woods. Curiously I edge further in toward a strong, thick tree with a giant fan of a canopy, all blues and glossy greens. Great streaks of iridescent lichen run down its white papery trunk, mingling with bulbous bubbles of golden sap. I move my face closer to its damp bark, so close the water streaming from above parts at the bridge of my nose where it meets the tree. I smell earth, water, bark and the living, breathing sap beneath its skin. The tree seems to pulse with energy, soaking up the endless Wet instead of drowning in it. I move my head back and look up, just above eye level.

There.

The markings are clear, despite the rain rushing down its long trunk. Scratched lines, all in neat rows, dug out by rocks or fingernails or flint. I reach up and trace my fingers along the ragged design, feel a buzzing rush into my fingertips with a hot snap. So similar to the markings I once left on a tree, but made worlds apart.

I don't bother to look for footprints as I move slowly away.

I walk from the River's banks through muted shades of grey, green and brown up the hill, water still streaming off my shoulders, to where Gammy sits slumped in her small circle of semi-dry. Her eyes are nervously searching through the Wet. She sits in the hollow of her tree with a dome of water around her. A little bubble of safety.

You once told me the world was our oyster, Gammy. Well, we went out into the world and you went and hid in the oyster. Whole bloody universe out here, wide-open spaces, and you manage to find yourself the one place with walls. I shake my head in amazement and she grunts in response.

Neither of us talks about lighting a fire, but instead pick up our little fish at the same time and bring them to our mouths, the pink tangy juices sliding down our necks to join the always moving mud below. We munch in silence and look out toward the heavy grey sky and blurred outline of canopies. I don't mention the markings on the tree.

She breaks the silence only once. 'My little water baby.'

I know, Gammy, I know. You're making me choke up. Shut up and eat your fish.

45.

'WHAT IS THIS ONE?' GAMMY TURNS OVER THE GIANT water snail, inspecting the swirling green spots on its back.

Dimwoo, Gammy. I grab the snail from her hand and put it back on the wet soil in front of the opening of the tree. Gammy is wedged awkwardly inside, one pale leg that doesn't quite fit jutting out at an odd angle. She looks like a crushed water spider. You sure are desperate to squash yourself inside that joint, Gammy. I shake my head in quiet amusement, little droplets of rain spraying from my hair.

She mutters something rude at me and points at a large fruit hanging from the nearest tree, plump and black. It is as round and big as my head. 'And that? What do you call that?'

Pingin. If you crack open a pingin, Gammy, the insides are juicy and sweet, with tiny little seeds inside. But see this?

I rise to my feet, walk into the wall of Wet, and pluck the pingin from the low tree branch. When I let the branch go it springs back with a wild arc of water.

See, Gammy? I show her the way the fruit's skin sucks in on itself. The minute you take it off the tree, it starts to wilt. You have about ten seconds to eat it before the liquid inside changes on you, starts to stink. That's why I never bring them back to the hut. Never used to bring them back, I mean.

I shove a muddy finger through the black, rapidly shrivelling skin, and then quickly hold the hole to my mouth, sucking the insides out through open lips.

I raise my eyebrows to Gammy, lift the fruit to her in offering, but she grimaces and shakes her head vigorously. Your loss, Gammy. I tip the rest into my throat then chuck the wilted skin onto the side of the hill, where it gets picked up by a little mud slick and starts to wind its way slowly toward the River.

I scan the small clearing on top of the hill we seem to have settled into. See, look here, Gammy. This one I bet you've never seen before.

I dive at the base of Gammy's trunk and sink my fists into the sludgy soil, and squeal in delight when my digging hand clamps around the cool shiny shell. I whip the grub out from the wet mud triumphantly, and wave it in Gammy's face, little specks of brown showering her leg where it rests outside of the protection of the tree. She wrinkles her nose in disgust and shuffles back further into the tree hollow, tries to jam herself deeper in.

What a whopper, Gammy! Isn't he beautiful?

'Looks like a shitty brown grub to me.' She flicks a damp strand of hair off her face dismissively, turns her eyes away from the wriggling grub in my hand and peers out at the heavy rain beyond my shoulder filling the valley below us.

Don't be an arsehole, Gammy. He is beautiful. Look – see those streaks of blue shining between the brown? And even the brown – look – there are hundreds of different colours in there. And he shines, Gammy, shines like the Wet.

She only glances briefly at the grub before resting her saggy cheek against the rough bark of her hollow and closing her eyes.

With a resigned sigh, she whispers more to the Wet than to me: 'What do you call that one, then?'

Um, these shitty grubs I call . . . Gammys. I peer at her from under my eyelashes, fighting the grin that threatens to split my wet face in two. She opens her eyes to narrow them, but can't dislodge herself enough from the hollow to give me the rap across the ears I know she wants to. My eyes never leaving her irritated face, I lift the squirming grub above my head, raise my face to the sky, then drop him straight in. With a loud crunch, he explodes in my mouth with a spray of liquid and gizzards. I smile wickedly at Gammy and rub my naked belly with a muddy hand. Mmmm, delicious, Gammy!

I think she actually might have gagged a little in that tiny space she has carved out for herself, and I am feeling mighty amused. You think I am disgusting, Gammy? Since you moved out of the Wet into that tree hollow, you smell like fucking shit. Like rotting fish carcases, your own filth. Smell like a bloody villager. Don't look at me like I am the disgusting one.

Her eyes flash angrily from the darkness of the tree trunk.

'What, you think you're special, kid? Think you're better than us?'

I don't see you lot coping very well out here, Gammy.

'I've got news for you, kid, there ain't nothing separating you from us. All the things you can do, you learned. Oh, I cried watching your beautiful soft baby body turning oily and hard in the rain. That disgusting waxy skin growing over you like a slithering reptile, changing you from a bub to a little kid before my eyes. And your little feet, your tiny little feet, started out as soft and weak as the rest of us when I first met you. Nothing you did made those feet scale over except years of fucking about in the mud.'

At least I changed.

'You aren't some bloody superhero, you're just a kid who grew up surrounded by water who learned to survive.'

Well, I think that makes me kind of special, Gammy.

She hawks phlegm and spits it out the side of the hollow. 'I didn't think you were going to last past your first birthday. Mummy with her milk at the bottom of the River, little baby with no one to raise you except me. You're only here because I looked after you, taught you to swim in shallow little pools, told you to hold your breath longer and longer, walked with you while I still could, kept you out of their way, got them relying on your food in case they decided they were sick of the sight of you.'

Sounds like you were kinda looking after yourself, Gammy. If what you have told me is true, they only kept me in case they needed some kind of sacrifice for the Wet. Thought you'd just wait until they chucked me in the River too, hey Gammy? What were you playing at?

She goes grey, and her face crumples.

'I kept you alive because I couldn't not,' she whimpers, more to the Wet than to me.

Whatever, Gammy. I kept myself alive, and now I am keeping us alive.

She shakes her head sadly, rests it backwards against the inside of her trunk and peers up through the hollow, ignoring me. I wonder what it looks like in there. I bet even on the inside the bark is a little wet, Gammy, just like everywhere else.

46.

GAMMY WATCHES ME SHREWDLY FROM ATOP THE HILL
without speaking. God knows what is going through her head.
She is crouched just out of reach of the Wet, peering down at
me thoughtfully.

I am ignoring her gaze boring into the back of my head
and playing with the boat I have just made. The only leaves dry
enough to make a boat were the ones resting under Gammy's
stale old arse; she had grumbled something chronic when I
demanded she shove over in her hollow so I could gather them
up from the dirty floor. But threaded onto a short slim stick,
they are the perfect shape and thickness for a steady sailboat.

I sail them at the base of our hill where the hundreds of tiny
streams meet in puddles before flowing into the River. When
the Wet is at its lightest, like now, the little streams propel the
boat around and round in a whirling slow dance, before they
are finally whisked away. They stand tall and proud despite the
little dollops of rain pelting down on their sails. I have been trying to see how long I can sail them before they get caught up in

the larger current; so far I have made a boat lap the base of our mound five times, and I swear as the most recent leaf speeds away and disappears under choppy foam.

I look up at Gammy to see if she is frowning at my language. She hasn't even reacted. You're losing your touch out here, Gammy. Back at the hut that would have earned me a smack on the back of the head.

She watches me intently as I thread a new leaf onto a stick.

I still wonder why they didn't just go to boats, when the Wet came?

Gammy finally opens her mouth and licks her dry, cracked lips. She's so weak she has to lean creakily on a protruding branch, resting all her weight as it sags. 'Boats are only useful if they have somewhere to moor,' she mutters down the hill. Unsatisfied with her response, I turn back to my tiny boat. I place it gently on the pool of water closest to my feet and, after a small pause, it takes off with a wobbly *whoosh*.

I leap to my feet and chase it around as it circles back and forward in a zigzag of little streams. With held breath I watch it tip sideways under water, and I jiggle gleefully from foot to foot as the boat rights itself again and continues snaking toward the River.

I think this one is going to be the winner, stay afloat the longest, but a sudden avalanche of water and mulch cascades down the hill and collects the little boat in its path, the whole bundle tumbling into the River and rushing away before I have time to catch it with grasping hands.

Turning to look up to where the surprise debris came from, I realise Gammy is standing atop the mound, foot still raised from where she kicked down the mud and water toward me. Her eyes are glinting wickedly and her stupid face is split in a nasty grin. An indignant stream of abuse leaves my mouth but she now is doubled over laughing, a side-splitting laugh, with tears streaming down her face. I stomp my feet in the mud, glaring at her through the rain from below.

You're a bloody arsehole, Gammy.

She wipes tears from under her eyes and continues to chuckle and congratulate herself as she creakily lowers herself back to sitting under her tree. I look around furiously for another dry leaf but I have used them all. I don't want to climb back up the mound to where Gammy is, that traitorous arsehole, but I don't have anything more to play with down here, so I stand on the spot with the Wet trickling down my forehead, looking and feeling useless.

'Boats,' she says, when she finally has finished laughing at me. 'Good for nothing but sunbaking and champagne and caviar. Fish eggs,' she explains when she notices my confused frown.

We eat fish eggs, Gammy.

'Not quite the same when they come from your filthy fist, kid.'

Bit fancy, are we now, Gammy? She motions to me to join her on top of the hill but I scowl in response, still smarting from her ruining my sailing game.

'C'mon, Gammy was just teasing,' she says, kindly this time, beckoning to me with a spindly, outstretched hand. Reluctantly I trudge back up toward her tree, head bowed sulkily, arms crossed over my bare wet chest.

When I finally stand next to her she shuffles over and pulls out another dry leaf from where her buttocks were resting before she slid out from her hollow, feels around until she locates a small twig among the dirt of the floor around us, and starts to thread it through the leaf. 'Here,' she shows me, 'if you thread it here, the boat will be steadier.' She hands me the new sailboat and I clamber eagerly back down the mound to test it out.

She calls down from the top of the mound. 'People starved on the boats, the idiots. They had to find food like the rest of us, had to wade through rain and mud on land just like the rest of us. In the end they all left the boats, ran to higher ground like we were told. Then higher, then higher still.'

And is that where we are now, Gammy?

She chuckles sadly. 'How the hell would I know, kid? You get up and move a million times over and the river and floods carve new worlds behind you so that by the time you look back, you have no clue where you are anymore. They just built the villages when they were sure they were high enough. No one had a fucking clue where we were by then.'

I launch the boat off and it is perfect. It sails strong and straight through the light smattering of rain and round and round where I stand, nine – ten times – before flying across the shallow water and out to the River. Did you see that, Gammy? I turn excitedly back to where she sits with a knowing half-smile. She nods once, and settles her back once more into the hollow of the tree, eyes closing, a satisfied look on her face. She gently falls asleep where she sits, while I fossick around to find my next boat.

47.

GAMMY IS SNORING A LITTLE, HER BREATH RATTLING near the surface of her little chest and tiny whistles punctuating the rush of the water. She is upright but slumped against the peeling, damp bark on the inside of her tree. Tiny bubbles appear at the corner of her mouth that pop when she breathes, the saliva joining to dribble down her prickly chin. It takes all my willpower not to take some mud on my longest finger, reach into the tree hollow and make markings on her saggy face, but I stop myself just in time. Who says I'm not growing up, Gammy? I snort in amusement to myself.

I'm not sitting in her hollowed clearing; it's too small and cramped under there and I need the heavy feeling of water on my shoulders. Smells like shit under there too. Gammy's body is bloating and distending, taking on the Wet in odd places, leaking out weird gasses and smells.

Any light in the sky is starting to fade, pale grey deepening to a darker blue-black. I am camped a few feet from her, sitting out in the open, a wall of Wet surrounding my naked body and pounding me from my head to my arse. I can see the whole way down our hill through a tunnel of grey, and behind me the water pressure is building, piling up on the small of my back before splitting around me and rushing past my thighs and down to the River below. The stronger it gets, the more relaxed I feel, like the flow is feeding into me in a way that all the reeds and fish and snails in the world never do. It fills me up and makes me feel powerful, bit like Gammy's kings and gods.

Straggly branches stacked with fat wet vines creak and groan and sometimes collapse with a whoosh of falling water and debris to charge into the River and be whisked out of sight. I am not facing Gammy's laboured whistles and sighs, I am looking straight into the choppy depths, twig-filled mud flowing either side of me and making a swirling black path down the side of the hill. I will follow that path later, down into the welcoming stormy River, catch some more fish, maybe even find an eel or two. Perhaps a slimy little frog with bowed legs like Gammy's.

Maybe we could make this our little home, Gammy. A new clearing, your little tree, a new part of the world?

Do you really think Gammy can make it out here? I push the thought aside and instead think about the firm, succulent fish I am going to sink my pointy teeth into. Gammy will be ok sitting in her little cave under the spreading canopy for now. I can keep her warm, maybe find some large branches to hold off the worst of the Wet, make a large fire to dry her sodden clothes, her sodden hair. Stop her shivering and spluttering and hacking coughing fits. We could last a while, out here, me and this old lady.

My stomach rumbles again at the thought of fish.

I am shocked when the grumbling in my tummy turns to a dull, painful kick in the middle of my torso. My loud swearing startles Gammy from her uncomfortable rest. She stares at me wild-eyed from her hollow as I double over, clutching my middle in agony.

'What the fuck is the matter with you?' Her eyes are showing all their whites, panic written all over her wrinkled grey face. Like my pain is deliberate, like I have done this just to wake up an old lady. I am in agony here Gammy; have some sympathy. The pain is throbbing and spreading through my lower abdomen, radiating down my legs.

She shuffles worriedly halfway out of the tree trunk, leaving a dry patch of dust in the space from under her arse, and beckons for me to come under her tree. I crawl slowly over, the Wet buffeting my naked side and the pain shooting and throbbing from my belly to my back. I haven't been in this much pain since the time I walked into a low-flung branch while I was hunting for snails, and stupidly not watching where I was going. This ache is deeper though, not caused by a stray boulder or branch. It sits heavy within me.

I slide under the canopy near the opening of her hollow and try to find a comfortable position for my poor body, shuffling my arse this way and that on the hard surface, when I realise Gammy is staring at my legs, her eyes wide with horror. I look down and even my heart skips a beat when I see the dark clotted blood smeared on my inner thighs, coming from deep between my legs.

Then, with relief, I remember all the stories Gammy told me about the changes, about growing up, and my hammering heart recedes. I laugh a little, reaching down and wiping the clots from my legs, inspecting the bright red mixed with rusty brown, and putting my hands out under the cascading water to wash the blood away. A small trickle of new red still makes its way down one leg to mix with the dry earth underneath me, and Gammy cannot stop staring at it.

To my disgust, a low moan starts in the back of her throat, like it is coming up from her own belly, her own deep place. The noise increases until a hoarse wail rises up from her mouth, piercing through the roar of the River below and the splashing of the Wet. Then she is on her knees next to me, staring at the blood, screaming and carrying on, tears and green snot streaming down her face.

I look down at her writhing body in shock, try to block the sound of her screams from my ears with my hands. For a mad second, through my palms, I swear I hear the screams of hundreds of other old ladies in her voice, circling around the canopy above us. Screams of despair and terror. I shake my head in confusion. Of course it's just Gammy wailing, her voice shrill and cracking, but alone.

I stand up and stare at her crumpled form next to me, her hands outstretched to the sky as if begging the Wet to take this new bloody gift away from me.

Fat chance, Gammy, the Wet knows what it wants. I look down at her shaking and hunched back for a moment, taking in her ripped and faded green cloak, identical to mine, and the shiny pink patches of her scalp through her straggly hair, then shrug and step back out into the grey water outside of our sheltered circle. The blackened blood trickling down my inner thighs instantly washes away and joins the torrents of clear water running down my body.

See Gammy? Gone.

She just kneels there and wails, trembling and shaking, a broken mass dribbling into the mud. Her hands are caked in wet brown soil, her arms splattered with sludge. Her body is filthy and mine is clean.

I don't need this carry-on.

I turn from her and stomp down the path made by the sliding black mud, and at the bottom of the hill I launch into the air, feeling strong and exhilarated despite the throbbing pain in my lower abdomen.

Because mingled with the pain is a new charge, like new blood is coursing through my veins. Gammy's wails are sucked into the air behind me as I slice through the water's surface, my ears filled instead with the low dark roar of the River. In its waters, the pain stops, and I no longer see any blood. I breathe out into its depths, the movement of the water pulling me this way and that, until I choose my direction and kick out strongly.

'I DID WONDER IF IT WOULD COME.' GAMMY IS SHATTERED when I return to her tree; shaking and exhausted, eyes red from weeping. I choose to ignore her frightened face and pretend nothing has happened – no bleeding, nothing to see here Gammy – a silvery fish in each hand and a pile of molluscs carefully secreted in my bulging mouth.

We both tear in, my pointy teeth doing a better job than her ragged old gums, thoughts of a fire long behind us. She is deliberately not looking at the blood that has matted parts of my dark pubic hair now I am undercover, concertedly avoiding the little rusty smears down the fleshiest parts of my thighs. The initial throbbing pain has receded, and I am stretched out lazily, long limbs half under the shelter of the canopy from Gammy's tree, half splattered with water from the darkening sky above, picking my teeth with a fish bone. Gammy is looking even smaller than usual, folding in on herself. Her features seem to be disappearing into the hollow the longer we stay out here, smudging into the blurred lines that are all around us.

'But you seemed so different; I thought you might be spared. It's a cruel joke of mother nature,' she whimpers slightly, her weak gums gnawing at the remains of her fish. 'That bitch gives you the power to survive in the Wet, then curses you like every other woman.' I shift uncomfortably: I feel like I am the one being scolded, not poor old mother nature.

I don't feel cursed, Gammy. I feel fucking brilliant.

She glances at me in surprise, like she is seeing me for the first time. Her watery eyes, hard to make out in the dark, take me in, my whole body languidly stretched out in the shadows, narrow hips and budding chest, one hand under the water like I always need it to touch me in some way. I do always need it to touch me.

She breathes out slowly and says nothing, but I hear a catch of recognition in her breath.

Something has shifted in the air between us. I see the silhouette of her shoulders unwind and relax, and her breathing steadies out. About time, Gammy, you barely have the strength to sit upright in this damn place, let alone have a hissy fit.

She clicks her tongue in mock outrage but I think I see a tiny gummy grin split her face. She throws her fish bones into the Wet and watches them spill down the muddy hillside.

'I thought they would keep us for sport.' Her voice is quiet, thoughtful; I can barely make it out through the rush of water around us in the dying grey light. 'Sport or breeding. But it turns out, when the world is sliding out from underneath you, all those needs disappear. The hierarchy of needs becomes a hierarchy of fear. The ones who were left, those poor broken bastards, they were so scared of us, and what they thought we had caused, that they were just consumed with getting rid of us. It thickened their minds and muddied their vision. Plugging up the encroaching River with our corpses to appease the gods and stop the Wet. The promise of an afterlife: that's all they could think about. They were frenzied by the notion.'

What if God was a she, Gammy, and they were just royally pissing her off by killing all the women?

She chuckles, but I don't think she is amused. I can barely make out her form in the hollowed trunk, the sky around us is so dark. It makes her look twice her size, like a shadowy Gammy tree monster. Or perhaps a tree with a shadowy Gammy parasite inside.

'It would never have crossed their minds, my dear. The Unbidden told them that women were the cause, our filthy deeds and acts, our bodies, just our very *being*, had brought the floods, so the women had to go. They only stopped the killing when the waters kept rising and it had made no difference. The Wet kept coming, the world flooded, they kept dying, the River still came after them. Only then did they wonder: maybe they were wrong all along. Maybe the killings weren't the answer. But the same desperate fear blackened their minds. So each ramshackle village now led by those men who tried to kill us all, each one had to take a little girl child born in the floods as a future offering for the River.'

She pauses to cough wetly, drops of pinkish saliva spraying from her thin lips. 'Poor suckers, you should have seen their faces. We were like angry she-demons to them, the cause of all their problems, the bringers of the floods, but in the end they thought just one more killing would ruin their chances of an afterlife. One more after the thousands murdered. So here you are, my little water baby, one of the only ones they were too scared to throw into the River. And the old woman to look after you because they couldn't bear to be near you.' I can only see the whites of her eyes now, suspended between the shadowy canopies overhead and the dark below. She looks like a bloody demon herself. I suppose she is, really.

'And look at you.' She laughs dryly but her dancing white mouth isn't smiling. 'Just look at you. The tadpole turned into the very monster they most feared: a little she-god running strong and wild and dancing and bleeding and laughing in the Wet, while they sink and scurry and die off one by one. Serves the bastards right.' Her white mouth is closed in a hard line now and I can barely see the shape of her in the dark anymore. The moon is cloaked by thick black clouds and funnels of midnight rain.

What you are saying and how your voice sounds aren't the same, Gammy, and I can't see your face to tell how you really feel.

'I miss the seasons,' she mutters.

I don't understand half the crap that comes out of your mouth, Gammy.

She gives a little snore in response, so, with a disgruntled sigh, I roll under the shelter of the tree branches, reach into the hollow and wrap my arms around her upright, damp body. She smells like mulch and shit and I breathe her in. She doesn't smell like Gammy anymore. I remember the dust and the oldness and her faint smell of decay. Now, she has the briny smell of the wet mud and the River and molluscs after I have taken them from their shell, and a putrid gas that I have never smelled before.

The Wet is seeping into her pores, and the tighter I hold her shivering body, the more I feel like she is melting into the mud slicks, like that pile of old black rags.

48.

I can't see, kid, can't breathe, can't talk, it's in my lungs, drowning, sinking.

Pack your bags and go. Move to higher ground. We'll see you there. But when we get there, how will we know how to find you? Where will you be?

Camp here, little makeshift camps. Move again, keep going, the waters are rising. Here, let's stay here. Make a life, make a village, try again. Make a go of it, make a mess of it, lose all of it. What's the plan?

Need an answer? I have answers, *it whispered,* all the answers. *They might die, but at least you dared, made a plan, not a great plan, but a plan.*

Truth or dare? No truth, make it up, find someone to blame, watch them all sink. I dare you, *it whispered. Waterlogged, water in the brain, weigh them down, watch them sink.*

Ready for the afterlife, friends? It's not there, friends, idiots, comrades, people, lovers, the water is all we have. Hunt them down, chase them down, think the river cares, think the river knows? River isn't playing your game, friends.

I see you baby, little one. Why me? You're all I have. Why you?

My skin itches, flakes, evaporates, smells of leaves, smells of death. Your skin fresh and young and sweaty and cool. Bit whiffy, even in the rain, kid, whiffy from the rain.

Close the walls kid, shut it out, shut me in. Wood at my back, shelter my poor head, keep the water at bay. Rising waters, always rising. Where will we go, kid? I don't know this place.

Where are you, kid? All I can see is the grey and all I can feel is the terrible weight of water crushing my bones.

49.

A WHITE FACE IN THE SHADOWS.

My heart lurches from my stomach to my feet and a wild
rushing fills my ears. I know I said I could feel the River even
with blocked ears, Gammy, but now I can't even feel my own
hands because the fear is thrashing through my veins, liquid
cold and fast, so fast.

As soon as I see it the face has gone and I am frozen in terror.
From the top of our hill, through the tangled canopies and thick
Wet and weak morning light, my eyes could have been playing tricks on me. Going batty out here. I am pleading with the
woods to admit they have played a grand joke, been messing
with me. How the hell would he have come this far otherwise?

Gammy is still breathing softly next to me where she lies
half-curled in her tree hollow, oblivious to my panic. I am craning my neck, craning now to see where he has gone.

Why the fuck did we stay, why didn't we keep moving? My
legs are wobbly and it takes all my willpower to jump from the
ground and stand between Gammy and the space separating us
from the face of the ghost I think I have just seen.

My throat is dry and coarse and a boulder has lodged itself behind my hammering heart.

Gammy. Gammy get up. I barely know if I have said it out loud or just willed her to hear.

The fear registers on her face before she opens her eyes. Her tiny body starts trembling in her hollow, blue veins pulsing on her temples. I can't afford to keep staring at her so I turn back down the hill to the forest and the River, my back curved forward, one arm stretched in front like I can stop whatever is going to come out of the shadows.

Where did he go? Where did he go? I'm frantic now, my back to the tree trunk, peering through the Wet behind every branch and rock and tree to find him, his hooded white face and black beard appearing everywhere I look with crazed eyes. Flashes of vines and shimmers of puddles play tricks on my searching vision. I can tell that behind me Gammy hasn't moved: she probably can't. It doesn't even sound like she is breathing but all I can think about is locating his face among the grey rain. It had appeared on the edge of my vision while I stared casually – like a fucking idiot – at the valley. A black-cloaked face staring out from among the trees. He vanished the moment I saw him, surprisingly swift. Or perhaps I was slow. My reflexes dulled by our stupid hill and Gammy's hollow.

Why did we stay?

Every crack of a branch through the rush of the Wet makes my neck prickle but my legs are somehow feeling steadier now, and my eyes have stopped darting back and forward. My uneven heartbeat softens.

Is it mad, Gammy, that I close my eyes for the briefest moment? I can feel your terrified presence behind me but in front of me, the forest feels like it opens up with a yawn when I close my eyes.

I take a deep breath.

When I open my eyes again, it is only a second before he lunges clumsily from the thick undergrowth below our camp. His wood-clad feet make sucking noises as he slops through the mud toward us, painfully slowly, but he doesn't make a sound himself. He holds a jagged stick in one hand and hauls himself toward us with the other, rocks and reeds giving way underneath his feet as he clambers upwards.

I take in his black cloak covered in mud and debris and a crisscross of wild red scratches covering every inch of exposed flesh; his skin hangs morbidly loose on his starved body.

He is eerily silent, black eyes fixed on us as he stumbles haphazardly, his open mouth gaping and gasping in the Wet. He is so slow – or maybe the world has slowed down as he enters our space. I don't move a muscle as he approaches.

Gammy squawks in panic behind me as he closes in.

When I imagined fights, Gammy, the fights from your stories, I saw visions of bloodcurdling yells and throaty cries, noise and chaos and aggression and blood. I have seen their faces when I have rained down blows on trees, on logs, seen their faces as I have sparred and thrown and cut. But our attacker is disturbingly silent except for grunts of exertion and weary sighs, his muscles thick in the mud and rain. This might be more terrifying than howls of aggression; his blank face focused on us, slipping and sliding toward us like a nasty eel.

It takes an age for him to cross the space between us and I would have let my arm down in impatience if I weren't so scared of his next move. As he inches forward I can't hold out any longer and with a scream to break the deafening silence I launch, ankle bell chiming wildly, throwing my naked torso in front of his progress and hitting out wildly with my arm. The first blow lands with a dull thud on his chest and he stumbles back briefly, before righting himself and moving forward again.

I had thought he would immediately fall – why didn't he fall? – and nausea rises in my throat at the realisation that I have to go back in again.

A whirring noise, higher pitched than the River, fills my mind as I lunge forward again, landing a heavy blow on his head. With a sickening crack his neck jerks back and he sprawls, landing heavily in the mud, silent still except for his wood-clad feet thrashing out from under his ragged black cloak. He is so close I can see his rotting green toenails and the patchwork of pink chafe across his white, blue-veined ankles. He has strapped the wood to his calves with old rags; they have scratched and scarred his legs to a pulpy, purple mess.

I'm not a god or warrior, propelled by strength and power when under attack, a flash of fight and aggression. Instead I stand desperately over his writhing body, willing him to stay down, and whimpering when he slowly pulls himself onto his hands and knees and shakily rises. His hood has fallen back off his slick head and his black, matted hair is plastered over his eyes. A trickle of bright red from my blow runs from a gash on his dirty scalp but is diluted by the water beating down on him. He gasps and wheezes as liquid runs down his face and into his open mouth and I know he can barely see through the thick grey wall of the Wet.

But still he rises unsteadily and lunges forward slowly, one wood-clad foot before the other. I am trembling all over and suddenly filled with revulsion at this empty vessel of a human, a man shaking and breaking and yet still inching toward Gammy and I, propelled by some unknown hunger. A need to destroy us, and nothing else. I hit him once more across his left shoulder and a sob escapes my mouth when he only falls back briefly, then fixes blank eyes on me and moves forward again.

Did I stop paying attention because I felt sorry for him, Gammy? I don't think that was it. I just couldn't bear to hold his empty gaze anymore. His eyes were hollow and deathly cold and didn't even seem to see me, despite my blows. He looked like a bloated fish corpse, glassy-eyed and grey, not a living, breathing human. That's why I look away for a moment back toward you, catch sight of your terror-struck face straining from inside the dark tree hollow.

In that instant, he raises his sharp-edged stick, landing a blow on the side of my head.

It is a weak strike but it causes me to lurch forward and drop to my knees in the oozing mud, and sends a searing bolt of blindness between my temples.

I know through my blurred vision that he is hurling himself forward through the Wet past me but I am briefly stopped in my tracks, unable to see or move. Old stick in the mud.

Scrambling sideways and willing my eyes to work, I frantically crawl toward the space I know I left Gammy. There are no noises of struggle, no screams of pain rising above the crashing of the Wet, but I feel panic pounding from my chest to my toes.

When the blurring of my eyes clears, I see him kneeling beside her prone body, her little white legs poking out from her green cloak – a woman's cloak – faded but still garish against his black rags. For a mad second I think he is helping her, so gentle is his posture, and I almost laugh at my own delirious confusion. Every action is thickened by the rain and mud and although his spindly hands are around her neck, somehow there is nothing violent in his movements.

The sick feeling in the pit of my stomach lifts and with sudden clarity I right myself and walk toward him, bare chest parting the sheets of the Wet before me. He doesn't even glance upwards as I reach down and lift his stick up from where he dropped it in the dank swirling mulch, and raise it above his head. Gammy's eyes are closed, her face alarmingly still above the pinched grip of his two hands on her throat. Two humans, I think, as weak as each other, trapped in a fruitless battle. If I left them here right now, would I come back and find them days later, in this position, in an endless posture of unfinished violence?

I feel a short burst of sympathy and something like disgust, which is quickly replaced with a grim determination that surprises me. I swing the stick toward the back of his hoodless skull and watch as it explodes in a mess of red and grey and hair. Without a sound he slumps to the side of Gammy and the hollowed tree, and the water starts to wash his broken head clean. In seconds, mud and mouldy leaf litter begin to creep up next to his black robes. It is only a matter of time before his pile of rags start to swirl slowly toward the greedy River, hungry as always.

The world is silent except for the crashing of rain.

I don't want his misshapen body anywhere near Gammy so without stopping I scoop her up and carry her almost weightless figure down the hill to the River's edge, one careful foot in front of the other, and place her under the scant shelter of a scrappy tree. Her eyes are still closed and rain runs like tears down her cheeks, but I can see her bony chest trembling a little under her ripped cloak. The man's soft hands barely left a bruise on her wrinkled throat. The River chuckles noisily at our side.

Only then does the cold feeling in my heart slip down to my stomach, and my cheeks flush with a nervous energy as I take in what has just happened. I kneel next to Gammy and put my head on her bony shoulder and breathe in deeply. She smells so much like the River now.

Little Gammy. Almost nothing of you left. I put my large scratchy palm on one delicate cheek and her eyes flutter a little.

I don't look back up the hill at the pile of black rags: I know by now the body will be slipping gently this way and that with water pressure building behind it, maybe snagging on an overturned tree, every little drop of water eroding him little by little. His corpse will be flattening already, softening, the steady drops of rain, so gentle by themselves, will slowly wear holes in his flesh until it parts and melts into the leaves and wet soil below. Soon enough there will be nothing to show he was there, not even a scrap of black material. All washed away. In a few days he will be gone.

Instead I look forward at the churning River at my side and let her noise rush over me and soothe my racing heart and trembling hands.

50.

SHE'S BARELY WAKING NOW, JUST DRIFTING IN AND OUT
of a restless sleep that is periodically interrupted by shuddering coughs.

The days are blurring into one. Gammy floats through
them in a state of half-sleep under her scrappy shelter, violent
dreams dancing across her lined forehead while she rests. When
she wakes I feed her small hunks of silky white fish and chewed
up reeds, her mouth opening like a gaping wound and closing
again gratefully. I cup my hand to gather cool water in my palms
and let it dribble on her lips, her grey tongue darting out like an
eel to catch the drops.

Leaning closely over her while she dozes, inspecting her
face, I can see her soft wet skin peeling in sheets. Angry red
chafe marks peek out from wherever her green cloak rests on
her skin. Her lips too, are surrounded by a crisscross of pink
cracks and white flecks of dried skin. It's strange how the wet-
ter her lips get, the more the moisture is sucked from them. She
looks like a shrivelled slug, pale and cracked with all the Wet

drawn out of her. Maybe it's gone to join the rest of the water dripping from the sky – not that it needs it, greedy old Wet.

Her cloak is more murky grey than green now, the colour seeping out and joining the leaves in the mulch piles surrounding us, and the silvery trunk she is resting against. Her eyelashes and eyebrows are almost all gone, a few white spikes surrounding ragged lids. Her eyelids are fluttering while she sleeps. What are you dreaming about, Gammy? Dancing in the world before? Dry clothes, dry feet, dry mind? Black cloaks and rising waters? Or are you just dreaming about your next feed, wondering how long we can stay in this little world we have created for you under this tree.

Even now, little streams of water are breaking through the canopy above and trickling down the trunk behind her back. Fat drops hit the semi-dry earth near where her peeling feet rest with their soft, ripped nails.

The bruises he left on her neck are yellow and fading. He barely made a dent on you, old lady.

We are almost out of time, Gammy. Her breath barely makes her thin lips flutter.

If I get really close, put my ear to her mouth, I can hear a soft whistle in and out.

Why the hell not, Gammy? I plonk myself next to her and start to whistle too. Long and low, the noises circle out of our hollow and through the trees and disappear with a hiss into the deep grey just inches from us.

The blood between my legs has slowed now, just a faint mark on my muscled thigh. The tight bands of pain along my back have receded, and my belly feels calm and clear.

Gammy doesn't smell like anything anymore.

I breathe in deeply and the Wet fills my lungs and rises through my chest. I swear, Gammy, I can feel the River's roar thrumming through my body, like if I stuffed my ears with mulch and all the rushing and raging noises of the currents suddenly stopped, I would still know exactly where the waters were in the silence. Second to you, Gammy, old Lady River is my only friend out here.

I can feel her presence more than yours now, really.

A little whistling fart escapes from her mouldy arse and I stifle a laugh. I might not be a kid anymore Gammy, but that is still fucking hilarious. I can't wipe the grin off my face as I draw my knees to my chin and peer down the hill toward the River, taking in the swirling grey currents and the frothy waves breaking on rocks, the low-flung branches and roots stretching to join the racing waters.

51.

AT THE EDGE OF THE VALLEY, I FIND THE CLIFFS. AS THE River winds its way from our tree, upstream of Gammy, upstream of the rotting pile of villager, it follows sheer rocky walls I can't see the top of, no matter how hard I squint. The faces of the cliffs are yellow, red, orange, brown. They look like they are on fire – two walls of fire shimmering through the Wet. The River has carved its way through the rock, must have started its journey well before the Wet came. There are no banks, no reeds, no little shrubs clinging to the rock face, just the River winding through this channel.

I have to strain my arms and legs to kick against her current, making slow progress. As I propel myself forward a few inches below the choppy surface, I can feel those cliffs looming toward the sky on either side of me, a nervous pricking on my neck. It feels like little eyes could be hundreds of feet above my head, watching my body slip upstream like a tadpole from above, and I would never know.

The channel starts to widen, opening up to the rainy sky, and the River eventually spreads once more into a large body.

I start treading water, listen to the roar of water I can hear just ahead, then swim again as the River turns into a great lake covering every surface of what is now a giant valley. The fiery outcrops, jutting out from the water below, encircle the entire edge of the valley except where the River winds its way downstream again. I float at the bottom of the cliffs, staring up the steep edges where they climb into the grey, circling clouds above.

I have never seen anything so incredible, Gammy. My admiring whistle is masked by the mad thrum of the waves and pounding rapids. There is a new wall of water before me, greater even than the Wet. Water rushes down every part of the cliff face in great frothy sheets, crashing in a mass of white and noise into the River that fills the entire valley below. A fine mist rises where the water running down the cliff hits old Lady River, which is then enveloped into the greater Wet. The air smells fresh, clean, wet and violent, its coolness coating my lungs and filling my veins.

I wonder briefly if I could swim up this vertical pathway of water rising above my head; fight the currents and pop up over the top like a flying fish. I chuckle where I bob in the choppy soup of the River at the base, the sound swallowed by the deafening roar of the waterfall.

Instead I swim across to a tree fighting out of the water only a few body lengths from the waterfall's base. Most of the lower branches have been yanked away by the currents, but straggly little forks have sprung up at the top of the thick trunk, covered in a mess of dark green leaves that glisten and shake in the rain. Tough little bastard, that tree, standing tall and strong despite the Wet coming from all sides.

I float a little closer, wrap my arms around its slimy trunk. Foam from the waterfall whips around the tree's base where it stands tall in the water.

Just above my head, I inspect the marked lines in the tree's thick brown surface. Neat little markings, all in rows. I still have to hold onto the tree with one arm as I reach up and run my fingers over the jagged lines; feel their hardness etched into the soft bark. So neat, so carefully made.

Then with a *whoosh*, I am whipped out into the centre of the white churning lake.

The entrance to the valley is at my back and I turn that way in the River, fighting the strong current to tread water in one spot. The waterfall rumbles behind me. Gammy probably doesn't even know I am gone. She barely registers my presence now, barely reaches for my arm. She doesn't even cough anymore, has stopped jumping when the wild flocks of birds crack open the Wet with their wings as they fly above her tree.

I wish you could see this, Gammy.

I float my way back down the River with the rocky walls of fire either side, toward our tree, back to Gammy, the sound of water filling my ears.

It's a real shame you won't.

52.

HOW LONG HAVE WE SPENT, GAMMY? WAITING ON THIS hill for something to happen? It feels like as long as our time together in the hut, but that is impossible, of course. That was a whole lifetime.

Could it really only be two days? Three? Already I see you planting your roots in this place. Something weird about your lot. Needing to plant yourself in steady ground, needing to make something solid in a world that refuses to be still. I see you, pressing into the mud, trying to make a space for yourself in the Wet, trying to etch out some room. Wriggling your flat buttocks into the ground to make a Gammy-shaped indent. You know it will just wash away, Gammy. Any mark you leave washes away.

When we were in the hut, it felt like we were the centre of the world, a warm pocket of light. It always felt bigger there than the two of us. Our world made a space in the Wet.

Out here, the world keeps swirling, dripping around us, and we stay still and almost silent now as the Wet takes up this space. Eats away at the edges of your little bubble, Gammy, takes a little more room from you every hour.

You are bunkering down. I am spreading out.

When I ask for something to happen, you tell me to be careful what I wish for.

53.

HOW SHE SLIPPED OUT IN THE NIGHT IS BEYOND ME. WEAK as piss one day, next morning flinging herself from under the canopy and slithering down last stretch of the hill like a mad old eel. I find her just above the River, snagged in a nest of dead branches like a splayed little crab, drenched and muddy and swollen eyes flickering, confused in the dim grey light.

Tiny bubbles of condensation cover every part of her, little shimmering spots of silver. Like you are covered in dancing moonlight, Gammy. Little moonlight Gammy. Little white person tangled in the reeds.

I gently untangle her from the sharp branches and fling them to the side, using my body to keep her from slipping straight down into Lady River. You're a fool, Gammy. What are you playing at?

Her upper body is out of the Wet at least but there is no other space for her down here, no way of keeping her safe. I use my naked bulk to keep the main rush of water off her, but little rivulets still drop onto her forehead and make tracks down past her ears and through her sparse white hair, which is growing steadily darker with mud and moisture. She gapes and gasps in the Wet, struggling to breathe despite my shielding the worst of the rain from her face.

I stroke her forehead absent-mindedly without looking down, my gaze drawn more and more up the River. From where we sit, perched on her banks, the River winds and runs slowly through a heavily forested channel, all smooth round corners and frothy waves.

I stare straight ahead, ears pricked, observing Lady River as she winds her way toward the waterfall valley.

Did you hear that, Gammy?

I start when I feel Gammy's hand on mine and I glance down. Her fingers are feather light, like they could float away like the seeds did back when we used to get sunlight.

It feels like such a long time ago, Gammy.

Her watery pink eyes stare up at me and she moves her dry cracked lips slowly. The words barely escape before being swallowed up by the Wet.

'My water baby.'

I lean down close to her and kiss her slimy white forehead, then place my lips next to her ear. The roar of water all around us fights with my whispered words, but I know she hears them.

At first she pauses, narrow mouth pursed together, but then I see a little light pass over her face. Your own little window of sunshine, Gammy. You did bring it with you.

I think she is starting to cough, but it's a laugh. A low cackle building deep in her heaving chest and bubbling up through her smile. The tears that pool in her eyes join the laughter and

I can't help smiling back at her, crazy old lady pissing herself laughing at the end of the earth.

When her frail little body can't manage her raucous laughter any longer she sighs quietly and gives my hand a faint squeeze – all she can muster. When she closes her eyes again, I barely pause before placing one hand on her green-robed shoulder and one on her sharp hip. I push her gently toward the edge of the River.

It doesn't take long for the swirling water and mud slicks around her to take the motion over from me and propel her over the riverbank, splashing into the brown waters below. I rise up and let the Wet envelope my naked body in a cold hug as Gammy slips and slides her way into the River's hungry mouth. For a short time, she bobs along the surface like my leaf boats, occasionally ducking up again then dropping below the surface around a boulder here, a wave of rapids there, until I can't see her at all through the wall of grey water in front of me.

When I turn and move upstream through the valley, the Wet moves with me.

Epilogue

DON'T BE SCARED GAMMY. I FEEL STRONG – SO STRONG. My heart flies thinking about what's up ahead.

Don't be scared. I know they blamed me, hunted me, because they think I brought the waters. But Gammy, I think they might be right.

I feel the waters deep in my belly, surging and raging. They are always with me.

Maybe I did bring the floods. They rise up from inside me like a mighty wave.

Goodbye Gammy. Don't be scared. I'm not. I feel strong, so strong.

Don't cry for me Gammy – I'm not alone. Just up ahead, if you listen carefully between the crashing of the water, you can hear it.

The sound of bells.

Acknowledgements

To Alfred and Madeline, for being my inspiration, always.

To Arts SA and the State Library South Australia for the once in a lifetime opportunity that came out of the 2022 Unpublished Manuscript Award. Thank you to Wakefield Press for the same: to my editor Maddy Sexton for her guidance, wisdom and cheerful marginal notes, and to Poppy Nwosu and Michael Bollen.

To Richard Rowe for his valuable feedback and encouragement on an early draft and to Chelsea Trinder for her early support and advice.

Politics sometimes gets a bad rap, but I have been fortunate to work with some of the best. To Ian Hunter and Jay Weatherill for my first examples of a sense of stewardship, particularly toward the natural world. And to Julia Gillard, for always putting theory into practice in supporting women, for her feedback on an early draft, and for her generous sharing of wisdom and friendship with myself and so many others. To Connie Blefari and Michelle Fitzgerald, for being absolute legends as friends and colleagues on this journey.

I have incredible friends who build me up even as they are out achieving brilliant things. To Hannah Stark for her refusal to tolerate my self-doubt, detailed feedback on drafts, and life-long friendship. To Shannon Schedlich, for her endless support, guidance, love, feedback on drafts, memes, and virtual hugs and laughs across borders. To Derek Pedley for being my writing buddy. To Serena Hawes, Catriona Hartigan, Mel O'Grady, Anne Romeo, Abbie Spencer, Alex Foster, and Ilze Teteris: I value our friendships so much.

To Julian, for his partnership, support, and kind encouragement over the years, which made this book possible.

To my family. To my grandmother, Wendy, for making me believe there were flower fairies at the bottom of the garden and for sharing her love of books and writing. To my father, Andrew, who taught me how to question everything, and for fostering my obsession with various end of the world scenarios. To my mother, Sally, for raising me to believe nothing was out of reach and instilling a love of literature – and to both parents for their boundless love and excitement regardless of the paths I walked. To Daniel for being the best brother.

Families come in all shapes and sizes and I have been lucky to have shared my life with many wonderful people. To Wayne Simons for his care and support. To Trent Goldsack, whose ongoing friendship and willingness to overlook my crap taste in wine means the world to me. To Ruth McCance, who came into my life when I was six years old, and with whom I shared three decades of love, laughter, conversations, hugs, hikes, canoeing trips, sunsets and silence that I will carry with me forever. Ruth's presence lingers in every page this book.

Wakefield Press is an independent publishing and
distribution company based in Adelaide, South Australia.
We love good stories and publish beautiful books.
To see our full range of books, please visit our website at
www.wakefieldpress.com.au
where all titles are available for purchase.
To keep up with our latest releases, news and events,
subscribe to our monthly newsletter.

Find us!

Facebook: www.facebook.com/wakefield.press
Twitter: www.twitter.com/wakefieldpress
Instagram: www.instagram.com/wakefieldpress